CAPTAIN GLOW

CAPTAIN GLOW

S.J. FLANN

CaptainGlow.com

Publishing services provided by Scrivener Books
Editor: Kathy Jenkins
Cover Designer: Holly Flann
Interior Print Design: Dayna Linton
Ebook Design: Dayna Linton

Library of Congress Control Number: Pending
ISBN: 978-0-578-55814-1 (Paperback)

First Edition: 2019; Updated Edition 2021

FOOTNOTE LINKS SUPPLEMENT

Numbered electronic footnote links for *Captain Glow*
The list below can be found on the www.captainglow.com website. The reader must go to the website to use the footnote links.

	Topic	Chapter & Page No.	Audiobook Locations
1	Power-to-Gas (Video)	Chapter 3— Page 46	Chapter 3— 15 min 27 sec
2	Power-to-Gas Hydrogen Pipeline	Chapter 3— Page 46	Chapter 3— 15 min 49 sec
3	Oceana Tidal Power Turbine	Chapter 3— Page 52	Chapter 3— 23 min 43 sec
4	Carinata Oil as Biofuel	Chapter 3— Page 53	Chapter 3— 24 min 42 sec
5	Build Your Dreams Electric Buses	Chapter 3— Page 57	Chapter 3— 31 min 24 sec
6	WAVE Wireless Bus Charging (Video)	Chapter 3— Page 58	Chapter 3— 32 min 24 sec
7	ASPIRE Electric Vehicle Lab	Chapter 4— Page 66	Chapter 4— 07 min 21 sec
8	IBM's High Concentration PhotoVoltaic Thermal (HCPVT) Sunflower	Chapter 5— Page 86	Chapter 5— 06 min 30 sec
9	University of California, Irvine— Water Resources (Video)	Chapter 5— Page 91	Chapter 5— 13 min 40 sec

S. J. FLANN

PART 1

THE SOLAR PV SYSTEM

CHAPTER

1

WILL CHAMBERS SHIFTED AROUND, restless and awake. On the bedside table, the glowing numbers of his alarm clock radio read 3:02 a.m. The lanky sixteen-year-old slid out of bed. Running his hands through his bushy, light-brown hair, he wondered why he'd woken up. The rest of the house was quiet. His mother and father were sleeping down the hall. Their newly arrived house guest, Audrey, was likely fast asleep in a different room. *Maybe that's it,* he thought, *that we have someone new in our home.*

Comox, Will's white husky, raised his head to look at Will. The dog lay where he slept every night—on a large, checkered floor cushion in the bedroom. The room had one other twin bed, which was unoccupied. "It's okay, boy," whispered Will, moving past a shelf of trophies and medals. The awards from regional science fairs belonged to Will;

science was his favorite subject in school. The other medals—for sports, mainly hockey and football—belonged to his older brother, Michael, who was now serving a church mission in Germany.

Hoping for a cool breeze, Will walked around the end of the bed to an open window and was surprised to see a car creeping along the street so late at night. He narrowed his gray eyes, trying to see who was driving, but it was too dark. The car stopped in front of his house, then pulled away, disappearing around the corner. *No big deal,* he thought. *Just an Aberdeen night owl out for a drive.* Comox had come to his side. "Hey boy," he said, ruffling Comox's head. Will crawled back into bed and went to sleep.

The following morning, a muscular man who looked to be in his early sixties stood in the blazing June sunlight in front of the zoo hospital in Aberdeen, Utah. He stared intently at the solar photovoltaic (PV) system on the roof; its twenty PV panels glistened in the sun. The back of his T-shirt pulled across his shoulders as he flexed his muscles. His eyes looked cruel. Glancing around to make sure no one saw him, he pretended to machine-gun the top of the building before dropping his arms and striding off.

Only a mile away, in the afternoon of that same day, Will Chambers was in a good mood as well, mostly due to the big turkey sandwich he was wolfing down. Finishing the last bite, he cleaned up the countertop and shoved the mayonnaise and butter back into the fridge.

Leaving the kitchen, he walked through a sunny, yellow hallway to check the mail for a fuel cell kit he'd ordered. The kit contained a small solar panel the size of a slice of bread.

When the panel was exposed to direct sunlight, it generated electricity to power the fuel cell. Then the fuel cell split water into hydrogen and oxygen. But the part that interested him the most, was how the fuel cell could reverse the process, recombining the hydrogen and oxygen to produce electricity. He pictured the process in his mind; either the solar panel or—the reverse process—produced electricity. The electricity was enough to power a small motor included in the kit. He was keen to get it and put it all together.

Stopping at the front hall table, Will riffled through the day's mail, which had piled up next to the phone. No kit—only letters and magazines. *Crud,* he thought. *Still on backorder.*

The phone rang. "Can you get that, Will?" his mother called from the kitchen. "If I don't leave now, I'll be late for my eye appointment!"

"Got it, Mom." Will reached for the phone and answered, "Chambers residence."

A somber-sounding voice asked, "Is this the home of Dr. Chambers, who works with the Aberdeen Zoo?" Will heard the back door slam and knew his mother had left.

"Yes."

"Warn the zoo! The new PV system will be damaged tonight! Do you understand? The attack will happen tonight!" With that, the phone went dead in his hands. Will slowly put it back into the cradle.

"Hey, Will, who was that?" A lively girl in jeans and a T-shirt was zooming down the stairs. She halted at the last step, holding on to the railing that separated her and Will.

Audrey, an agile sixteen-year-old with a head of copper hair, was a longtime family friend who was now staying with the Chambers family. She paused, seeing Will's odd expression.

"That was strange," he said. "Some guy just told me the zoo hospital's going to be attacked."

"Attacked?" said Audrey. "By who?"

"Don't know. He just said it's going to be attacked tonight and to warn the zoo. And then—bam! He hung up!' Audrey didn't move. "I have to call my dad," said Will. The doorbell rang. They could see a shadow through the diffused glass of the front entry.

Opening the door, Will was happy to see a tall Asian American teenager holding a bike helmet.

"Hey, Darius, come in!" Hearing Will's greeting, Comox bounded from the kitchen and Darius dropped down to scratch the dog's ears.

"Glad you're back!" said Will. "Hey, something weird just happened and I gotta call my dad." The young man threw Will a puzzled frown and then smiled, his dark eyebrows shooting up.

"Okay," he said.

Will remembered well how their friendship had started: Will had intervened when Darius was about to be beaten up in middle school. When the two met up afterward, they found they lived only a few blocks apart. From then on, they were friends. Now they biked or drove together to Aberdeen High, a school where they were both in the same grade.

Darius had been away for two weeks, and the Chambers family had missed him. They were also missing Will's older brother, Michael, who'd left two and a half months earlier for Germany now that the pandemic was over. With both Michael and Darius gone, life had gotten dull.

But with the phone call Will had just received that had ended. Will shut the door. "I gotta call my dad. But first, you two need to meet each other—Audrey Carter, this is Darius Cheng, my wild-man-friend and neighbor. Darius, this is Audrey Carter, a family friend who's, who is . . . staying with us now . . ." he trailed off. He'd almost added, "who's a total knock-out," but opted for a less embarrassing introduction.

Will had known Audrey for almost ten years but during that time had seen her only periodically when their two families had been camping together. He'd always considered her nothing more than a friend. Things were different now—Audrey had blossomed, and Will found it hard to think of her as the same mud-covered, frog-catching girl he'd known in years past.

Darius stuck out his hand. He was tall and thin and looked quite a bit like Will, except he sported hair that was bushy, thick, and black. His eyes had a lively spark, making it impossible not to smile back at him. Audrey reached out, and the two shook hands.

Will continued, "Her folks are working in Santiago, Chile—"

"So the Chambers got stuck with me this year," interrupted Audrey. Will pulled out his cell phone.

"Gotta call the doc," he said, and Audrey nodded.

"What's going on?" said Darius, taking in their expressions.

Will motioned his friends toward the kitchen. "You explain, Audrey." His father picked up on the second ring. "Hi, Dad—you at the hospital?"

"As ever," answered Dr. Lloyd Chambers. "I'm currently being mauled by a ferocious man-eater."

"Mauled?" asked Will.

"I'm treating a junior *Panthera tigris altaica*."

"A baby tiger?" asked Will, distractedly.

"Yes, a baby tiger—who's happily chewing on his bottle. He's got a fractured tail, courtesy of his bouncy older brother," said the doctor. "Reminds me of you and Michael."

Dr. Chambers, head physician at the zoo hospital, was in good spirits. He much preferred to be with the animals over wrestling with administrative work.

"Dad, I need to tell you something—it's important."

"Hold on," said his father. "Let me give this cub to Laura." His father called to one of his medical staff, a smart, blonde nurse who was more than capable of handling a squirming baby tiger cub.

"You have my full attention now," said the doctor.

Will explained about the phone call.

More somber now, Will's father asked, "Could it be one of your friends playing a prank?"

"No, Dad. It wasn't anyone I know. The guy sounded serious."

"Right, then," said Dr. Chambers. "I'll contact Tom Varcheko to get extra security. And I'll instruct Laura and Dan to lock up carefully, although they always do." He paused. "Maybe someone's after some choice medications." Then he sighed, "Our zoo director won't like this, but he'll act on it. There are people who have fewer brains—"

"I know, Dad," interrupted Will, having heard it a million times, "fewer brains than a termite."

"Right."

"See you later."

Prank call? thought Will as he hung up. *What would be funny about a phone call like that?* He found Audrey and Darius in the kitchen, where Audrey had told Darius about the caller's message.

"Talk to your dad?" Darius asked. Will nodded. Audrey looked up from a blissful Comox, who was having his back scratched.

"What did he say?" she asked.

"They'll bring on some extra guards," he said, then wanting to lighten the mood, he went on, "let's head to the game room!" It was early June, and Will knew the summer break would go by fast.

Heading downstairs, the three entered a simply furnished family room on the lower level. It was a good-sized room with a couch, two overstuffed chairs, a bookshelf, an aquarium, a video game system, a DVD player, a projector, and a large white wall.

"Hey Darius," said Will, waving a dance video game in the air, "any chance you been trying this out?" He knew Darius liked the game, but since Darius and his mother had been staying with his elderly aunt, the answer was most likely *zero* this time.

"No; messed around with Legos mostly," said Darius, whose devoted aunt showered him with Lego sets on every occasion. "I know I'll be terrible," he said. Darius was a perfectionist who liked doing all things well.

Turning to Audrey, Will said, "Darius makes Lego structures like Henry Ford set up assembly lines: pure genius." Turning back to his friend, he said, "What'd you build this time?"

"I did Rodin's sculpture of *The Thinker*. Here's a picture of it." Darius pulled out his phone and showed the photo to Will and Audrey. "My aunt went gaga."

"Whew!" whistled Will.

Audrey stared at the Lego creation. "That's . . . wow." She was clearly impressed.

"I still think Australia's Sydney Opera House was my best, but someone else had already done it, so no big deal."

"Yours was better," offered Will.

"Nah. Maybe . . . I don't know," said Darius, embarrassed, but still enjoying the praise.

They booted up the electronics.

Darius turned to Audrey, "So where're you from?"

"San Diego," answered Audrey, studying the list of songs offered on the game menu.

"Nice. Why are your folks in Chile?"

"My dad's a structural engineer, and my mom's a plant biologist. He's doing serious earthquake-proof building design there. It's a two-year project. When my mom was offered a great research project on medicinal plants . . ." she rolled her eyes, "they couldn't pack fast enough, so—now they're in Santiago."

"You have any brothers or sisters?" Darius asked. He was an only child and was curious to know whether she was too.

"I have a sister, Bette, who's eight. She's with my folks; she's probably loving it."

"And you're here in the states so you'll be able to graduate from high school," said Darius.

"Exactly," nodded Audrey. "My dad would really admire your Lego structures."

Will, who liked Audrey more than he cared to admit, pretended to make a long face and said, "Having her here is such a pain." Audrey flipped an orange pillow at him. He caught it and tossed it back. "Nah, it's good that you're here, Audrey. With Michael gone and then Darius taking off for the last two weeks, it was way too quiet!" He turned to the dog. "Right, Comox?" The husky wagged his tail and barked, making them all laugh.

"I'm going to be useful around here," said Audrey in mock solemnity, "and try not to be too horrible to poor Will." She smiled at him. His heart gave a leap. "As for Santiago—maybe I'll go there after I graduate."

"Cool," said Will. No matter what the far-off future held, he was glad she and Darius were here now.

The dance moves were challenging, but Will managed a perfect rating on the second song.

"No way—five stars on 'Funkytown'? You must be cheating!" said Darius.

Will's heart was thumping. "Nope. Your turn, Audrey."

She jumped up. "I'll do an early Beatles song." She swept her hands in front of the reader and selected "Love, Love Me Do."

She's so different now, thought Will, and he glanced at Darius, hoping his friend hadn't noticed anything different about *him.* But Darius couldn't have cared less; he was watching Audrey.

After an hour and a half, they finished up and shut down the system. "It's fish-feedin' time," said Will, crossing the room to a twenty-gallon tank. The Chambers' gray cat, Hudson, was balanced on the edge getting a drink. The cat, who was older than Comox, was king of the house.

"Yuck, Hudson," said Will, shooing the cat off the tank and opening up a fish-food container. One of the goldfish was the size of a small banana, and it splashed up to the surface as soon as Will dropped the pellets into the water. "All done here," he said.

Audrey scooped up the soft, gray cat and followed Will and Darius upstairs.

Mrs. Chambers, back from her eye appointment and errands, was rushing around the kitchen. A medium-height blonde, she was Canadian by birth. In a cheery mood and nicely dressed, she was preparing supper while talking with her husband, who'd walked in a few minutes earlier.

She turned to Will, quizzing him about the strange call. "Are you sure it wasn't one of your friends playing a prank?" Will had almost forgotten about it.

"No, Mom, it wasn't—"

Mrs. Chambers turned to her husband. "Lloyd, what about tonight? Should we cancel?" The couple had tickets to a touring production of an extraordinary play called *War Horse* and had been looking forward to it for months.

"Well, Janet, Tom Varcheko has two extra guards posted outside the hospital; that should be enough." He paused, "I can't think of anyone who'd have a reason to attack the place. There's nothing to gain. I think we should go."

"Good! I'm thrilled!" said Mrs. Chambers. She made a sweeping gesture over the table, which was now full of food. "You kids have everything you need." She smiled at her husband and said, "Lloyd and I are going out for dinner and a show."

As his parents' car pulled out of the driveway, Will looked at the food. A feeling of appreciation swept over him regarding his mother's cooking skills. There was steaming, hot chicken in a buttery sauce, cucumbers with ranch dressing, and a mouthwatering fruit salad, which Darius was already scooping up. Audrey took a plate for herself and handed one to Will.

After they'd finished eating and put the leftovers away, they walked Comox to a park, where the three of them threw a tennis ball that Comox endlessly was willing to retrieve. At dusk they headed back.

Sitting down at the kitchen table, they pulled out a favorite board game called "Branium." Audrey won the first round, barely defeating Darius. They began a second round as the sky darkened in the window. Will molded a blob of clay into a flat shape. After several wrong guesses, which included a dirty sock and a piece of beef jerky, Will molded a small clay pillow and a tiny flap, which he opened and closed.

"Sleeping bag!" Darius guessed correctly, giving two points to Will and one to him.

It was Audrey's turn when the home phone rang. Will picked it up. "Chambers residence," he said, putting his used game card down.

"Who am I speaking with?" It was the same voice as earlier.

"Will Chambers."

"Did you tell the doctor about the attack?"

"Who is this?" asked Will, motioning to Audrey and Darius that he was speaking to the same caller.

"Did you tell someone at the zoo about the attack tonight?" the man asked, ignoring Will's question.

"Yes. I told my dad, and he told the zoo director, Mr. Varcheko."

"Did Varcheko listen?"

"He posted two extra guards," said Will.

"I hope that's enough," the voice growled. "I can't get there in time! Will, the attacker's name is Sainos, and he is a *real* problem. His nickname is 'Insaino,' and it's a name he earned. Two guards might not be enough."

"Why would this Sainos guy attack the zoo?" asked Will.

"Because he hates my guts," said the man. "Did your dad or Varcheko ever talk about an unknown donor who funded the zoo's solar PV system?"

Will paused. So much for the prank idea: funds had been donated three months earlier.

"Yes . . ." said Will.

The caller went on. "Well, that anonymous guy is me, and that's why Sainos is going to smash the PV system to bits."

"Who are you?!" asked Will.

"Can't answer that," the man replied.

"How can I help, then?" asked Will. "My dad and the police'll want to know." With that, Will heard a sharp intake of breath on the other end of the line.

"I'd rather not contact the police."

"Why?"

The man's voice became quiet. "They'll want to find me."

Will wondered whether the man was in trouble. *Could he take back the funding?* Will measured his words. "I—look, I don't want to find you; I just want to know who you are."

The man groaned, then laughed. "Call me Captain Glow . . . all right, contact the police. Otherwise, that solar-PV system'll be in pieces by tomorrow. And try not to mention this call."

The line went dead.

Audrey and Darius stared at him. He set the phone into the cradle and told them everything.

"Captain Glow?" repeated Darius. His eyebrows furrowed in concentration. "Has your dad ever mentioned that name?" Will shook his head. "Have you ever heard it before?"

"Nope. Jeez, Darius, I would have remembered a name like that."

"What does *PV* stand for?" asked Audrey.

"Photovoltaic," said Will. "It's a solar photovoltaic system." He paused at Audrey's muddled expression. "You know, the big, dark, flat panels that produce electricity from sunlight?"

"Oh—on rooftops? Of course! I see them all over San Diego," said Audrey, her face reddened.

"This guy's the anonymous donor who funded the PV system for the zoo!" Will thought of how highly prized the PV system was. He and Michael had helped with the publicity campaign when the system was installed and began providing power. He made a decision.

"I'm going over to the hospital."

"Whoa," said Darius, "to the zoo? Don't you think you oughtta call the police?"

Will paused. "That's what the guy wanted me to do, but he wants to be kept out of it . . . I wonder why he's avoiding the police?" He wondered again if the man could take back the funding. Will wasn't sure why the next words tumbled out. "Look, I—I think that going over there is the right thing to do."

Audrey's eyes widened. She and Darius waited.

"This guy, this Captain Glow," said Will, shaking his head, "whatever that means, feels the solar PV system is at risk, even with the guards in place. If I had a way to contact them, it'd be different, but I don't, so—I want to check it out."

"Well," Audrey countered, "he did say to call the police."

"If I do and there's nothing to it, then I'm stuck. They'll be aggravated if I can't explain why I thought I needed to contact them." Will's pulse was pounding. "You guys should stay here and—"

"No, going alone is a bad idea," interrupted Darius. "It's common sense for me to come. We'll take my jeep."

"I'm coming too," said Audrey. "I can be a lookout."

"Then Comox is coming too," said Will. He pushed the board game aside.

Darius biked home to get his gold jeep and within minutes was back and pulling in to the driveway. His three passengers climbed in. From here it was only a mile to the zoo.

Arriving at the parking lot, they drove to the corner closest to the hospital entrance. Will told Comox in a stern voice, "Stay, Comox. Quiet."

Audrey looked troubled when she realized Comox was being left in the jeep. "Shouldn't we bring him?"

"No, not yet," said Will. "I don't want him to startle the guards or the zoo animals. We'll come back and get him if we need him." They left one of the jeep windows open, providing a large gap that would give Comox plenty of air.

Walking onto the grounds through an opening in a thick hedge, they trotted down a narrow pathway and up to a side gate just outside the tan stucco building that was the zoo hospital. Will entered his father's security code into the numeric keypad on the locked metal gate. The bolt on the gate clicked, and it swung open. Will studied the area, looking for the guards in the shadowy grounds surrounding the zoo hospital.

"Don't see anybody," he said, motioning for Darius and Audrey to follow him. They crossed a small terrace to the back door of the zoo hospital. "What!?" Will froze outside the door. It was slightly ajar, its lock broken and covered with black powder marks.

"Stop!" he whispered to the others. "The door's been blown open. You wait here, I'm going in." He pushed the door open.

CHAPTER

2

"WILL!" HISSED AUDREY, TERRIFIED. He motioned for silence and moved forward. The dimly lit room revealed a woeful sight. A guard lay motionless on the ground with a syringe beside him. *I need to see if he's okay,* thought Will, going farther into the room.

Will was startled by a soft mewing sound coming from a corner pen in which a tiger cub watched with wide eyes. Will bent down, placing his fingers on the side of the guard's neck. To his relief, the man had a strong, regular pulse. Turning back to the door, he gave Darius and Audrey a thumbs up. *Should he turn on the lights? Where was the intruder?* Then he heard a sound from above. He looked up.

"Darius," he whispered, "Someone's on the roof!" Will came back through the door.

Motioning Audrey to stay back, Will and Darius edged slowly around the building. A ladder was propped up against the outside wall. They looked at each other and then in a single movement, they stepped forward and lifted the ladder away from the building, letting it fall. The clattering noise split the night air as the ladder hit the ground. Will yelled to Audrey, "Get Comox and call my dad from my phone! Prop the gate open!" He tossed his phone onto the grass. She scooped it up and ran to the gate. Will turned back and looked up, expecting to see a face appear. But nothing happened.

Darius breathed, "Where did he go?" Suddenly a loud, rhythmic, thudding noise sounded from the other side of the building. Will moved around the hospital's edge with Darius close behind. A rope dangled from the roof. A man of medium height raced away from the building, and Will and Darius sprinted after him. Only when they were passing by the elephant enclosure did they realize that the path ahead was empty.

Gasping for air, Darius asked, "Where did he go?"

"Don't know!" said Will, coming to a full stop. They'd lost the runner in the maze of buildings and shadows. They could hear Comox barking far behind them.

"Go back?" said Darius, and Will nodded.

Audrey was standing outside the hospital with Comox at her side. She'd turned on the light. Her face flooded with relief when she saw them.

"Were you able to reach my dad?" asked Will.

"No, it went to voice mail!" she said unhappily. "Is—is the guy still up there?"

"No," said Will. "He climbed down and took off. We followed, but he got away."

Darius went around the corner to where the chase had started.

"I'm going to check on the guard," said Will, thinking that if his father was here, he would do that first. Commanding Comox to sit, he and Audrey entered the building.

Darius came back quickly. "Our intruder was prepared," he said. "He rappelled down."

"Wow, that is—prepared," said Will, as he knelt down to check on the guard. His name tag read *Hillstrom*. He was fast asleep and smiling like a baby.

A syringe lay beside the guard, and Audrey poked at it with her shoe. "Careful with that!" Darius cautioned her.

"Maybe it's a sleeping drug," she said, studying the guard's face.

Will stood up. "I want to check the PV system."

Going back outside, they looked around, finding wire cutters and a sledgehammer on the ground not far from where the ladder lay. Darius whistled. "He was definitely looking to cause some damage."

"Let's see if he did," said Will. He and Darius grabbed the ladder and put it back up. Will climbed up first, got onto the roof, and began an inspection. The panels looked good, and the small DC-to-AC inverters underneath each panel were all unharmed. The wires going down to the power meter were fine. The entire system was intact. The knot in Will's chest loosened.

A canvas bag and anchoring equipment were attached to the rope on the other side where the man had rappelled down. Will, Audrey, and Darius must have arrived just moments after the intruder had gone up on the roof. *Would the man come back? No, not while we're here*, thought Will. He climbed back down.

"I'll call Dad. Audrey, do you have my phone?" She gave it to him. This time his dad answered, since his parents were just leaving the theatre. Will told him about the guard and everything that had happened.

"I'm on my way now," said his dad. "I'm calling an ambulance. Will, make sure you and the others are safe! Got it?"

"Yup," answered Will. He put his phone away. Suddenly he remembered that his dad had said earlier there would be two guards. *Where was the other one?* Will told Audrey and Darius about the ambulance and then about the other missing guard. "Audrey, stay here with Comox and wait for the ambulance. Darius and I are gonna look for the other guy."

They headed outside. "That building's closest to the hospital," said Darius. "Let's start there." The monkey house was a short distance across a large concrete walkway. In front stood a metal sculpture of a tree with a spider monkey swinging from its branches.

"That's eerie," said Darius. In the dim light, the sculptured monkey had a menacing look.

Suddenly Will jumped. "Do you hear that?"

"Yeah," said Darius, "it's coming from there." A thumping noise issued from the recessed entrance to the building. Will and Darius cautiously approached; then they raced forward.

A pair of bound feet were pressed up against the doors. The missing guard was lying on the ground, trying to get free. He was gagged with duct tape and bound by layers of rope tied to a post next to the door. His face was sweaty, and he had a bloody welt on his forehead. They knelt beside him. An orangutan's calm face peered at them as she watched from a large window that looked outward.

Will spoke to the man in soothing tones, "It's okay, we're here to help." Will looked for other injuries and was glad not to find any more. "Let's get that duct tape off."

"Right," said Darius, loosening the edge of the tape on the man's mouth. "This could hurt," he said and then he ripped the tape off.

"Ow!" said the guard. Then he started taking huge gulps of air. Will used his pocketknife to cut away the ropes that bound the man's torso, feet, and hands.

"You all right?" Will asked.

"I think so," said the guard. "Is Hillstrom okay?"

"Yeah," said Will. "He's in the zoo hospital building. He's been drugged, but he seems fine."

"It's like he's having an awesome nap," said Darius reassuringly.

"Who—who are you guys?" asked the guard, rubbing at the raw skin on his wrists.

"My dad's Dr. Chambers; he runs the hospital here. I'm Will, and this is Darius. Um—an ambulance is on the way."

The guard put his hand to his forehead, smearing the blood from the cut. "Jeez," he muttered. His name tag read *Johnson*. "I saw two figures moving. When I circled around from the back, someone jumped me. Then, bang, right on the head! Next thing I know, I'm tied up and I hear a dog barking."

"Mr. Johnson," said Will, "your cut doesn't seem deep, but we should be careful. Is anything hurting? Are you able to walk?"

"My head hurts, but I'm okay to walk," said Johnson.

"Let's head back to the zoo hospital."

"That," Johnson replied with irritation, "is what I'm supposed to be guarding tonight. I know I saw two guys; one's an average height and the other is big and tall." Darius and Will exchanged looks; that meant there were two assailants.

Which one did we chase? thought Will. *Probably the smaller one—he was so fast!*

"Glad we didn't meet the bigger guy," muttered Darius.

"Let's get you up," Will said to the guard. He bent down and lifted one arm; Darius took the other. They heard a siren getting closer.

When they got to the hospital, they eased Mr. Johnson into a chair just as Dr. Chambers arrived. He identified the syringe used on Mr. Hillstrom as a sedative. "It's not harmful," he said. "He'll sleep it off." Then he went to Mr. Johnson and cleaned the guard's wound. "You shouldn't need stitches; let me check for a concussion, though." He stated that he was relieved Mr. Johnson didn't have dilated pupils, a condition that would suggest a possible brain injury.

With lights flashing, the ambulance arrived outside the door, having used the service entrance. Dr. Chambers showed the emergency medical technicians (EMT) to the guards.

"We're taking you to Aberdeen Regional Hospital," said Dr. Chambers to Mr. Johnson. "We want to make sure you're okay."

"Dad," said Will, "can I talk to you for a minute?" They moved off to the side. Will chose his words carefully. "Do we need to call the police?"

"I already have." Will's face made Dr. Chambers pause. "They have to know, Will. People have been injured, and we have to check for other damage."

"No, Dad, I checked the PV system and it's fine."

"Was this about the PV system?" Dr. Chambers looked puzzled. "And why don't you want the police involved?" Will squirmed.

"The man who called this afternoon called again. He's the anonymous donor; the one who funded the PV system." His father registered the new information.

"And? Go on."

"The caller said that he was the donor and that the system would be attacked, but he didn't want the police to know anything about him."

There was a moment of silence. "Uh, I don't see how we can leave that out."

"He doesn't want the police looking for him . . . He wanted to stop the attack, but he was too far away." Just then the EMTs interrupted, wanting to know whether they were waiting for the police.

Dr. Chambers exhaled. "Yes, we are." Mr. Hillstrom was now resting on a gurney. "Let me do a quick check around here to make sure nothing is missing."

The baby tiger had settled down. A serene anaconda, a permanent lodger of the hospital, balanced at the top of his cage, watching everything. The only damaged article was the small case that contained the syringes. One had been used on the guard and another was missing.

"Well," said Dr. Chambers, "it could have been worse." More police sirens sounded in the distance, and he snapped to attention. "Let's hope they find the assailants."

"Dr. Chambers," Darius spoke up, "The criminals left some tools and other stuff."

"Dad, if you'd like, I can stay and talk to the police," Will said, knowing his father wanted to go to the hospital with the guards.

"Okay," said his father, "but you'll have to lock up."

Remembering the darkened metal, Will said, "Dad, the side entrance lock is broken."

Darius jumped in. "I'll call Seever's Lock Repair and give them the type and model. My mom had one fixed at the store and they did the whole thing in fifteen minutes."

"All right," said Dr. Chambers, "have them bill the Aberdeen Zoo, attention to me." The doctor turned to the seated guard. "The police'll want to talk with you, Mr. Johnson. I'm afraid Mr. Hillstrom'll be under sedation for a while." He turned to Audrey and Will. "Go meet the police in the parking lot. Keep your hands visible and high; be very calm. Bring them directly here."

Will and Audrey met up with two police officers. They quickly explained the situation to a tall, dark-haired officer named McGuiggan who asked, "Do you think the intruders are still here?"

"We don't know," said Will.

Arriving at the hospital, the officers made a quick search around the building then came back.

"There are a lot of places to hide here," said Officer McGuiggan as he began his report. Darius showed them the damaged lock, and the officers took photos, checked for fingerprints, and gave the okay for a locksmith.

After questioning Mr. Johnson, Officer McGuiggan allowed the EMTs and Dr. Chambers to load the two guards into the ambulance.

"Will," said the doctor as the driver started up the vehicle, "I'm not sure how long I'll be at Aberdeen Regional. Call your mother and explain what's happened. Tell her no one's seriously hurt. The Lundstroms gave her a ride—she'll be home already." Then he left to follow the ambulance.

Will answered further questions from Officer McGuiggan and his partner. Hesitating, he left out any mention of the second phone call.

Darius and Audrey went to meet the locksmith in the parking lot. The officers headed into the grounds with Will and Comox. Their powerful flashlights swept across the walkways. They moved along the path where he and Darius had chased after the man. Except for an occasional shriek from a monkey or a bird, all was quiet. Comox didn't growl once.

After a long search that yielded nothing, Will and the police returned to the zoo hospital. Audrey was speaking softly to the baby tiger. Darius was with the locksmith, who'd finished installing a new lock and was packing up to leave. The police took the damaged lock as evidence.

Officer McGuiggan gave Will a sharp look. "Do you think the attackers are people you know? Someone you go to school with?"

"No," answered Will, and Darius also shook his head. The officers accepted their denials. The police packed up the lock, the syringe, the ladder, the tools, the anchoring equipment, and the ropes. They planned to keep surveillance on the zoo hospital until morning, and they gave Will, Audrey, and Darius permission to go. Will called his mother, keeping it short. The three friends and Comox exited through the hospital door with the officers waiting outside. Will locked up and was pleased to hear the dead bolt click smoothly into place.

Escorting them to the parking lot, the officers asked, "Any of you need a ride?" The teenagers said no and pointed to the gold jeep. Will gave them the gate code, and the officers headed back into the grounds.

When they got to the jeep, Darius groaned. The tire on the rear driver's side was slashed wide open. The vehicle leaned to one side.

"It wasn't like that when I came back for Comox!" said Audrey.

"They doubled back," said Will, holding tight on to Comox's leash.

"To make sure we couldn't follow?" said Darius.

"Or maybe," said Audrey, "to show us that we shouldn't mess with them."

"Look, I know we have to report this," sighed Will, "but for tonight, can we just go home?" The others nodded. Then he clapped Darius on the shoulder. "Man, I am so glad you're the kind of guy who has his spare tire ready to go." Suddenly they were laughing, the tension draining away. They quickly removed the slashed tire and put the spare in its place.

Then Darius called home. "Mom, I know it's late—I'll explain when I get there," he said being very calm. He'd missed four phone calls, all of them from her. Will and Audrey could hear Mrs. Cheng's voice, and she was anything but calm. "I'm dropping off Will, and I'll be right home. Bye." He gave his friends a grin. "She'd go crazy if she knew what'd happened tonight."

Arriving at the Chambers home, Will asked Darius not to say anything to Mrs. Cheng about the second warning phone call, or even the first if he could manage it.

"I'll try," said Darius. "She'll either chase me off to bed or want to know every detail. I'll yawn a lot so I can go right to my room."

At Will's home, Mrs. Chambers was standing just inside the front door, waiting with an ashen face.

"Mom," said Will, "we're fine, Dad's okay, and the hired guards are too. One was drugged and the other was tied up, but nothin' serious happened. We got there before the guy could do any more damage."

"You shouldn't have gone at all!" she said. "What if you or Audrey or Darius had been hurt, eh? Will, I—" she broke off as Will gave her a big hug.

"We're okay, Mom!" he said. She turned and began to fuss over Audrey.

"I'm fine, Mrs. Chambers," said Audrey. "I was never in any danger, and Comox was right there with me. The police came, and they're searching the grounds now; they're going to catch those men."

"Men?" Mrs. Chambers looked stunned. "There was more than one?"

"We saw only one," said Will, trying to downplay what had happened. They moved Mrs. Chambers into the kitchen and sat her in a chair, the same way in which they'd helped Mr. Johnson.

"Why did you go at all?" she asked.

Audrey looked at Will. She knew he was trying not to mention the second phone call because of the captain's request and to safeguard the donation.

Will dodged the question. "We did end up saving the PV system, Mom. That's what the guy was after." He could have hugged Audrey for what she did next.

"Mrs. Chambers," Audrey said with a huge yawn, "is it all right if I go to bed? I'm beat!" That looked true enough—Audrey had dark circles under both eyes.

"Of course! We all should!" Lucky for them, Mrs. Chambers believed in early to bed, early to rise. "Your father just called; he'll be home any minute. We can sort this out in the morning."

Comox was tired too. He'd lapped up most of the contents of his silver water dish and had flopped down on the kitchen floor. He happily headed upstairs to his checkered cushion.

As Will climbed into bed, he heard the garage door open for his father's car. He thought about how he hadn't mentioned the second phone call to the police. It made him feel uncomfortable, but he couldn't ignore the stronger feeling that he'd done the right thing.

Call me Captain Glow, the voice had said. If the captain hadn't called again, two guards would be lying on the ground at the zoo and the solar PV system would have been smashed to bits.

PART 2

THE ELECTRIC-VEHICLE LAB

CHAPTER
3

A FEW DAYS LATER, WILL, Audrey, and Darius met with the officers once more, this time at the Aberdeen Police Station. Darius told Officer McGuiggan about the slashed tire. Will still avoided referring to the man who'd called himself Captain Glow but decided to share one more thing.

"Officer," he said, sitting with Darius and Audrey in the sparse gray interview room, "there's something I left out." The officer looked up from his laptop. Will went on. "I'd forgotten. The guy on the phone mentioned a name. He said the attacker was called—uh—'Sainos.'"

"Sainos?"

"Yes. He goes by the nickname of, well, "*Insaino*."

"Insaino?" said Officer McGuiggan pointedly.

"I—he, he only mentioned it once," answered Will. "Then he hung up."

"Have you heard that name before?"

"No," said Will. Officer McGuiggan added it to the report.

"Okay, thank you for your help." Relief flooded through Will's body. They were free to go.

As they left the police station, Darius turned to Will and Audrey. "I gotta get a new tire."

They drove five blocks, parked the jeep, and entered a medium-sized one-story brick building that bore a sign advertising Quality Tires. Crossing the gleaming showroom floor, Darius went straight over to a long, beige countertop.

"I need a Crawler KM2 tire for a Jeep Wrangler," he said to the tall, burly man behind the counter. The man began scrolling through information on a computer.

Darius was comfortable doing this. For the past few years he'd helped to handle his family's car maintenance and many other things due to sad circumstances. When he was only three, his father, a well-respected geologist, was killed in a climbing expedition. An avalanche on Mount Rainier had claimed the life of Darius's father and two others. After the accident, Darius and his mother moved from Seattle to Aberdeen, Utah. They lived there with Darius's Auntie Lin and then found a home of their own. During the sad years that followed, Mrs. Cheng had poured great love and affection into her only child.

Four years ago, Darius's aunt had completed nursing school and moved back to Seattle during the pandemic to accept a job there. Darius and his mother had decided to stay in Utah, liking the vibrant, friendly small-town atmosphere of Aberdeen.

Mrs. Jing Cheng was now quite a popular salesperson at a local furniture store. Her eye for beauty and design made her a favorite among Aberdeen's well-to-do. Darius, now sixteen, had grown up with the support of local friends and teachers.

Through Will and Darius's relationship, the Chambers family had come to know the Chengs well, and they helped Darius and his mother find good car mechanics, plumbers, and physicians. Darius was now comfortable taking care of his jeep and his mother's Toyota and was confident about getting the repair done today.

The shop displayed stacks of large, new tires. "Will you have to pay for this yourself?" asked Audrey, sounding indignant.

"Calm down, Audrey," Will laughed. "Darius has auto insurance and it covers vandalism. The police report's filed and Darius just needs to get the tire and submit the receipt."

"And that's what I'm doing," said Darius. "But your plea for justice is most appreciated."

The muscular man looked up from his computer screen. "We have that tire in stock. Here's the cost, plus labor charges," he said, turning the monitor around so Darius could see the display.

Darius looked it over and said, "That's fine. Please put the new tire on the rear of the driver's side and have the spare remounted onto the back."

"Will do," said the man with good cheer.

"Hold on," came a jeering voice from behind them, "who's that talking?" A large young man with a trashy-looking T-shirt and low-hanging, baggy jeans came around from behind a tall stack of tires. He looked about the same age as Will, Darius, and Audrey.

Sauntering up to the counter and pointing to Darius he asked, "What's this guy doing here?"

Darius stiffened. It was Fletcher Stiles, who was a year older than Darius and the others, but in the same grade at school.

Six years earlier, when Fletcher and Darius were in the same fourth-grade class, Fletcher had begun to bully the younger boy. Fletcher punched and tripped Darius, calling him names like *squarious* or *squinty-eyes*. Fletcher often said, "It hurts me to look at you."

More than a few times, teachers reprimanded Fletcher. By the time they were in fifth grade, Fletcher got a week's suspension due to his derisive behavior. After that, he merely simplified things by bullying Darius when no teachers were around.

By sixth grade, Darius was top in every academic subject. At first Fletcher didn't care, but as time went on, he seemed to take this success as a personal affront. Fletcher was also a troublemaker in other areas, sometimes damaging school equipment, but he was always crafty enough that he didn't get caught.

One of those sixth-grade bullying incidents introduced Darius to Will. It was springtime, and Fletcher, who was taller than most other sixth-graders, had a baseball bat. The weather was mild and sunny, a perfect day to practice hitting the ball. Instead, Fletcher chose to corner Darius at the bike rack.

Will, who was getting his bicycle nearby, looked over. There was no mistaking the fear on Darius's face or the cruel smile on Fletcher's. Will did the only thing he could think to do: he lifted a dangling whistle from his pack and blew.

Fletcher froze. He stared at Will and then spat through clenched teeth, "Stay out of this."

Will responded by blowing harder. Fletcher glared. The exchange gave Darius enough time to back away from the bike rack. Two older boys who were twenty paces away had also looked to see what was happening.

Fletcher, feeling the older boys' gaze, decided to back off. He'd gotten in a lot of trouble for that suspension and didn't want to risk it. He smacked the baseball bat down hard on the seat of Darius's bike.

As the two older boys came over, Fletcher tossed the bat vertically in the air, caught it in the middle, and trotted away. The four boys watched him go. Darius thanked them for their help.

Will and Darius rode home together, keeping a sharp eye out for the bully. That's when they discovered their homes were only five blocks apart, and from that day on, they were friends.

The summer between sixth and seventh grade, the two took a Green River rafting trip and a camping trip with Michael and Dr. Chambers. They took a Tae Kwon Do class and rode their bikes together everywhere. During the school year, Will and Michael were usually with Darius during free time and finally Fletcher reached the conclusion that it was easier to leave Darius alone.

But today, when their paths crossed again, Fletcher's usual antagonism flared.

Will stepped in. "Just buying a tire, Fletcher. That's all."

"Is that so?" Fletcher sneered. "The stupid creep run over something pointy—like his head?" Audrey's sharp intake of breath made Fletcher look at her. His face changed. He paused then said in mock wonder, "Now why would a girl like you wanna hang out with these creeps?"

The man behind the counter spoke sharply, "Fletcher, go out to the shop and give Kyle a hand."

"Just havin' fun, Jim," Fletcher shot back.

"Do I hafta call your dad?" Jim's eyes flashed.

"Nah, not worth it!" snapped Fletcher. He crossed behind the counter and went through a door into the back. Jim looked annoyed and then relieved.

"Sorry," he said. "My nephew is . . ." he rolled his eyes, suggesting he'd had trouble with Fletcher before. He resumed a professional manner. "Your jeep will be ready in twenty minutes. Do you have the keys?" Darius handed over a single key attached to a key ring with a rubber sea turtle on it.

They sat in chairs in the middle of the room. Audrey quietly asked, "Who was that horrible person?"

"Fletcher Stiles," muttered Will. "Not anyone you want to know. His uncle Jim runs this place. He's okay, but Fletcher's not."

"Rotten to the core," said Darius. The two young men explained the past events to Audrey and then eager to move on, they scanned a travel magazine and played a short game on Will's phone.

Minutes later Jim Stiles called out, "You're all set." Darius went to the counter and ran his debit card through the reader. He punched in his PIN and the transaction was approved.

Jim gave Darius a receipt along with his key, and the three went outside. There was the jeep, its spare tire back in place.

In the days that followed, all was quiet. To protect the zoo hospital, Dr. Chambers and Tom Varchecko purchased a new sophisticated alarm system. It was installed two days after the failed attack, and the zoo hospital posted extra guards for several weeks.

With everything in place, Dr. Chambers told his family and Audrey, "Thankfully, there have been no strange occurrences and no buildings have been broken into. We might not have any more trouble."

———

In mid-june, will approached his parents about his science fair project.

"I'd like to do a study about electric bikes."

At the mention of electric bikes, Dr. Chambers' face lit up.

"I know a fellow at the university, who—wait, his name is . . . Professor Larry Sheffield! He runs an electric vehicle (EV) research lab there. Look him up and send him an email."

Will did. The following day he had a short meeting with Professor Sheffield, who approved the design for his project. He came back from the lab hopeful and a bit overwhelmed. As they sat around the supper table that night, Audrey expressed curiosity.

"Why are you interested in electric bikes, Will?"

"E-biking could be a great low-cost substitute for a car that often just sits in a parking lot all day," Will explained.

She pressed him. "Anything else?"

He gave her a smile. "Yes, professor—an e-bike is emission-free and doesn't take much electricity to recharge."

"And . . . do you think all vehicles should be electric?"

He liked being asked these serious questions. He sat up taller. "No—to power heavy equipment, you'd probably need fuel cells or conventional combustion engines. For example, an electric bulldozer would need a ton of batteries, and they'd drain too quickly."

"Charging systems for electric cars are seeing great breakthroughs, though," Will continued. He'd been following several interesting car battery industries on the web. "The most competitive design is . . . uhh . . ." he had to work to get it right, "rechargeable, lithium-ion batteries that can power a car for more than four hundred miles on a single charge."

"Oh, wow. How long do they take to recharge?" she asked, thinking of her phone.

"Depends on what car you have and what level charger you're using," he shrugged. "If the vehicle is a Tesla, they just rolled out a supercharger that can give you a 250-mile range in fifteen minutes. The ratio is one thousand miles of range per hour of charge. They use liquid-cooled cables to make the fast charge possible."

"That's impressive," said his dad. "How about the others?"

"The other electric vehicle (EV) automakers also have rapid DC chargers for sale, but it's more like thirty to forty minutes to recharge."

"And if you're not at home?" asked Mrs. Chambers.

"There are public charging stations with Level 1, 2, or 3 chargers. Level 3 is the fast DC charger. Level 1 is the slowest, with a full recharge taking eighteen to twenty hours, and—" he had to stop and think, "Level 2 takes four to eight hours for a full recharge."

"Are there lots of charging stations?" asked Audrey.

"EV makers would like to see a lot more," he grinned. "The makers might have to build some. But businesses that sell gasoline are starting to put in charging stations too."

"And when you recharge at home?" she asked.

"At home the standard outlet of 120 volts is the Level 1 charger. The good news is most people in the United States drive only thirty to thirty-five miles per day, so the battery's not going to need a full charge every day. That means a battery could easily be recharged overnight on the Level 1 charger."

"What about natural gas vehicles instead?" Audrey probed.

"Oh, right—CNG—compressed natural gas," Will nodded. "Some companies have switched their fleets to natural gas, but natural gas engines could be . . . just transitional until EVs or fuel-cell vehicles replace them."

Dr. Chambers chimed in, "Things change daily, but in looking at converting zoo trucks to natural gas, Mr. Varcheko found that replacing natural gas tanks can be costly—they have to be re-certified every five years, and when the tank's expiration date is reached, that's it. You have to get a new tank. It's for safety reasons, but it can be costly—from $600 to $3,000 dollars."

"And," added Will, "burning natural gas still puts particulates in the air. True, they emit fewer particulates, but having no particulates at all would be best."

Then Mrs. Chambers, who'd been silent until then, said, "I hope you don't mind these scientific discussions we have, Audrey."

"No," said Audrey, "I like them; they're interesting!"

Mrs. Chambers continued, "Another concern is natural gas wells. First off, the drilling process called fracking can cause earthquakes. Second, experts say that 20 percent of wells end up with cement casing jobs that will leak! But worst of all, fracking uses a huge amount of fresh water and then creates an *astounding* amount of wastewater—which is full of toxic chemicals. Leakage from the cement casing plus the wastewater does contaminate our below-surface water; we don't know how much, but we know spills and contamination happen."

"Yup," Dr. Chambers agreed. "Above-ground water flow, such as rivers, is well-mapped, but we have much less of an understanding of our underground water systems, aquifers, and how they connect. The National Ground-Water Monitoring Network probably doesn't have the funding it ought to—I'm referring to our geology people." He beamed at his wife.

"Lloyd's right. Geologists are the protectors of our groundwater systems," said Mrs. Chambers. "My dad's a retired geologist, and he supports rigorous monitoring of groundwater."

"Absolutely," said Dr. Chambers. "Looking on the bright side, there's something new called power to gas, where synthetic natural gas is made safely aboveground."[1] The doctor stuck his spoon enthusiastically into his rice pudding. "Refined natural gas or synthetic natural gas are the same thing: methane. Right now leaky methane pipe systems put a sloppy excess of particulates in our atmosphere." He took a deep breath. "Fortunately, there are proposed national standards that could, for the first time, directly regulate methane emissions." He stopped and smiled. "Basically, we have to plug the methane leaks. And with this new[2] power-to-gas technology, it's clear that creating natural gas above ground offers more protection to groundwater. My father always said, 'Never risk anything you can't afford to lose'—and we can't afford to lose clean water."

"Agreed," said Mrs. Chambers.

"So, what are we looking at?" the doctor continued. "We know burning fossil fuels damages clean water and air. We like nuclear power advancements such as a traveling wave reactor (TWR) because these burn up discarded radioactive fuel from the old outmoded reactors. But still,

1. For Footnote Link go to Captain Glow Website
2. For Footnote Link go to Captain Glow Website

traveling wave reactors are in the development stage and could take awhile."

He looked around the table. "I don't say change is easy." Voicing respect, he added, "We thank those old industries for the past century they gave us—we're grateful! But it's time we see new inventions make their contributions!'"

Audrey smiled at Will as Mrs. Chambers gave her husband's arm a loving squeeze.

———

TWO WEEKS LATER ON a sunlit morning in the last week of June, all four were finishing up breakfast. The doctor took a last bite. He was due to prep a miserable, sweet hippopotamus named Little Pete for dental surgery on his touchy, impacted molar. Rising from the table, the doctor grabbed his notebook, gave his wife a peck on the cheek, and raced out the door.

The others finished their eggs and sausages and then began to clear the table. Mrs. Chambers scooped up the pineapple juice as Audrey handed dishes to Will, who loaded them into the dishwasher.

"Will," said Mrs. Chambers, looking at a big paper calendar on the wall, "you're going to the university today, right?"

"I'm leaving now," answered Will. "Audrey, you wanna come along?" He hoped she'd say yes.

"Definitely!" she answered. She'd already been there twice.

He grabbed his backpack. "Let's take the double-bike. It needs air in the tires, anyway."

"Please do!" his mother urged. "Your father and I rode it just the other day, and we were puffing like old geezers." Will and Audrey laughed. "I know we're not young, but I think those tires are almost flat."

"Sure about that?" teased Will. "Maybe you *are* old geezers."

Mrs. Chambers protested, "We've got a few good years left!"

"Of course you do!" said Audrey. Will grinned and called to Comox. The plan was to inflate the tires and then meet Darius at his home.

"We can go to the 7-Eleven. They have an air pump there," said Will, jingling the four quarters in his pocket needed to run the air compressor. Entering the garage, they grabbed the purple double-bike and backed it out into the driveway.

"What can I say? Your double-bike . . . it's—it's a classic!" giggled Audrey as she hopped on the back.

"The 'purple-people-eater'? Ha! Maybe—but it can be embarrassing when your folks are riding around on it," said Will over his shoulder as he steadied the handlebars.

"Oh, your folks are great! They're fun!"

"Right . . . heel, Comox," said Will, pushing the pedal down. Off they went, Comox loping alongside.

At the 7-Eleven, they parked the bike, and Will slipped the quarters into the air compressor. The pump roared to life. He unscrewed a plastic cap from the front tire valve and pushed the metal nozzle into it. As air began to flow, the tire stiffened up. He did the same with the back one. He felt the firmness of the tire sides. Satisfied that they were close to the correct pressure, he put the plastic caps back on, wound up the hose, and hung it on two large hooks attached to the side of the compressor. At that moment, two girls came out of the convenience store with a carton of eggs.

"Hello, Will!" they called out.

"Hi!" answered Will. "What are you guys doing?"

"Getting eggs for Mom. She's making her fab-u-li-cious flourless chocolate cake again," said the taller of the two girls.

"Great! Save me a slice," said Will, remembering the scrumptious cake from a school party.

Jackie and Margaret Clayberry, two lively sisters who were rarely seen apart, were close in age: Margaret was in Will's class, and Jackie, just one year older, was entering her senior year. "Where're you going?" asked Margaret. She was a brunette with a ready smile and dark-brown eyes.

"Over to the university." Will introduced Audrey to his friends, explaining that she'd be coming to Aberdeen High in the fall.

"Great," said Margaret. "You'll like it; it's an awesome school."

Audrey, who was entering her junior year along with Will and Margaret, asked, "Are you taking precalculus?"

"Have to," said Margaret, her brown eyes twinkling. "I want to become a nurse practitioner, so I need the math."

"I took it last year. It can be a slog," said Jackie, throwing back her blonde hair. "But if you do the work every night and get help when you need it, you'll be fine." Margaret rolled her eyes, indicating she'd heard this lecture before.

"What's happening at the university?" asked Jackie.

"I'm working on an electric bike project for the science fair."

"Wow, you're starting early," said Margaret. "What's it about?"

"I'm going to collect data from thirty electric bike riders, cyclists—then I'm going to use a GPS app to measure the distance covered and the electricity they've used."

"And after you've collected all this data, what're you going to do with it?" asked Jackie.

"I should be able to calculate what size solar PV micro-grid any facility would need for x-number of electric bikes. The micro-grid would charge up the bikes at a school or at any business.

"Cool," said Jackie.

Just then Margaret got a text. "Oooh, Jackie, we'd better get home with the eggs; Mom's waiting. Good luck with your bike stuff—and it's great to meet you, Audrey."

"See you guys," said Will. He, Audrey, and Comox moved out into the bike lane. Just then a large red truck came barreling around the corner.

"Look out!" screamed Jackie. Will yanked the bike back, throwing himself and Audrey onto the grassy boulevard. The silver-haired driver whooshed past, missing them by inches. He didn't stop or even slow down. The plates on the back were dealer plates, so there was no way to identify the driver.

"What a jerk!" said Margaret angrily. "You guys okay?"

Will nodded and looked at Audrey. "You?" She nodded. They patted Comox, who wagged his tail. Will yanked the double-bike off the ground. He and Audrey climbed on, and Audrey gave the two girls a wave.

"Heel, Comox," called Will. Five minutes later, they were at Darius's house where he was waiting with his new bike. It was electric and Darius already loved it. His data would be part of Will's science project.

The weather was perfect and soon the teenagers arrived at the university's new engineering building, which housed the electric vehicle (EV) lab on the main floor. They locked their bikes onto a bike rack and secured Comox under a shady tree.

Entering the building, they moved along the main hallway, which was lined with research posters and two large electronic screens that also showed research projects.

"This one's interesting," said Darius, stopping at a poster on hydrokinetic power. It featured a cylindrical, multi-finned device that converted the energy of waves, tidal currents, ocean currents, or river currents into electricity. The device had completed successful trials in Alaska, and the project was seeking investment dollars. Darius read out, "These submerged systems will provide significantly cheaper, cleaner electrical power to remote Alaskan villages that are not able to be on the grid. In these remote locations, the cost of diesel-generated electricity can be over ten times the cost paid by grid-connected customers."[3]

"Reduced cost is good," said Will. "My dad really liked the lower electricity costs for the zoo hospital. The monthly summer bill went way down."

At the end of the hallway, they pushed through a set of blue double doors. Though it was summertime, the lab was full of people coming and going from the research areas. Dr. Larry Sheffield, the professor in charge of the lab, turned around as Will, Audrey, and Darius walked in.

"Hello, Will. I see you've brought your friends again," said the professor. He turned to Audrey as he said, "Your mother is a botanist doing plant research in Chile, right?"

"Yes," said Audrey, blushing slightly.

"Hmm," he paused thoughtfully. "The Chilean seaweed biofuel work ran into a huge cost barrier. But I suppose she's not involved in that."

"No," nothing with seaweed," she said.

---

3. For Footnote Link go to Captain Glow Website

"Well, we're looking here at *carinata*, a mustard seed strain that can be mixed with jet fuel,"[4] said the professor, simultaneously checking an instrument reading and then moving to a rack of beakers. He took one out, looked at the cloudy contents for a moment, put it back, and lifted another one. "I believe the carinata seed can deliver benefits. The Chilean problem was that seaweed is worth *more* left as seaweed!" He smiled and added, "Finding workable solutions for the world's fuel needs is a challenge, but I think we're up to it."

"Professor Sheffield?" they heard a voice call. Mrs. Cottle, the lab secretary, was peering around the lab-room door. "A gentleman just stopped by your second-floor office and left something for you."

Professor Sheffield looked surprised. "Did I have an appointment with him?"

"No, but he said it's urgent that you look at the paperwork he left for you."

Professor Sheffield put the beaker of slurry back in the rack and left. Will crossed the room to a bulletin board and signed in on his project sheet. Then he headed through a door and down a hallway with Audrey and Darius at his heels. Opening a side door, they entered a computer lab, where Will put down his pack and logged in. Today he planned to finish the initial design of his experiment.

---

4. For Footnote Link go to Captain Glow Website

"You can show Audrey the lab where they're growing and processing the carinata strains," he suggested to Darius. Will's friends left him to work.

When Will was almost finished, he mumbled to himself, "I think that'll work—"

"What'll work?" a friendly voice interrupted. Will swiveled around to see his friend TR Bartson. TR was tall and fit with smooth brown skin the color of caramel.

"Hey, TR, when did you get back?" said Will.

"Two days ago. And Yellowstone was great!" TR, who was named after the well-loved American president Theodore Roosevelt, was a high-school student heading into his senior year. He was employed part-time at Professor Sheffield's lab working on the carinata project. Will stood up to stretch and just then Darius and Audrey returned.

"Audrey," Will said, "This is TR. He's a—"

"Let me handle the introductions. You finish your stuff," urged Darius. Will agreed and sat down to put the finishing touches on his design worksheet.

"TR Bartson, this is Audrey Carter," said Darius. "She's going to be a junior. She's staying with Will's family and is going to school in Aberdeen while her folks are in Santiago, Chile. Audrey, this is TR Bartson—also known as Theodore Roosevelt Bartson—who is also known as the man with the incredible green thumb."

TR laughed. "It's really the magic of water, sunlight and soil." His smile radiated confidence.

Darius continued "His mother is a fearsomely able math teacher at Aberdeen High who tolerates no goofing off."

"Amen," said TR. "My mom's mother was good friends with Eleanor Green Dawley Jones, one of the first fifteen African-American women to get a PhD in mathematics. My mom's pretty fired up where math is concerned."

"And," Darius went on, "you'll probably have her for precalculus."

TR broke in, "I sweated over every math test I ever took, but I passed! I'm not sure I have my mom's math gene, but if you need help with plants—I'm your guy." Audrey laughed.

Darius said, "He's serious. You should see the pumpkins he grows. They're bigger than Comox!" They talked about the work that TR was doing for Professor Sheffield. He was trying to decide what university program to choose as he entered his senior year.

"What are you going to study in college?" Audrey asked.

"Either landscape architecture or a focus on engineering and biofuels," he said. Then his face lit up. "Say, Darius . . . are you guys available to help me finish some landscaping around the new outdoor stage at the high school?" He gave them a winning smile. "It'll only take a couple of hours."

Darius laughed, "He's persuasive too."

"I can help," said Will, who'd put his notebook into his pack and rejoined the group.

"I'm in," said Darius. Audrey agreed to come too.

"Well," said TR, "let's get lunch and plant some trees."

"Trees!" exclaimed Will.

"They're just little ones, Will. Small cottonwoods—the kind with no fluff. Fast growers."

"See what I mean about Mr. Green-jeans?" said Darius.

They left the computer room. Coming into the main room, they heard the excited voices of Professor Sheffield and a bearded, barrel-chested professor named Zubner. Both seemed overjoyed.

"We've just received a huge cashier's check!" Professor Sheffield was telling Zubner. "It's a gift from an unspecified donor. The only stipulations are that the money be used *only* for our clean energy research—no problem there. And as there are no other strings attached, the donor does not wish to be contacted or mentioned!"

"Wunderbar!" said Professor Zubner in his native German accent.

"And I was assured the funds are from a legal source," Professor Sheffield added. "It's mind-boggling." He was clearly overwhelmed.

"Vhen did zis happen?"

"Less than an hour ago! He left the check with Mrs. Cottle, along with specific legal instructions. He left before I could meet him." Professor Sheffield halted, noticing the presence of the students.

Will had frozen when he heard the words *unspecified donor* and *does not wish to be contacted or mentioned.* Those were the same instructions for the PV system last spring when it was offered to the zoo hospital. *Captain Glow again?* Will couldn't ask Professor Sheffield questions—it wasn't any of his business.

Professor Zubner chortled. "Now ve can pay off zee new parts to convert ze diesel bus! Zis is great news, dear students!" Delighted over the funding, he gestured broadly. "An IMC system iz zee perfect choice. Please, I vill explain. IMC iz zee letters meaning in-motion charging. Vhat iz good about using in-motion-charging electric buses? Zey do not make air pollution!" Glasses askew, Professor Zubner bounced on the balls of his feet. Christmas had come early to the biofuels and electric vehicle research labs.

At Professor Zubner's urging, TR snatched up a brochure wedged under a *Bus Technology Today* magazine. The brochure was from a company that makes electric buses. TR quoted from the front cover. "By keeping the air clean and being cheaper to run, our buses make the quality of life better wherever they operate."[5]

"But buying ze brand new bus does not educate. So— our goal is to buy zee parts and convert a diesel bus to become an IMC electric bus."

---

5. For Footnote Link go to Captain Glow Website

"What makes an in-motion-charging bus work?" asked Will.

Professor Sheffield answered. "An IMC electric bus has onboard batteries that hold enough charge so that the bus can operate away from the charging pads. The charging pads are either overhead or under the road surface."

"Under the road surface?" asked Darius.

"Yes, the pads can be under the road surface. The bus only needs to be recharged at intervals from those pads."

"It's like an electric toothbrush—where it has power even when it's not at its charging source," said TR, who knew something of this technology already.

Professor Sheffield nodded. Then he turned to a computer screen and pulled up a video link that showed an IMC bus in operation.[6]

"Impressive," said Darius after watching it. Will, Audrey, and TR grinned.

"And," Professor Sheffield added, "we'll be taking a portable system out for demonstrations. We use several electric go-carts and a charging pad." He pointed to a diagram on the wall that showed an electric car that got its charge from a pad beneath it.

---

6. For Footnote Link go to Captain Glow Website

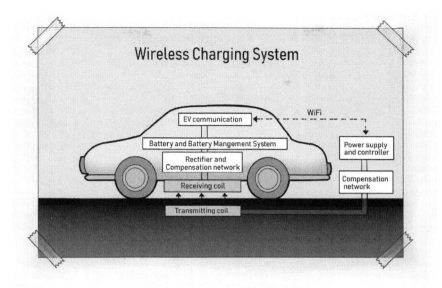

TR's eyes lit up. "So that's what my brother, Benjamin, and the other lab guys are working on."

"Yes, yes, but don't spoil the surprise, TR! We're keeping it under wraps until the STEM picnic."

"The what?" said Audrey.

"We'll tell you about it over lunch," said TR. "Come on, let's go."

Will signed out on the project sheet and said, "That's great, Professor Sheffield! We won't say a word." Then he hesitated. *Should I mention the anonymous donor?* He decided he wouldn't.

CHAPTER

4

Two weeks later, the high school held its annual science, technology, engineering, and math picnic, also known as the STEM picnic. The event was popular with students and their families. It was always held on the high-school grounds and started at five in the afternoon. July was hot in Utah, but the tall cottonwood trees bordering on the grassy areas provided lots of shade.

The school's math department was in charge of the food, the science department was in charge of the games, and the music department was in charge of the entertainment. Lorna Bartson, TR's mom, was a talented and energetic math teacher. She was also one of the STEM picnic supervisors. She bustled about, making sure there was ample table space for all the food. Desserts and salads were donated by those coming to the picnic.

Will, Audrey, and Darius surveyed the new outdoor stage that was being used for the first time that day. Audrey trotted over to look at a particular small green bush.

"Our landscape work turned out great!" boasted Darius.

Will snorted. "I think TR has the bragging rights to that, but yeah, we helped."

"Will!" called Audrey. An older man in the distance heard her, and he fixed his gaze on Will. He wore a slouchy hat and turned his head away when Will noticed him staring.

"Will, come here," called Audrey. "Look!" Will walked over to her. "The barberry plant has perked up." She beamed, gently touching a small leafy bush she'd planted only two weeks earlier. Will thought she probably had a talent for growing things, just like her mother and TR. He noticed that when he looked at her, his stomach sort of did . . . a flop. Right now, with her shiny auburn hair, she seemed to sparkle in her clean white T-shirt, blue tennis shoes, and jeans cuffed just above her knees. *Flip-flop.*

TR bounded over holding a cluster of green grapes. He wolfed some down and offered the rest to his friends. Margaret and Jackie Clayberry turned up with five of their mother's famous, delicious chocolate cakes, along with ripe strawberries to go on top.

"Put them over there, girls. Thank you! They look scrumptious!" said Mrs. Bartson, hurrying to their side. "There's some space on the table with the yellow cloth." She turned to Will. Her hair had frizzed out a little and her face shone. She was having a great time. "Are your mom and dad enjoying their conference in Hawaii?"

"They're lovin' it," said Will, and he pulled out his phone to show her the pictures. "See? Swimming with turtles . . . going to the Polynesian Cultural Center."

"Good for them," said Mrs. Bartson. "Heaven knows your father works hard. He deserves a vacation!" Just then they heard the twang of a guitar.

A three-piece band was setting up on the bottom level of the newly constructed stage, which was designed to look like a huge natural-rock formation. It was really a giant welded superstructure of steel that supported yards and yards of glass fiber-reinforced concrete (GFRC). On either side of the massive structure were stairs that looked like they had been hewn from rock. Only the stair railings hinted that the formation had not been made by nature.

There were four performance levels at differing heights, and all were rendered in colors of reddish-brown rock. At the uppermost tier, a gently rounded, huge boulder shape, was set at the very back, forming the rear wall needed to complete the topmost platform.

On the stage's second-highest area, set back to the right, were three rows of simple stone ledges that also looked sculpted from rock. The proportions were perfect for sitting on. The largest area was the bottom stage, in the center. Electrical outlets were hidden throughout and were designed to blend in. Will thought it looked as good as any Disneyland creation.

The young trees and shrubs that had recently been planted surrounded the formation. In time they'd give the immense stage an enchanting, majestic quality.

The three-man band began playing. The crowd swelled toward the stage, and the picnic was officially underway.

The Aberdeen High School principal, Mr. Parker, bounded onto the stage and stepped up to the mic. He was thirty-something with a crew cut; built like a football player, he had a square jaw, intelligent eyes, and a look that said he wouldn't tolerate nonsense for long.

He welcomed the picnic goers and introduced the band, The Haywires. Along with the rest of the crowd, Will, Audrey, Darius, and TR sat down to eat hot, fried chicken; chunks of honeydew melon and watermelon; warm, buttered carrots; and a green salad with slices of cucumber. They had their choices of desserts: gelato, apple crumble, ice cream, or a cold treat called Dreamies—which came on a stick—and, of course, the chocolate cakes. The kids made sure to grab a slice each, knowing the cakes would disappear quickly.

The musicians played rock-ballad music, and the audience loved it. At the side of the stage, the high-school band lined up, getting ready to play show tunes they'd been practicing in the spring. For the next two hours, there were games, potato-sack races for children, relay races, an ultimate Frisbee competition for the older kids, water-balloon battles, and even a tug-of-war tournament.

After a rousing fiddle group's melody got everyone up and dancing, applause rang out, and the music portion was over. Principal Parker took to the stage and thanked all the musicians for their performances.

Two figures ascended the stairs on the right. One was Professor Sheffield; the other was a science teacher, Mr. Bentley, a young man in his twenties who'd been at the school for three years. He went to the mic.

"Welcome, students and families. I'm Mr. Bentley, and I teach some of the science classes at Aberdeen High. Students, it's not too soon to start thinking about what you'd like to do for the science fair this coming year. Some of you might want to contact our local university to get ideas. If you already have an idea you're excited about, go for it!" He paused, looking at Principal Parker, who stood off to the side with a serious expression.

"Of course, we'll always proceed with great caution and care. We remember how Marty Dudeck's test-tube fire set off the alarms, but no harm was done! He had his safety googles on! And his eyebrows have almost completely grown back." Sitting in the front row, Marty Dudeck held up his arms in a triumphant muscleman pose. His eyebrows did still look a bit sparse.

"Moving on," said Mr. Bentley, "please welcome Professor Sheffield, an accomplished scientist and educator from

Aberdeen's state university. He has something special to share." The picnic goers applauded as Professor Sheffield stepped to the mic.

"Hello all! Thank you for inviting me to your excellent STEM picnic! I'm very pleased to be here. The food and music have been great. Having said that . . ." He cleared his throat. "Tonight, I'm here to share something different in the way of science! I'm in the engineering department at the university, and we have a new vehicle transportation system to show you. This exhibition will be given right now by our university's very own hardworking electric vehicle challenge team!"[7]

Professor Sheffield paused, and right on cue, the band-leader had his trumpet players do a fanfare. Members of the Aberdeen electric vehicle team, wearing navy-and-white T-shirts, lined up in front of the stage. Professor Sheffield boomed proudly, "Our team is going to demon-strate an electric vehicle transportation system over in the west parking lot. We've got a portable charging pad and two electric vehicles that will show clearly how an electric vehicle in-motion charging system works. He looked over the crowd. "Are any of you students thinking of going into engineering? If so, you'll be able to learn how these new IMC vehicles work and assist in converting an inter-nal combustion bus into an electric IMC bus. Please join

---

7. For Footnote Link go to Captain Glow Website

me and the team as we head over to our demo site." The professor left the mic, came down the steps, and merged with his team in front of the stage. Students and teachers followed them over to the parking lot.

A team member called out, "Mom, Dad, look at this—a vehicle that runs completely on electrons!" A man with a small child perched on top of his shoulders and his wife walked over to join their son. Professor Sheffield gave a few more remarks and launched the demonstration. The small electric one-person cars were guided by their drivers over the portable pad, which was laid out on the ground. The vehicles received a recharge for their onboard batteries, which would keep them going for a significant amount of time. The two machines glided elegantly around the large parking lot, where orange cones had been set in place to create an oval track.

Will noticed how TR's older brother, Benjamin, was using a large poster of the same diagram he'd seen in the lab, which displayed how the transmitting coil in the pad induced a charge into the receiving coil of the vehicles. Catching Will's attention, Professor Sheffield motioned him to come over.

"Will," he said, pulling away to speak more privately, "I have a grant application due and the deadline's tonight. So I just need to run back to the lab and quickly finish it up. Could you and one of your friends come by and pick me up from the lab and give me a ride back here, oh, say . . . around . . ." He looked at his watch. "Eight o'clock? That way, when I bring the demo system and the trailer back to the lab, I'll have my car there."

"Sure, I can do that," said Will.

"Great," said the professor, and he turned back to answer a student's question.

Will found Audrey, Darius, and TR. They were helping Mrs. Bartson return empty food platters to picnic goers who were leaving. Will was explaining how Professor Sheffield needed a ride when Mrs. Bartson motioned for him to come over and speak with her.

"Will," she said briskly, "could you please take these unopened Dreamies and potato salad tubs to the food bank? A man named Bill Beck is there, waiting to put them in the refrigerators, so could you go now?"

"Yes, I can do that," said Will.

"Bring your car to the curb and we'll help you load up." She beckoned to Audrey, Darius, and TR. They began transferring the unopened food from coolers to empty cardboard boxes. "Hey, you three," cajoled Mrs. Bartson, "I could use your help with some of the cleanup. Can you stay for, say, forty-five minutes?" They agreed.

Will headed to the car. As he approached the eastern parking lot, he saw Fletcher Stiles dart out from between two vehicles. Fletcher was with Delbert Korbelak, a thin, gangly youth who often hung out with him. As Will reached his mother's car, he saw Delbert and Fletcher move to a section used for driving instruction. Eight well-worn, slightly battered cars were parked in a long row near a chain-link fence.

The cars, which were used to teach students how to drive, sat near a section of the parking lot where the dark asphalt surface was painted with bright-yellow patterns. These were utilized by students to practice turns, signaling, backing up, and the dreaded parallel-parking maneuver.

Will saw Fletcher and Delbert approach one of the driver's ed cars and try the doors. Will came closer. *Should I get a teacher or just go?* As he hesitated, the car emitted a piercing noise. The alarm had gone off.

Fletcher and Delbert howled with laughter and dashed off, disappearing through an opening in the fence that led to the football field.

"What do you think you're doing?!" roared a voice behind Will. It was Mr. Robinson, an industrial-shop teacher who was also one of the driving instructors. The alarm continued to blare.

Panic rose in Will's chest as the large man charged him like an angry bull.

"I didn't do anything," said Will, looking back at the football field. Delbert and Fletcher were long gone.

"Don't move!" Mr. Robinson shouted, going over to the shrieking car and unlocking it to reset the alarm. He relocked it and came back. "What's your name?" he growled.

"Uh, Will Chambers, but sir, I didn't touch the car; it was—"

Mr. Robinson was in no mood to listen. "Stay away from these cars," he interrupted. "Understand?"

"I do; I mean, I did! I *was* staying away!" Will protested.

"Well," said Mr. Robinson, mopping his brow, "maybe it wasn't you, but whoever it was, tell them these cars are *off limits*! Got that?"

"Yes, sir," said Will respectfully. The driver's ed cars were clearly a serious concern for the man. With a final scowl, Mr. Robinson stomped off.

Will went to his mother's car, got out his keys, opened the door, and slid behind the wheel. He started the car and checked the gas-tank reading. It was almost full, which was good—because the gas float was off. The gauge showed a quarter of a tank when the tank was actually empty.

Mr. Beck, a lanky middle-aged man with wire-rimmed glasses, was waiting in front of the food bank. Together they unloaded the boxes from the car and into the building. With an expression of thanks, Mr. Beck waved Will off and disappeared into the building. Will looked at his watch. It was 7:46 p.m. and time to go to the engineering lab. As he pulled into the parking lot, he heard the familiar ding that meant he had a text message. To his astonishment, he read, "Sainos trapped inside Zubner's office. Dangerous, do not go near. Call police!"

Heart thumping, Will dialed 911 for the first time in his life. Police dispatch answered. "I'm reporting a break-in at the university," he said, "at the engineering building. The guy who broke in is still inside." The dispatcher took his name and number and confirmed that university police were on their way.

Will looked at the message again. "Dangerous, do not go near." *Well, too late for that,* he thought. He looked around. The empty parking lot was eerie in the twilight. He opened the car door and got out. *Should I wait for the police or go in?* Then, at the far end of the building, he saw a shadowy figure emerge from a single door. *Was it Captain Glow?* It was a man, but in the failing light, he couldn't make out any details.

A university police car skidded into the parking lot. Will watched the shadowy figure bolt through trees that hid a trail along the river. It led to a residential area, and Will knew if the man had parked his car there, he'd be gone in a moment. The university police car pulled up beside him.

"Are you Will Chambers?" asked the officer who was driving.

"Yes, I am." The officers shut their car off and got out. "The intruder's inside; he's trapped in an office."

"I'm Officer Holmes," said the man who'd been driving, "and this is Officer Dixon. Do you know anything about the intruder—is he armed?"

"No, sir, I don't," said Will, "but I can take you to Dr. Zubner's office."

"Is that where the intruder is?" asked Holmes.

"Yes, he's in an office on the second floor—on the east side."

"If everything looks clear, you can come with us as far as the second floor," Officer Holmes instructed. "You can point us in the right direction, but then we go alone. Understood?"

"Yes, sir."

The officers produced keys to the building and entered. As they climbed the stairs, Officer Holmes asked, "How did you know about this?"

Will showed them the text message on his phone.

"D'you know who this is from?" inquired Holmes.

"No."

The officer handed the phone back. "We'll check it later." They'd reached the second floor.

Will pointed down the hallway to the blue double doors. "It's through there—second door on the left." They could hear loud banging noises from inside.

"Let's go," said Holmes. The two officers approached the double doors cautiously. As they pushed them apart, the noise grew louder. The officers entered. Will held his breath and moved closer. He pushed one of the doors open. *Would Sainos fight back?* He watched as Holmes and Dixon pulled a tightly wedged chair from under the doorknob of Professor

Zubner's office. When they opened it, a man tumbled out. He was blindfolded, bound, and gagged.

It was Professor Sheffield. He had obviously been roughed up and had a red welt on his cheekbone. Officer Dixon lifted him from the floor.

"Wait—that's Professor Sheffield," Will said, rushing in. "He works here!" The officers looked from Will to the professor. They removed the man's gag and blindfold along with the tape that bound him.

"I *am* Professor Sheffield," he gasped. He had a lump the size of an egg on his forehead but otherwise seemed unharmed. "When I arrived, I heard noises in Zubner's office. That," he said, pointing to the fallen chair, "was wedged under the doorknob. Someone inside was banging on the door. When I answered him, he quieted down and said he'd been the victim of a prank, so I removed the chair. When I entered, he clubbed me from behind! With *that*, I suppose." He pointed to a gray paperweight whale that lay on the floor. "It almost knocked me out!" He rubbed the lump on his forehead gingerly. "Next thing I know I had a blindfold on and all this idiotic tape." The lab director was clearly embarrassed.

"Did you get a look at your assailant?" asked Officer Holmes.

"No!" said Professor Sheffield. "This is infuriating! I have no idea why he did this!"

"Any reason he'd be here?" asked Officer Holmes, looking around. "Petty cash? Anything worth stealing?"

The professor looked around the room and then said, "Nothing seems out of place. We don't have petty cash . . . but I'd like to check the other lab rooms. We do have valuable research equipment."

"Dixon, see if you can do a trace on that text message while the professor and I look around," Officer Holmes said to his partner. Will handed his phone to Officer Dixon as Officer Holmes left with Professor Sheffield.

The policeman, a large brown man with thoughtful eyes, made a few quick taps and then shook his head. "Bad news: the text is from a blocked number." He looked at Will. "So you really have no idea who sent it?"

"No," answered Will truthfully, "I'd like to know too."

Officer Dixon handed Will's phone back.

"Why do you think you got the message? And who's this Sainos?"

"I've no idea who Sainos is, but . . . I think I got the message because my phone number's posted right there." Will pointed to the bulletin board where his project sheet was tacked up. His cell phone number was right at the top. "I don't know why he had me call 911. Maybe the guy didn't want to get involved. But when Professor Sheffield arrived before us—"

"He freed the guy we were supposed to find," said Officer Dixon.

"Right," said Will. At that moment the blue doors burst open. It was TR, along with his older brother, Benjamin, and two other students.

"Hi, Will," said TR in surprise, looking from Will to Officer Dixon. "We brought the trailer and the demo system back. Where's Professor Sheffield? Everything okay?" Before Will could answer, Professor Sheffield was back with Officer Holmes.

"Thankfully," said the professor, "nothing's been damaged or taken." In the next few minutes, Will and the professor explained to TR and the other students what had happened. Officer Holmes said he'd like to check for fingerprints.

"The man was wearing gloves; of that I'm sure," said the professor. "I felt them on my arm. But you can check for the other person—the one who blocked the door in the first place."

Will flashed back. *Had the man who left the building been wearing gloves? That man was either the captain or Sainos.* In the twilight it had been impossible to distinguish much more than the broad shoulders.

At Professor Sheffield's request, Benjamin and the other two students went back to the first-floor garage to put away the trailer, the electric vehicles, and their charging pad. The professor pressed a towel filled with ice to his forehead. He assured the policemen and Will that he felt fine and could drive himself home. The officers told Will they had no more questions, so Will and TR headed back to the high school. TR needed to help his mother with the last of the cleanup, and Will had to pick up Audrey.

He parked his car at the curb where they'd loaded up the food. Audrey sprinted over. She climbed in, and as she pulled her seatbelt in place, Will explained all that had happened. When he finished, she was openmouthed. Then she asked, "Can I see your phone?" She'd had a smartphone for a very long time. She made some rapid taps and then said, "This number's blocked. How frustrating!" The phone rang and she almost dropped it. Will took it from her, expecting it to be TR or one of the policemen. It was the same quiet voice he'd heard a month earlier.

"Did they catch him?"

Will tensed up. "No. Professor Sheffield got there first."

"Sainos got away!?" said the captain.

"Yeah; he jumped Sheffield and then tied him up."

"Blast!" said the captain. "I was so careful tracking him! When he entered Zubner's office, I grabbed a chair and jammed it under the doorknob." His voice was tight with anger. "I grabbed the explosives and cleared off—the police could have had him!"

"Explosives?!"

Audrey was silent; she'd guessed who the caller was.

"Explosives," repeated the captain. "So Sheffield must have opened the door, and then Sainos knocked him down and cleared out."

"Was Sainos going to blow up the lab?"

"Now you're catchin' on," growled the captain. "He plays a high-stakes game. We won the last round. I guess we halfway won this one. But you've got to understand," his voice was full of anger again, "Sainos lives to destroy things!" Then he sighed. "I'm sorry. It's not fair to blame you. Did you tell the police everything?"

"I showed 'em your text, but—but I said I didn't know who you are—which is true. And I left out that I'd spoken to you before." *Now was the time to ask.* "Did you give the funds to the lab?"

"Yes," said the man, "I did—and thanks for not mentioning me." His relief was obvious. "I just want Sainos caught. I took the explosives in case he got the door open."

"Were you still in the building when you sent the text to me?"

"No, I'd already left."

"I saw a man leave just as I got there," said Will, "it must have been Sainos."

The captain was calmer now. "Will, I can't prevent the police from tracking me if I contact them directly. I don't want to be found." He let out a sigh. "That's another reason I grabbed the explosives. It would have brought in the FBI." He paused. "It's hard to avoid the authorities these days if they want to find you."

"I suppose."

"Listen, Will, there *is* someone—a police detective—who could help, but because of a connection to Sainos in the past, it could put him and his family in danger. I want to avoid that. You see, I'm the guy Sainos is really after. I make a move, he makes a move, I move to block him—it's always been that way. I'm sorry to involve you.

As it stands, Sainos hasn't linked you to me, and that's good!" The captain let his breath out. "I drove by your home a month ago, late at night . . . wondering if I should even make any kind of contact. And then later I had to. Anyway, I have to go. Sainos nearly got caught, so I hope he's given up and this is the end. Thanks for your help."

"Wait," said Will, but the call was over, and there was no way to return it.

PART 3

THE PV HOT-WATER SYSTEM

CHAPTER
5

THREE WEEKS LATER, ON a bright summer morning in August, Sherrie Lionetti parked her silvery-green car in front of the elegant beauty salon she owned. Grabbing her purse and sunglasses, she slid out from behind the wheel and shut the door with a flourish. The shiny, new vehicle was a present given to her by her thoughtful husband, John Lionetti, to celebrate the salon's grand reopening after extensive renovations.

"Good morning, Holly," Sherrie called to one of her stylists, who had just pulled up in a bright-red Prius.

"Hi, Sherrie. Let me get these supplies," said Holly, "and I'll be right in." She reached around for a sack of multicolored boxes in the back seat.

Sherrie unlocked the salon. Its name, Beyond Hair, was emblazoned on the front door. The official reopening ceremony had taken place the day before. Along with the beautiful new interior, they also had a valuable new exterior feature.

Next to the large single-story building and taller than the roof, were shiny new solar PV panels affixed to the top of four steel poles. The panels provided electricity for the salon's curling irons, straighteners, and hair dryers as well as for an electric hot-water heater of the latest design. Hot water was very much in demand, being used to launder towels and wash away shampoos and other hair products.

Next to the entrance to Beyond Hair was a wide patio with flower pots and several wrought-iron chairs. Ahead of that was an expansive terrace dotted with brightly colored umbrellas and outdoor tables at a restaurant known as Café Salsa.

Miguel and Rita Cardena owned the popular establishment. Huge stone pots and hanging flower baskets decorated the restaurant's sunlit patio. Clients from the salon often stopped there to eat after getting their hair done. Both businesses were doing well and were happy to be neighbors in the same building.

A few weeks earlier, before her trip to Hawaii, Janet Chambers had been at the salon getting highlights when a curious exchange had taken place. A mysterious woman had entered. She'd stepped around a pile of boxes next to a flowery sign that read *Please excuse our mess; we're getting a makeover!* Stopping at the front desk, she'd asked Kara, an attractive, platinum blonde, to point out the owner. Kara obliged, and the visitor walked straight over to Sherrie.

The woman's hat brim was pulled down, and Mrs. Chambers couldn't see her face. The woman spoke clearly, making Sherrie an offer she had already made to the Cardenas: to install a solar PV system at no charge. She'd promised Sherrie that the money was lawful. Sherrie had scanned the one-page document, noting the place where the Cardenas had already signed. She carefully read it a second time and then also signed. The woman thanked her and left. Immediately, two of Beyond Hair's best customers, Maureen Nelson and Brenda Doxey, began buzzing.

"Sherrie, what did you just agree to?" asked Brenda. Janet Chambers listened as she waited for the conditioner in her hair to process. Sherrie explained about the new solar PV system while bending a piece of foil into Brenda's hair.

"Interesting!" said Holly, whose fingers moved with lightning speed. She was giving Maureen hair extensions for an anniversary cruise intended to fan the flames of romance. Holly and Maureen looked in the mirror, and their expressions indicated that the extensions were an improvement.

Then, referring once more to the solar PV system, Holly said, "Heavens, Sherrie, you'll be an innovator!"

Sherrie laughed. "Not sure about that! But I do like saving money."

Maureen nodded in agreement, making her now longer hair swish.

"It won't cost us a thing," Sherrie explained. "That's what the contract said."

Within a week, two local companies, Canyonland Plumbing and Solar-Go, came in for several hours of planning. The system went up quickly. A Powerwall battery from the Tesla Company was installed so any excess electricity would be stored for future use. When everything was finished, the salon and the restaurant each had a new hybrid-electric hot-water heater that was twice as efficient as a conventional one. Thrilled to have lower energy bills, Sherrie and the Cardenas were also pleased when the invoices came. They were marked *Paid in Full,* in accordance with the offer made by their mysterious visitor.

———

A FEW DAYS AFTER RETURNING from Hawaii, Janet Chambers saw an announcement in the *Aberdeen Courier,* their local newspaper, about the café/salon project. Janet was serving up breakfast while her husband scanned the headlines.

"I was right there—sitting right there—when Sherrie signed the papers! It was peculiar! I'm sure that woman was a professional of some kind; she was so polished." Arriving at the kitchen doorway, Will caught part of the conversation. Audrey was right behind him.

"Come in, breakfast is ready," said Mrs. Chambers. She turned back to her husband, who was still reading. "The document must have been clear, because Sherrie signed it right away."

Dr. Chambers poked at his omelet. He'd wanted more bacon, but Mrs. Chambers, who was health conscious, had given him only two pieces—not enough, in his opinion.

Mrs. Chambers went on, "Sherrie said it surprised her that there hadn't been a request for free advertising. Maybe that'll come later, eh?"

"Janet, sweetheart," said Dr. Chambers, "would you like to have lunch at Café Salsa today?"

"I would love to!" The zoo was close to the café, which was a favorite spot of theirs for lunch or dinner. Will, now curious, looked at the newspaper's photo of the new PV system.

"Dad, why put the panels on a pole and not on the roof?"

"You can do it either way. Maybe they get more sun that way, or they didn't want them on the roof. Our roof at the hospital is tar and gravel, and there's plenty of sun up there, so it made sense for us." His eyes twinkled. "I'm a full supporter of 'occupy rooftops' for solar PV. But you have to keep in mind that you could gain more sunlight by using a pole or a nearby slope."

"How'd you know that, Lloyd?" asked Mrs. Chambers.

"Our installer had some brochures" he replied. "Interestingly, people who want a system to heat a building or a big swimming pool can use a large parabolic dish that will track the sun. Our hippos would love one of those."[8]

"An even bigger heated pond? Oh, I'm sure they would, Lloyd!" his wife said, laughing.

"What heats their pool now?" asked Audrey.

"Little Pete and Angel's water pond is heated by natural gas," said Will.

Mrs. Chambers pointed to the paper, "You kids should join us for lunch! Then you can see the system for yourselves."

"That'd be great, Mom," said Will, looking in the fridge for more bacon. "We're going over to the lab, then Darius, Audrey, and I can come to the café." He paused. "You aren't going to have an argument with the Cardenas about . . . too much cheese, are you?"

Mrs. Chambers' sharp intake of breath meant she just wasn't sure. She was reading a nutrition book called *You're Not Bad; You Just Eat Badly*. It addressed the growing awareness that people couldn't burn off the many starchy and fatty calories they were consuming. It recommended fruits, vegetables, lean protein, and only small amounts of corn, grain, sugar, and dairy products. She always said that

---

8. For Footnote Link go to Captain Glow Website

large amounts of cheese were a problem because cheese contains so much salt and fat.

They all knew that breakfast cereals high in sugar were on her do-not-ever-bring-into-this-home list, and the good doctor knew to either not buy them or else to hide them. Her family understood that she wanted them to have good health, but they teased her for being such a zealot. Avoiding Will's question, she said, "Agreed then? We'll meet at twelve-thirtyish for lunch."

Just after twelve noon, the high schoolers finished at the lab and left for the restaurant. Audrey and Will rode on "the purple-people-eater," and Darius rode his electric bike.

"It's like flying," he said, "and it's so quiet. It's an awesome machine."

Will's e-bike project for the science fair was going well. A company had donated five bikes for use at Aberdeen High and Will had enlisted more riders from the surrounding area. For his rider data, he was using one of the bikes; in addition, he had four other students; Darius; twenty-four e-bike riders from Moab; and riders in St. George, Salt Lake City, Provo, and a few in Pocatello, Idaho.

As Will thought about the state science fair, he hoped more and more that he could walk forward to shake hands with the university's dean of the College of Science to accept one of the first-place awards. The distinguished computer company INTEL sponsored an enormous international science fair each year in May, and the local state winners were invited to attend. He hoped his project would be good enough to win a spot to compete at this exceptional event.

"Man, I'm hungry!" Will called over his shoulder to Audrey as they pedaled toward the café.

"Me too. I think I'll have the fish burrito," she said. "Your mom says they're incredible." Arriving at the restaurant, they locked their bicycles onto a brightly colored bike rack.

Dr. and Mrs. Chambers waved to them from a patio table that was well shaded under a striped green-and-orange umbrella. The waitress had already brought out cups and water. Will sat down next to his dad and took several gulps. The outside temperature was eighty-seven degrees Fahrenheit, but a wide umbrella and nearby hanging plants provided enough shade to make the patio entirely comfortable.

After scanning the menus, Dr. Chambers ordered enchiladas. Mrs. Chambers chose a fajita dish with no cheese, and Darius did the same. The Chinese foods he had grown up with had no cheese products in them, and he didn't care for it. Will and Audrey got the fish burritos, which passed Mrs. Chambers' standard for healthiness. When the food came, it smelled delicious, and they got right down to the business of eating.

Suddenly, from across the courtyard they heard a whooping noise followed by a child's loud complaint. In the distance, Mrs. Bartson dragged her soggy eight-year-old son, Denzel, away from a small garden pond at the patio's far end. Mr. Bartson, TR, and Benjamin had gotten up from their table with amused looks on their faces.

"Mom!" bellowed Denzel.

As she came nearer, they could hear her say sternly, "You put them back, right?"

"Yes, but why can't I—"

"Because they live in the pond, that's why!" his mother sputtered, her face flushed with heat. Denzel was dragging his feet, and his tennis shoes made a squishing sound. Mr. Bartson and Benjamin were laughing, and TR grabbed Denzel's other arm. Denzel looked longingly over his shoulder at the small, iridescent pool. The Bartsons, having already paid their bill, picked up their things and were going past the table where Will sat.

Will couldn't resist. "TR, what's up with Denzel?"

"Snails," said TR, rolling his eyes. "He's in love with the pond snails, and Mom says he has to leave them there."

"Leh' me alone!" Denzel pulled his arm away from his brother. "There's a million of 'em in there; no one would care!"

"DENZEL!" Mrs. Bartson's voice rose. "They belong to the restaurant, and that's the end of it!"

Mr. Bartson gave his wife a wink and said, "Son, remember that skateboard you were talking about?"

"Yeah, Denzel," said TR, helping to change the conversation. "You can't ride around on a snail, but a skateboard—"

"Okay, but it's gotta be a decent one," said Denzel, still sulking.

"Ah, children," Mrs. Bartson said comically to her friends. "I know why guppies eat their young." Then she brightened. "Did you see the newspaper article about that new PV system here?"

"Yes, we did," said Dr. Chambers, swallowing the last bite of his enchilada. "We looked at it when we first arrived." Then he paused, "I think the company making these electric hot-water tanks is just over in Eden."

"It is!" said Mrs. Bartson enthusiastically. "One of my former students works for them and the build site is in Eden."

A cheery voice interrupted their conversation. "*Hola!* Hello—hello!" the voice called over Will's shoulder. It was the owner, Mr. Miguel Cardena, looking delighted to see his café so full. "Did everything taste good?" His hands moved expressively. Everyone nodded that yes, the food was great.

Stepping forward, Mrs. Chambers said, "Delicious, but I did want to talk to you—"

"Mom," interrupted Will, warding off a conversation about cheese and nutrition. "Look how busy the restaurant is."

"Yes, Janet," said Dr. Chambers, catching on. "See how well the restaurant's doing?"

"Oh, that's fine," said Mr. Cardena. "If she wants to ask about our new PV system, I'm not too busy. Lots of people read today's article and are curious." He smiled and slipped his arm around his wife, Rita, who'd just come over.

Rita said, "Miguel and our daughter Lorina are both thrilled that we have this now."

"Oh, Lorina was one of my best students," said Mrs. Bartson. "Remind me, where is she going to school?"

Mr. Cardena smiled proudly, "She's at Water UCI,[9] which is a brilliant research lab at the University of California, Irvine, and she's loving it."

Mrs. Cardena added, "She was delighted to learn we have a solar PV system supplying electricity for our hot-water heater.

"It's the solar sensation, sweeping the nation," quipped Dr. Chambers, using a jingle he rather liked. At that moment Denzel Bartson jumped into the center of the circle. He asked Mrs. Cardena a question that had nothing to do with cheese, the sun, or a new PV system. He was quickly given the okay to take home some snails.

Dr. Chambers glanced at his watch. "I've got to go! There's a baby penguin due for his fish paste; I'm afraid his mother has rejected him."

"Oh, poor thing," said Mrs. Chambers.

"He's actually doing very well. In fact," Dr. Chambers continued, "he really perks up when he hears show tunes."

---

9. For Footnote Link go to Captain Glow Website

"Oh, Lloyd, why would that be?" teased Mrs. Chambers. "Is he hearing them played at your hospital?"

"I, uh . . . yes, he is," said Dr. Chambers, his cheeks reddening. Will, Darius, and Audrey grinned. They knew the doctor had a fondness for musicals and that he whistled popular tunes and listened to them often. "He eats better when the music's playing," he said with a straight face. His wife and friends laughed, and he joined in. "Time to go."

"I'll catch the bill," said Mrs. Chambers, and they waved him off.

ON A SUNDAY NIGHT two days later, Janet Chambers raced around, packing for a trip. Comox, who knew what suitcases meant, watched with interest, wondering whether he'd be going along. He would not; Dr. and Mrs. Chambers were heading off to a zoo conference in Denver, Colorado. As Mrs. Chambers put the Aberdeen newspaper with the article on the new PV system in the recycling bin, she returned to the topic of the mystery woman who'd visited Beyond Hair. "Hmm, there was no mention of that nameless donor in the article," she said, stuffing the newspaper in with the others.

The hair on the back of Will's neck stood up. He gave Audrey a meaningful look as she handed Mrs. Chambers some clean socks from the laundry basket. Audrey looked puzzled then comprehended. She said nothing, and Will flashed her a look of gratitude. *Why bring up anything that would alarm his parents?* When the captain had said, "I hope this is the end," Will had felt the same way. He hadn't mentioned the captain's involvement at the Electric Vehicle Lab to anyone but Audrey and Darius. He didn't want to be back at the police station. Professor Sheffield had concluded that his assailant had been part of a prank, and he had moved on.

Will thought of the mysterious woman. *Is it possible that Captain Glow is a woman? No.* He pushed all thoughts of the captain aside and offered to take his parents' suitcases to the car. He carried the luggage down through the kitchen and out to the garage.

They had a quick supper that evening. Will finished before the others, savoring the last spoonful of the strawberries and gelato. His father was at the zoo hospital finalizing the talk he was giving at the conference in Denver. Mrs. Chambers was heading out to pick him up and then they'd make the short trip to the Salt Lake City International Airport.

Will and Audrey both insisted Mrs. Chambers let them clean up. When they'd finished, Audrey went upstairs, and Will walked out to the backyard. He flopped onto an oversized hammock that hung between two large maple trees. Comox lay in the grass by his side.

Just as Will started to relax, he felt a premonition—something that was not at all typical for him. When his phone rang, he looked at the caller ID. It was blocked.

"Hi, Will. Can you relay a message?" The man sounded tired. "Sainos is going after the system at Café Salsa, and it's most likely happening tonight."

Will was surprised at the exhilaration he felt. "Do you know the woman who paid for it?" he asked.

There was silence. Finally the man on the other end of the line said, "Just—forget that woman—it's not important! Sainos is planning to wreck that system and I'm six hundred miles away."

"How do you know Sainos?"

"We're running out of time—"

"Before I do anything," interrupted Will in frustration, "you have to explain a few things!"

"Like who I am?"

"Yeah!" said Will.

"Well, I can't. Maybe later, but not now. I have to do it this way."

"Why?" said Will.

"Forget it, then. I'll—"

"Okay, if you can't tell me about you, tell me about Sainos!" said Will, desperate for anything that would help him know he was doing the right thing.

Captain Glow paused. "Fair enough." He was calmer now. "You've done a lot to help."

Finally, thought Will. He saw his mother push the curtains aside in the kitchen window. He nodded to her as she waved goodbye and blew him a kiss. He waved back, hoping she wouldn't spot his fake cheerful look. She vanished from the window. "Go on," said Will.

The captain spoke rapidly. "I'll start with why this is happening. Go back in our planet's history to the first moon landing in 1969. Just imagine the joy, the pure thrill of seeing two human beings make that journey. It was a whole new era."

Will watched his mother's car move out of the driveway and head down the street.

The captain went on. "Go forward three years. I guess I was sort of a hippie type back then. We didn't have internet or cell phones, but we had powerful coverage from three television networks. They delivered troubling footage of a long war—the Vietnam War; you might have heard of it. The news also reported on college students across the U.S. and other parts of the world, protesting the war. One of those college students was me. Finally, the war in Vietnam ended and the troops came home—change-A-lleluia! The country wasn't committed to war as the grand solution anymore, and it felt like progress. Afterward, some of us moved on to what we thought was even more important: seeing our world, this earth, the same way the astronauts saw it—as one planet, a home to everyone we know, everyone we love. Could we be better people? Treat each other and the earth right and not blow ourselves up? If yes, maybe we could explore beyond earth."

Will listened, watching maple leaves rippling in the breeze overhead.

"That same year we saw pollution so bad it actually caused a river to start on fire. So people got their heads together and passed the Clean Water Act, and that improved things. My parents, who were connected to the Aberdeen Zoo, worked to get the Endangered Species Act passed. People were now realizing that certain corporations were making huge profits but didn't pay a cent for the trash they put into the air or water. 'Follow the money' was the phrase. Look up the Love Canal[10] mess sometime—that's a perfect example.

"But to be fair, my age group had our own problems too. I guess we had what I'd call the good-hippie/bad-hippie problem. The good hippies had the 'make a better world vision,' and it was going to take a lot of work. I admit, most of the good-hippie 'visionaries' were privileged—too intellectual at times—and the line between these two groups wasn't clear. Anyway, the good hippies became impatient with the lack of focus and what I'd call the bad hippies' commitment to having an endless party. Things began to fall apart. A lot of bad stuff happened; families were fighting— the drug scene was horrible—" His voice had become heavy.

"What about Sainos?" Will broke in. "What about him?"

---

10. For Footnote Link go to Captain Glow Website

"Yeah, well, he was part of a spin-off group, which included me—we were at a commune outside of San Francisco. It was clean, healthy, no drugs, 'do good work'—all that stuff. But Sainos came for one reason. There was someone there he wanted to be close to—that's when I met him. That's when our rivalry began."

"And then?" said Will.

"Sainos is attracted to explosives . . ."

"Yeah, I got that part," muttered Will. "What about the 'someone'?"

"Skip that," said the captain. "We're talking about Sainos. He's an anarchist with no compassion; he hates authority. His half brother showed up and started accusing Sainos of taking money and blaming him for it. Sainos punched the kid and hustled him out; no love and peace there.

"Soon after that, Sainos said our group should blow up the oil refinery down near the bay. Most members wanted him gone. He backed off, saying he was only joking, and that he supported the goal of building our own power and energy systems. That's where the money we were putting into the group was supposed to go. Then Sainos proposed an idea for getting a large amount of money—it was a bad idea, but at the time, I didn't see the lie."

The captain sighed. "There were complications. In the end, Sainos didn't get the money. The key people in our group, the 'visionaries' you'd call them, left the commune and it fell apart. The seventies ended, the computer industry came to the rescue in the eighties, the economy was saved, and the new vision? Well, it got blurry . . ." The captain gave a hollow laugh. "But one thing is certain: Sainos didn't forget me. We are lifelong enemies. And that, Will, brings us to now. He ruined part of *my* life, but he thinks I ruined *his*. So, every time I fund a clean-energy project, he tries to destroy it. If he's blocked, he moves on to the next one. What matters to him is that I'm the one funding them."

"How does he know that you're the backer?"

"I'd like to know that too."

"Why should I believe you?"

"Because it's *true*."

"Okay . . . okay." Will *did* believe him. "What do you need me to do?"

"Contact a man named James Clayberry. He's a police detective."

"Clayberry? I—I know his daughters."

"Yes, that's him. He's a really good guy. I didn't want to pull him into this, but—tell him Sainos is behind these attacks. He'll know who you mean." He paused, "It's likely Sainos is out of explosives for now. Maybe that'll delay him. Try to reach Clayberry now. But if you can't, Will, just stay put 'til he contacts you."

"Why aren't—"

Before Will could finish his question, the phone went silent, and Will realized the captain had ended the call.

Immediately Will called Darius. "Hey, Darius, can you come by with the jeep? It's an emergency; I'll explain when you get here." He heard Legos sliding across a table.

"Be right there."

Will raced into the kitchen. Audrey was putting dog food in to Comox's dish. "Darius is coming over." Then he remembered he had Margaret Clayberry's phone number on a school directory list. He dug through a kitchen drawer, pulled out the list and found her number.

"What's going on?" said Audrey as Will hurriedly tapped the number into his phone.

"The PV system at Café Salsa might be damaged tonight."

"Oh, no!" She looked frightened. "Did he call you again?"

He nodded. "I can handle it," he said. *Would Clayberry be at home?* He thought of how the Cardena family would feel if the new system was destroyed. *What was that quote about evil succeeding if enough good men do nothing? Anyway,* thought Will, *the captain said the only person Sainos was after was the captain himself.* He jumped when Audrey placed her hand on his arm.

"Will, we should call the police!" Her voice trembled.

"Yup! And the captain gave me the name of which one to call." He hoped that would reassure her. "I'm doing it now." He tapped the number in and hit the call button. Not surprisingly, Margaret Clayberry answered when the call connected.

He asked, "Is Detective Clayberry there?" He didn't give his name. *No sense complicating things.*

"I'm sorry, he's gone 'til later," she said. "Can I take a message?"

He spoke in a tone that was lower than usual. "Yes." He gave her his cell phone number. "There's going to be some vandalism at the Café Salsa restaurant tonight. This next part's important," he spoke carefully. "Tell him Sainos is involved. Got that?"

"Yes, I do," she said. "I'll try to reach him." Will ended the call abruptly.

Just then Darius rang the front doorbell, and Will took him to the kitchen where Audrey and Comox waited. He explained about the phone call.

"Why doesn't this . . . captain just call Detective Clayberry himself?" said Audrey with concern.

"He didn't want to involve Clayberry—so here's what I think. Three weeks back he mentioned knowing 'someone on the police force.' Then he said that because of a connection to Sainos in the past, that man could get hurt. Since the captain doesn't know how Sainos is getting the information that he's the one funding these systems, I think he's not contacting Clayberry directly in order to protect Clayberry. If Sainos knows both of them . . . maybe Sainos is doing some surveillance on Clayberry and so is able to know if the captain contacts him. But the record of a call coming from me, just looks like I'm calling my friends. Make sense?"

"Yeah, I can see that," said Darius. "So, what's next?"

"We should wait for Clayberry's call," said Will. They went to the family room, played a video game, and then watched a classic suspense film, *The Fugitive*.

Three hours later when there was still no phone call, Will changed direction. "I'm not going to stay put," he said. "I want this guy Sainos caught. Maybe I can get a photo of him!" He jumped up from the couch.

"I'm coming with you," said Darius, following Will up the stairs.

Audrey was right on their heels. "I'm coming too!" Will turned to object, but the look on her face told him it was no use. They piled into the jeep along with Comox and headed to the café.

CHAPTER
6

WHEN THEY ARRIVED AT the café, everything was quiet. The PV panels looked fine. They drove around back and parked. The jeep was mostly hidden by a large, sky-blue dumpster and a long, wide countertop left over from the remodeling. They turned off the motor. The back of the building was a quiet place with two large trees and a long alley that saw very little traffic.

Within minutes, a slow-moving, unmarked white van pulled into the back-parking area. All three teenagers held their breath. Even Comox was still. The driver got out of the van and approached the building. Will and Darius slid out of the jeep, but Darius's foot skidded on a stone, making a loud noise.

The man spun around. Then he dashed over to his van and grabbed a pipe wrench from the front seat. He brandished it like a weapon. The three came to a standstill.

"Why are you here?!" Will demanded.

"What!?"

"You here to cause trouble?"

"No! No!" the man stammered. He was in his late twenties at the most. *Not the right age for Sainos,* thought Will. The man kept the pipe wrench pointed at them.

"Why have you come here tonight?" asked Darius calmly, realizing the man was just as rattled as they were.

"I'm an apprentice plumber and I heard this place had a new system. I finished a job nearby, so I came to see it." Will and Darius stepped back, and the man lowered his pipe wrench. Then he asked, "Why are *you* here?"

Will answered awkwardly, "We're just here—uh—to guard the place. Sorry we startled you."

The man relaxed. "I thought I was going to be mugged." The pocket on his blue shirt read *Jensen Plumbing.* Still a bit shaken, the guy put out his hand. "I'm Roger Larson." Will stepped forward and shook it.

"I'm Will Chambers, and this is my friend, Darius Cheng."

"I gotta ask," said Roger, "what are you guarding? Expecting trouble?"

"Sort of," said Will.

"Well then, I'll stop by another time."

"Yeah." Will nodded. Trying to sound friendly, he said, "Stop by for lunch; the café has great food—they'll tell you all about the new system."

The man put his pipe wrench back in the van. "That was just in case," he said. Then he walked to the driver's side and climbed in.

"Sorry about earlier, Mr. Larson" said Will.

"Nah, never mind—and just Roger," smiled the man. "I'm not *that* old." He started his engine and pulled away.

"False alarm," Darius told Audrey. He and Will got back in the jeep.

They sat for a long time. Darius looked at the cell phone watch he'd gotten from his Auntie Lin. "We've been here more than two hours," he sighed.

"Audrey," said Will, "if something does happen, you and Comox stay with the car to make sure we don't get slashed tires again, okay?"

"I'd really like it if that detective called," she said stifling a yawn.

"If not, Audrey, just think, we might be able to ID the guy," said Darius. "Picture this: we're looking at a lineup. You stand up, point to him, and say, 'That's him, officer. That's the man who tried to blow up the beauty salon and café." Audrey giggled. "And look at this," he said, changing the topic; he showed her a Lego model on his phone. "It's my version of the Seattle Space Needle." The tension in the jeep melted away.

Will grinned. "I'm glad you both came along."

"We are too," said Audrey, rubbing Comox's ears.

More time passed. It was a quarter to three. Even though his jeep windows were partially down, Darius finally whispered a protest.

"Can we get some air in here?" As they opened the door closest to the blue dumpster, they heard a loud, clanking noise. Will looked at his friends.

"Show-time," he said. Comox started making low growling noises, and Will cautioned him to be quiet. Will motioned to Darius, and the two young men slid out of the jeep. Audrey soothed Comox, keeping a firm hold on him. Will and Darius moved quietly around the right side of the building, staying low. Peering around the corner, they saw a huge, red truck parked on the patio. In the shadows, a man in dark clothing was pulling something metallic and noisy out of a box. Darius grabbed Will's arm and pulled him back.

"D'you hear that?" Darius said. They moved back to the rear of the building.

"Look," Darius whispered. A brown truck had pulled into the parking lot where the jeep sat.

Quickly Will moved back, trying to see who was in the brown truck. Maybe it was Clayberry.

"Oh, no," Darius groaned. It was Fletcher Stiles and Delbert Korbelak. They'd pulled in beside the long countertop. They both got out and started pulling the long, heavy piece of laminated wood toward the back of their truck.

In a commanding voice, Will said, "What are you doing?" The young men jumped, and the countertop crashed to the ground.

"What're *you* doing here?" hissed Fletcher, recognizing them. Then he spotted Audrey in the jeep as she held on to a growling Comox.

"You still with these losers? You should come with us. Right, Del?" He gave her a nasty leer. "We're a *lot* more fun." Delbert laughed. Audrey shrank back, and Comox growled louder.

"Get outta here, Fletcher!" said Will, moving toward him.

"Make me!" Fletcher shot back.

A loud clanking noise caught all of their attention. "What's that?" asked Delbert.

"Probably the police!" answered Will. "We called 'em."

"Aahh, right," Fletcher sneered.

"We did!" said Audrey. Just then Will's phone buzzed. He ignored it.

"And you were stealing that," added Darius coolly, pointing at the countertop.

"Come on, Fletcher," called Delbert, who was running back to the truck. "Let's get outta here." He and Fletcher climbed in. Fletcher jammed his truck into gear, backed it up, and raced away past the front of the salon. Will and Darius ran to the other side of the building. As they came around, the red truck pulled away, but they were able to see the license plate number.

"Six forty-two *X-B-H,*" said Will, and Darius typed it into his phone. The truck sped off, nearly colliding with a fire hydrant. Fletcher had spooked the man when he and Delbert had cleared off. Will and Darius surveyed the scene. Several large metal hooks were scattered on the ground, and a tall wooden ladder was propped up against one of the poles. Will froze. Large chains had been looped around the panels. If the chains had been attached to the truck, the panels could have been torn from the poles.

"Whew . . . this is one bad dude!" said Darius. They moved closer.

"Don't touch anything," said Will.

"If that idiot Fletcher hadn't shown up, we could've gotten a photo," Darius fumed.

"He moved pretty fast."

"Fletcher?"

"No, Sainos," said Will, feeling low. "Well, at least the panels are okay. And," he added, "we've got a license plate number. Maybe the police can find him."

At that moment, another car pulled in. *Friend or foe?* thought Will. The anxious face of Margaret Clayberry peered through the passenger window. *The man behind the wheel must be her dad*, thought Will. Margaret and the man got out of the car.

Will and Darius lifted their hands to show they didn't have weapons. The detective spoke first.

"Are you Will Chambers?"

"Yes, sir," answered Will.

"I thought it was you," said Margaret. "So I convinced Dad he should bring me along."

"Sir," Will cleared his voice. "This is my friend, Darius." Then he pointed up at the panels. "We didn't bring that ladder or the chains—we scared off the man who was trying to—"

"Stop," interrupted the detective. "Who's that?" Audrey and Comox had come around the corner.

"I'm Audrey Carter, sir, and I'm with them."

"Comox," said Will, "sit." Comox immediately obeyed.

Audrey's face brightened when she saw Margaret. Then she spotted the dangling chains and her mouth fell open. "What—did he get away!?"

"Do you mean Sainos?" said Detective Clayberry. "My daughter told me a man named Sainos is involved. Is that right?"

"We think so," said Will.

"And, sir," Darius added, "we got the license plate number off his truck."

"Six forty-two *X-B-H,*" said Will. Detective Clayberry pulled out a notebook and jotted it down. Then he quickly called the Cardenas and Sherrie Lionetti, the two building owners. Mr. Cardena arrived first, followed closely by Sherrie and her husband. The two owners and Detective Clayberry checked the doors to the two businesses. The doors were still locked and, to the owners' relief, no damage had been done.

"We're so lucky you kids were here," said Sherrie, "and that you prevented that crazy man from wrecking anything." Then she paused. "Why were you here?"

"Uh," Will halted, caught off guard; luckily, Darius had an answer.

"We saw some other guys we knew, and we followed 'em around back. They're known for causin' trouble, so we thought we'd check it out."

Audrey added, "I think they were going to steal that long countertop that's out back, but then—"

"We heard noises coming from this side," said Will.

Detective Clayberry was surprisingly quiet, not mentioning that Will had called him earlier to alert him of the possible attack.

The detective put on gloves and carefully removed the chains. He also gathered the hooks and then made out a report, taking down everyone's contact information. Then Mr. Cardena and Sherrie and her husband left, leaving the teenagers with the detective.

"How about if we drive over to your house and finish up there?" Detective Clayberry said to Will.

"Darius has his jeep out back," answered Will, "we'll pull it around." He turned to go.

Detective Clayberry called after him. "Did Sainos talk to you? Did he see you?"

"No on both counts," said Will, "but, sir, I'll tell you who I *have* been talking to."

"Good," said the detective. "Margaret and I will follow you."

As they drove to the Chambers' home, Audrey hugged the dog and cooed softly, "Good Comox."

"Finally," said Will, "I can tell a policeman what's been happening."

"And," said Darius, "it sounds like he knows these people." He pulled in to the Chambers' driveway. Detective Clayberry pulled up to the curb.

"Should I get us something to drink?" asked Audrey.

"That's a great idea," said Will. "Get the lemonade out of the fridge."

"Yes," said Darius, "I'm parched!" Comox felt the same way. As soon as they entered the kitchen, he lapped up half the contents of his water dish.

Audrey, Will, Darius, and Margaret sat down at the kitchen table. Detective Clayberry preferred to stand. He flipped open his notebook. "Tell me everything that's happened up to now."

Will began with the first phone call, when the zoo system was the target. He relied on Darius and Audrey for help. When they'd finished, the room was quiet. The detective looked over his notes.

Finally, Will said, "Who's been calling me?"

The detective was evasive. "I think . . . well . . . for you to understand, you'd have to know there was a third person involved." His face saddened. He was older than Will's parents, with a head of silvery hair. Margaret pulled out a chair for him, and he sat down. "It's complex. This other person is—was—Marylou Hansen. We were students together at Yosemite University. Marylou was bright; truly special. She was one of the first women accepted into the California Fisheries and Wildlife Program, and that was no surprise . . . but further back is when . . ." he paused, looking for the right words, "the trouble began. When Marylou Hansen and Sainos were fifteen, they met at a summer camp in Maryland—Camp Carthage, I think. It was for affluent kids. Each summer its activities changed. The first year was deep-woods hiking, the second year, sailing. Things like that."

Audrey offered him a glass of lemonade, and he gladly accepted it. After several swallows, he put it down and went on. "From the very start, Sainos challenged authority. Marylou said that it was exciting at first. Sainos's father owned the Blooming Armored Car Company, and he boasted openly about his family's wealth, but still . . ."

He took another swallow of lemonade. "It wasn't just a money thing. Sainos could hike farther and pitch a tent faster than most of the Camp Carthage staff. In the second year, he took a strong interest in Marylou." He grinned unexpectedly. "She was fun. She didn't cause trouble though; she was interested in life and just—made things happen. I'm sure she had friends there right away. Not hard to understand Sainos's attraction to her. Her parents were also well-off; they had a California olive grove or something . . .

"At first, Marylou was flattered. But the final summer at Camp Carthage, when they got into rock climbing, she said things had changed. He was controlling. He angered too easily—like the time he busted up some wooden chairs after losing a chess game. In that last summer he was put in detention after pulling a cruel trick on the cook's dog. She said detention meant staying at a remote cottage far away from the main camp and higher in altitude, up where they did the rock climbing."

The detective rubbed his chin. "The offender would be locked in with a great view and the whole night to realize causing trouble wasn't worth it. So, this is where Sainos earned his nickname, *Insaino*. He smashed out a window, pried open the equipment shack, strung rope together, and rappelled down a sheer cliff all by himself. He had to drop the last ten feet. Exciting guy, right? But by that time, Marylou said he scared her. Later she reflected how it bothered her that his father had just sent the camp more money instead of addressing his son's behavior. Anyway, when she registered for Yosemite University, Sainos registered there too."

"Dad," said Margaret, "that's where you went to school. Did you meet Sainos and Marylou there?"

"Yes. I hadn't met your mother yet." He sighed. "I believe Marylou's the reason Sainos is causing all this trouble. You see, he and another man both loved her." The detective's face became grim again, but he shook off the emotion and went on. "Marylou and I both belonged to a student organization called the 'See-Jays'—short for 'Students for Ecosystem Justice.' S-E-J, you see? Like this." He wrote the letters *SEJ*. "We had some really good people in that group."

"What happened to Marylou?" said Will. The detective looked uncomfortable.

"Not sure. She left the Green Valley Project and I never saw her again."

"The what?" Darius asked.

"The Green Valley Project—a student community. Well, all right . . . it was a commune. Most of the people there had been part of the See-Jays. I was there, along with Marylou, and Sainos was also there." He looked away, "That was a long time ago."

"Dad!" said Margaret, shocked. "You were in a commune?"

"Yes, I met your mother later. In defense, our commune had some bright hard workers." He laughed. "Probably why we didn't grow much. We weren't into partying and drugs, and we really weren't political. One guy's uncle had worked at Bell Labs, where the first solar cell was developed.[11] That interested us. Anyway, to answer your question, Will, about Marylou—she went missing. It was tough on her parents. Really terrible . . . in fact, that's part of why I became a policeman."

"Oh, Dad," said Margaret, touching his arm.

"By the time we were at the Green Valley Project, Marylou was very cautious around Sainos. We didn't realize it then, but today we would say that he was stalking her.

---

11. For Footnote Link go to Captain Glow Website

It was before the term was coined, but that's what he was doing." The detective sighed. "No surprise it ended badly."

"Who's Captain Glow?" said Will.

"Captain Glow isn't a person."

"What!?"

"Captain Glow was just an idea. We were working on a primitive solar PV system and getting ridiculed for it, so bundling our projects under the name Captain Glow Incorporated was a—a morale booster!" His face brightened. "We put a micro-hydro system in a fast-running stream, and it worked great; it powered the lights for a whole barn. Anyway, the name *Captain Glow* stuck. It was a replacement for 'Old King Cole,' and it gave us a connection.

"Did you incorporate?" asked Darius.

"No," laughed Detective Clayberry, "we were too young; we didn't know anything about incorporating a business."

"Who's the guy who's been calling me?" asked Will.

Detective Clayberry stiffened. "I'd rather not say." He put his notebook away. "Otherwise, a real injustice could occur . . . I'll run those plates in a minute. If we catch Sainos, that's all we should need." He looked at the four teenagers. "Can you live with that?"

"Well—" Will was taken by surprise, "I'd like to know more than we do now."

Darius sat bolt upright. "Yeah, like who is this captain guy?" The detective turned away.

"Darius," said Audrey, looking from Margaret's face to that of the older man, "Detective Clayberry must have his reasons. Anyway, it's four a.m., guys." With that, Margaret and her father stood up.

Will changed his approach. Following Margaret and Detective Clayberry to the front door, he asked, "Can we help?" The tall man turned around.

"I'm sure there's a warrant out for Sainos; hopefully our law enforcement will catch him, prove him guilty, and then . . . I'd just want to close the case."

PART 4

THE GROUND-SOURCE HEAT-PUMP SYSTEM

CHAPTER

7

WILL HOPED THAT BY providing the license plate number, Sainos would be caught. But almost immediately, Detective Clayberry received bad news. The plates belonged to a donut truck recently smashed in a highway accident. The report stated that the truck had been taken to a local scrap yard called Ropelato's Parts and Salvage. Detective Clayberry headed there to investigate.

The owner, Mr. Ropelato, was a spirited, older man with a head of bristly, white hair. His blue eyes sparkled in contrast to his red-and-black, checkered shirt.

"Lucky break for that driver," he said cheerfully, referring to the wreck. "His airbag blew up in front an' his cream puffs came up from behind! What a mess! Wasn't a scratch on him, but the donut truck? Totaled!"

"Yes, Mr. Ropelato, that was lucky for him," said the detective, "but the plates on the truck—what happened to them?"

"Yeah, uh, well, we were gonna remove the plates—and I told my yardman, Stoney Korbelak, to take the plates off, but he didn't get to it." He pointed to a smudgy door just behind him. "You can go talk to him if you want; he's out back."

Pushing through the door, Detective Clayberry walked into an open area where cars were towed in and weighed. Beyond it stretched long rows of crumpled, abandoned vehicles. He started down the path to his right, where he saw a man in the distance. The yard was hot and smelled of oil and dust. He could hear buzzing from a wasp's nest, hidden in a vehicle somewhere.

Stoney Korbelak, a large and surly-looking man, was in his midforties. He was oddly dressed for a yard man; instead of overalls, he wore a shirt and trousers. His collar lay open, exposing a heavy gold chain. The man kept his eyes down, intent on cleaning his fingernails with a pocketknife.

"Sorry, don't know where they went," he answered irritably when Detective Clayberry questioned him. "Can't tell you anything." He waved toward the rows of broken cars. "The plates were here one day, gone the next."

"Would you know a Delbert Korbelak?" asked Detective Clayberry.

Stoney's head snapped up. "He's my kid. Why? Is this about the Café Salsa business? He's been cleared. He was in the neighborhood, that's all." Stoney's eyes glittered. "And I have nothin' to add."

Detective Clayberry sighed. "All right. About those missing plates—any strangers hanging around here when they were taken?"

Stoney shrugged, shook his head, and went back to cleaning his nails.

"Thanks," said Detective Clayberry. Going back inside, he slid his business card across the counter to Mr. Ropelato and left.

Given his other police workload, it wasn't until late September that Detective Clayberry was able to meet again with Will, Darius, and Audrey at Will's house. The school day had ended, and Margaret came with him. In a frustrated tone, the detective explained, "The license plates are a dead end. We can't find a connection between them and the red truck."

"Hmm," mused Audrey. "Isn't it curious that the plates on the truck have something to do with Delbert Korbelak's father?"

"If there is a link," the detective's voice was flat, "we won't learn about it from Stoney Korbelak."

"Did you talk to Delbert?" asked Will, disappointed about the plates.

"Yup," answered Detective Clayberry, pushing the notebook back into his pocket. "Both he and Fletcher Stiles said they didn't know anything about the PV system or the driver of the truck. They also said you three were stealing that countertop from Beyond Hair."

"Ha!" muttered Darius, "*They* were the ones stealing it."

Margaret leaned over to her dad. "Those two are often in trouble at school."

"Well," said Audrey, "it makes sense that Delbert didn't know anything about it, or he and Fletcher would have stayed away."

"True," said Will. "And the noise from the chains is what scared them off."

"Yeah—they probably didn't know about it," said Darius.

"Any fingerprints?" asked Will as Detective Clayberry stood up from the table.

He shook his head. "Not a print anywhere. Sainos was careful."

"You're sure it's him?"

"Only because of the phone calls you've gotten," said Detective Clayberry pointedly. "Time to go." Will, Audrey, and Darius walked outside with Margaret and her father.

"Bye, guys," said Margaret. "Sorry it wasn't better news."

The detective looked at Will. "If you're contacted by this Captain Glow again, let me know right away."

"Yes, sir," replied Will.

After that, the questions surrounding the captain and Sainos were pushed aside. High school was giving Will and his friends plenty to do. Their junior year of precalculus and physics called for hours of studying. Darius and Will were taking the same subjects, and Darius often got the highest marks in the class. Will had always worked to get good grades, but now, he admitted to himself, something had changed. Audrey was working intensely for top marks, and it made him try harder too. It was fun to be in her company. He liked the person she'd become. She was confident but not pushy, hardworking yet able to laugh at herself. He liked how well she got on with his family.

He thought back to the first time he'd met her. She was missing two front teeth, and the resulting lisp made her sound like a cartoon character. Will and Michael teased her without mercy, imitating her every time she talked. Audrey didn't complain, but finally Will's mother scolded them, saying, "Knock it off, you two."

Now it was different; Audrey made life at the Chambers' household much more interesting. She was playful, and he couldn't help noticing little things, like how nice she smelled. Not perfume-y—just clean, like fresh laundry. It nearly drove him crazy sometimes. He wasn't going to share that with a single soul, however, and it embarrassed him to think his mother might have caught on. Mrs. Chambers had a Sphinx-like look on her face whenever she noticed Will gazing sideways at Audrey, but she never said a word. *Thank you, Mom,* he thought. Just getting through his junior year was enough for him to think about.

CHAPTER

8

THREE WEEKS LATER, ABERDEEN shone in the splendor of autumn. Maple and aspen trees glowed in dazzling colors of red, orange, and yellow, and the October sky was a sparkling blue. Pumpkins appeared on doorsteps, and the grocery stores exhibited colorful racks of Halloween costumes. The Aberdeen High School football team was also in its glory, having trounced several top-ranked Utah teams, including the Bonneville Lakers and the Brighton Bengals. But a good football team wasn't the only interesting thing happening at Aberdeen High.

Trucks, trailers, and construction vehicles were laid out side by side on the eastern edge of a large field that bordered the football stadium. The project employed scores of people, most of whom wore the familiar garb of the construction worker: a plaid shirt, a white or yellow hardhat, blue jeans, and work boots.

As they arrived for school one Monday, Will, Darius, Audrey, and TR watched the vigorous activity on the large field. Workers laid out wooden stakes as others with blueprints in their hands pointed to various locations on the huge field where the work was being done. Large drilling equipment, laying horizontally on gigantic flatbed trucks, rolled past them to the parking lot.

"Interesting. I wonder what the drilling equipment's for?" said Darius, scrutinizing the machines.

"To do some drilling?" razzed TR as the four of them crowded through the door with the other students.

"Well, obviously they're gonna drill," said Darius, rolling his eyes, "but what are they drilling *for*?"

"You could ask Dr. Kanakawa," said TR over his shoulder as he headed off to his senior English class.

"I think we *should*, Darius" said Will, stuffing his jacket into his pack.

Dr. Kanakawa was the physics instructor at Aberdeen High. Will, Darius, and Audrey took their seats in her orderly classroom. When the last bell rang, she stood up from her desk and called the students to attention. The day's lesson was interesting. It covered Generation 4 nuclear power and included a short video of the prototype design for the traveling wave reactor (TWR) and a longer video on Molten Salt Reactor Fundamentals.[12]

---

12. For Footnote Link go to Captain Glow Website

They learned how Generation 4 reactors are sodium cooled, making these systems vastly safer than the outdated water-cooled reactor designs of Fukushima, Chernobyl and Three Mile Island. When class ended, Audrey, Will and Darius had no time to ask unrelated questions.

At lunch over roasted turkey, broccoli, steamed rice, and apple crisp, Darius, Will and Audrey talked about the drilling rigs. "Tomorrow I'll ask Dr. Kanakawa what's happening," said Darius, shoveling in the last bite of the gooey dessert.

"Or you could ask Mr. Bentley," said Audrey.

"Or even Principal Parker," offered Will, looking over Darius's shoulder, "except—there he goes." The principal had left the lunchroom after checking the bright orange 'This Exit Blocked' sign that kept students from going out into the construction area from the lunchroom.

Later that afternoon in English class, Mrs. Keller stood up to give them a reminder. "If you're debating, remember to drop by Mr. Compton's room today after school's dismissed." It was time for Aberdeen High's annual Halloween activity: The Great Alien Debate. This debate had taken place for nine years now and was always held on a Friday evening, usually two weeks before Halloween.

Mrs. Keller donated one day of fall class period to speech writing and debate in order to support it. "Remember, any proposition must have a science component involved," she announced, pointing to a poster advertising the event. The artwork showed a man and a woman gazing from the window of a spaceship at an unfamiliar planet; two moons glowed in the distance. Mrs. Keller went on, "Today, those of you who signed up to debate will choose the proposition from the ones that have been submitted."

Two weeks earlier, a sturdy wooden-and-brass suggestion box with paper and pencils had been placed on the activity table in the lunchroom. Since then, students had been writing down suggestions and stuffing them into the box. There had also been a sheet tacked up where students could sign up to take part in the debate.

Today Mr. Compton, the debate coach, and the students participating would choose the topic for The Great Alien Debate. On the evening of the actual event, the proposition would be affirmed or negated by ten costumed members of a theoretical "Intergalactic Federation." Darius and TR were returning veterans from the previous years' debates, and this year Will, Margaret, and Audrey had signed up to do it also. After school today, along with choosing the proposition, they would form two separate teams: one for the proposition and one against.

"Remember, class," said Mrs. Keller, putting down her copy of *Rhetoric & Readings*, "there will be a vote on which team makes the best argument, along with two trophies and two cash prizes for the best speech and best costume. Keep in mind the audience can ask questions, so if you'll be an audience member, listen up and think of some good ones!"

When the last bell of the day rang, Audrey called over to Will and Darius. "We have the Great Alien Debate meeting today, remember?"

Will gave a thumbs-up; tossing pencils and books into his pack, he said, "How long do you think it'll take?" He wished today's precalculus assignment wasn't so big.

"I suppose it depends on how long we take to choose the proposition and form two teams," she said.

"Wait," said Darius, frowning, "I want to talk to Mr. Bentley about the drilling project—especially before I see TR. Do I have time?"

"Sure," said Will.

"Just go quickly," said Audrey, pulling her pack onto her shoulders. "We'll tell Mr. Compton you're on your way." Darius sprinted in the opposite direction, disappearing into a flood of students in the hallway.

As they walked to Mr. Compton's classroom, Will couldn't resist. "Audrey, what kind of costume are you making?" Audrey and Mrs. Chambers had been on several mysterious errands the week before getting items for the extraterrestrial character Audrey would be in the debate. Her parents had even sent her a cardboard tube all the way from Chile, which had immediately disappeared into her room.

"Uh-uh, no good. You have to wait. It's a surprise," she said mischievously and then paused. "What are *you* going as?"

"Oh . . ." he stammered, realizing he hadn't given it a thought. "My dads got a tiger costume—I could wear that."

"And what galaxy are you from?"

"Uh, the jungle galaxy?" answered Will.

"Oh, you can do better than that."

"Yeah, I can," he said. "I just gotta think about it." They turned through the doorway of the debate teacher's classroom.

Mr. Compton stood writing at his whiteboard. The suggestion box was open on his desk, all papers unfolded and their contents revealed. His classroom displayed posters of famous authors, screenwriters, and filmmakers ranging from Charles Dickens to Steven Spielberg, the latter of whom had a caption below his photo reading, "I dream for a living."

TR was already in the room. He had a forest-green armband that he'd started wearing on September 19. It depicted a white map with large printed words. At first Principal Parker wasn't sure about the armband, and he called TR into his office to discuss it.

"My armband is a statement of mourning for damaged ecosystems and lives in the Gulf of Mexico," TR had explained. The map was an actual image of the gulf itself, and the words written across the image were *Crude Awakening*. TR's commitment stemmed from an older cousin of his who lived just outside New Orleans and was a member of the Coast Guard. He'd been a first responder to the horrendous explosion of an oil rig in the Gulf of Mexico. It was the largest known marine crude oil spill in the history of the petroleum industry.[13]

The accident occurred in April a few years earlier, and for the following three months oil flowed unrestricted into the gulf. It was *completely* stemmed on September 19 of that year, four months after the oil rig blew up. The loss was huge. Even now, years later, dolphins in the area of the oil spill died at a higher-than-normal rate, and autopsies of their lungs showed signs of oil poisoning. TR's cousin said that tar balls were still washing up on the beaches that had been hit with the worst of the contamination, given that the oil had sunk and was still buried beneath the sand just offshore.

After hearing what TR's armband represented and realizing there was nothing in the dress code that forbade it, Principal Parker gave TR the go-ahead. TR said he planned to wear it for a month to raise awareness of the fragility and beauty of marine ecosystems.

"It's not just about the people who were killed and the damaged sea life—and the mangrove islands, which my cousin Marshall says are almost wiped out," TR explained when people asked him about the armband. "It's that now we have other options. We don't have to keep punching holes in the bottom of the ocean. We have to advance the other potential sources of energy." Instead of seeing

---

13. For Footnote Link go to Captain Glow Website

the armband as a sign of disrespect, friends and faculty accepted the armband as exactly the opposite: a reminder to defend life on earth.

"Hey, TR," Will called out, "know what galaxy you're coming from?"

"Hmm," TR looked up. "Space, the final frontier. I'm not sure yet. First, I wanna know what the proposition is, then I'll choose my galaxy."

Next Margaret arrived followed by five other students.

"Darius is coming, Mr. Compton," said Audrey. "He had to see another teacher."

Mr. Compton turned around. He was a tall man with bright, gray eyes and a quick wit. He tossed his dry-erase marker onto the ledge of the whiteboard. "Let's begin, folks. Here are the choices." On the whiteboard he'd written out five potential topics.

"Is that all of them?" asked TR.

"Well, all the ones related to the debate. There was a rude one about school lunch—and a few others that were just ridiculous," Mr. Compton grinned. "Shall we get cracking?" He stood back from the whiteboard and they all looked over the list.

- *We aliens should take over leadership of Earth's technology corporations for a decade to improve their technology.*
- *We aliens should secretly test new drugs on humans to help them and all intergalactic species.*

- *We aliens should take knowledge scrolls from the Celestial Library and allow Earth's top scientists to have them for ten weeks before returning them.*
- *We aliens should appear to Earthlings as supernatural life-forms to give them guidance.*
- *We aliens should show humans exactly how WRECK-reational drugs harm a human body and lower Intelligence Quotient (IQ).*

What do you think, folks?" Mr. Compton continued. "Any of these you like? Any you don't?"

"I don't like the one that has to do with secret drug testing," said Margaret stridently. "It's unethical because the humans wouldn't have a choice. It would be done to them in secret, and that's wrong."

"Okay, then. Do we have anyone who wants to keep it?" Nobody objected. He turned to the whiteboard and drew a line through it.

"Yes! Thank you!" said Margaret, satisfied. Mr. Compton asked, "How about the remaining ones?"

Jace Spurlock, a rugged, handsome senior, sat with his friends Chris Craddock and Matt Simons. He spoke next. "I really like the one about supernatural life-forms."

Lynette Goodhardt, a lively blonde, swiveled around in her chair. "I can see its attraction, but it's also very . . . um, how to put it? It's a sensitive topic! You'd have to define supernatural *very* carefully. Like, what are you talking about? Does the ghost of Walt Disney appear to you or something?"

"Now that you mention it," said Jace, teasing, "he does, all the time!" He grinned at Chris. "Our best ideas for animation come from him." Mr. Compton and the other students knew that Jace had a popular YouTube account where he posted humorous animated videos. He and Chris generated the videos together and had a social following of more than a hundred-thousand subscribers, a few of whom were sitting in the room at that moment.

Matt, a lanky, thoughtful person and the quietest of the bunch, spoke next.

"Supernatural does sort of, hmm, tread on the sacred ground of loved ones who've passed on . . . it would have to be handled with sensitivity."

"Oh, I see your point," said Jace. "Not my greatest quality. Okay, we can skip that one." Lynette beamed at him.

Natalie Porter, a dark-haired senior and good friend of Lynette, piped up. "The one about taking knowledge scrolls from the Celestial Library sounds intriguing."

Matt grinned, "That's mine." He sat back, folding his hands behind his head. "The proposition is that we take knowledge scrolls from the Celestial Library to share with Earth's scientists, and the scientists have to return them before they get angry and cause death, destruction, and—that stuff."

"Keep going," said Will, "—and why do they do that!?"

"Because the top dog Celestial librarian doesn't share. He's kind of a grandmaster guy—it'll make him mad."

Matt continued. "The knowledge scrolls contain technologies that humans would want."

"Like what?" asked Chris.

"Like—a successful fusion reactor—or a functioning space elevator to carry things out of Earth's gravity," said Matt.

"Like mining Helium Rain!" said Jace diplomatically.

"You mean Helium-3. *Helium Rain* is a videogame," said Will.

"Right, Helium-3," Jace grinned.

"That would fit right in—Helium-3 moon-mining that works," said Matt. "Humans would like to have that ability, right?" He looked around the room. No one objected.

"What about the first one," said Mr. Compton, "the takeover of Earth's corporations?"

"Does Earth have anything to offer aliens that would make it worth their while?" Jace said, snorting.

"So true," said Chris. "And aliens could actually make things worse if they didn't understand trade relations, global patent law, and marginally educated workforces."

"That's us, right?" said Jace.

"Hey," said Mr. Compton, holding up his hand. "No, you're not marginally educated!" He ticked off his fingers. "Sports rules, religious constructs, Google search methods, online video streaming, complex phone applications—not to mention what you might've picked up at school." The students laughed.

"You're right, Mr. Compton," conceded Jace. "We'll put that knowledge to good use."

"Bingo," said the teacher.

"Mr. Compton," Audrey piped up, "the topic of technology leadership is good—it's just that . . . debating over leadership is like—career planning. Someone in here will likely *be* a corporate leader one day."

"Yes!" said Chris zealously, "And if so, remember your bright high school friends who can do great public relations work for you!"

"Yeah!" said Jace, and he and Chris did a fist bump across the aisle. Then it happened. Jace winked at Audrey, and she smiled back. Will's stomach plummeted.

Chris continued, "On that topic, while technology leadership *might* benefit humans, that proposition does lack adventure. I'm leaning toward raiding the Celestial Library."

"I don't know," said Mr. Compton. "Having an eleven-foot-tall red alien in charge of the Lawrence Berkeley Labs could be very interesting!" But when they took a show of hands, the students voted no on that one, and—on the one about aliens posing as supernatural life-forms. Mr. Compton drew a line through both suggestions. Just then, Darius bolted into the room.

"Sorry I'm late, Mr. Compton," he said, sliding into a desk. He looked at the propositions on the board and saw that they had been narrowed down to two: taking scrolls from the Celestial Library or educating humans about WRECK-reational drugs. Darius frowned. His suggestion had been crossed out. "Hey, why not the one on technology leadership?"

Margaret explained its lack of appeal.

Darius spluttered, "Aliens could be great with global patent law!" but gave up when he saw that it had no support.

Next the WRECK-reational drug idea was vetoed because, as Natalie Porter said, "We have an awareness project ongoing about how the legalization of pot is only so that criminals are put out of business and very sick people are able to eat."

"She's right. Health class is all over that," said Chris. He pointed to a poster on the wall. It was titled "The Harmful Effects of Marijuana" and showed how the brain, the reproductive system, the lungs, the immune system, the heart, and many other body parts were damaged by marijuana use.

The final choice was made. The students liked that it was completely different from the previous year's proposition, which had been to take all of humanity off of the Earth so that the Earth could recover from pollution. In an unexpected outcome, the audience had voted in favor to do so, after a persuasive speaker gave a concise, well-crafted argument to support it. She'd suggested that putting humans on a different planet would *protect* them and make them healthier.

She was well prepared, spoke clearly, and wore a pale-blue gossamer wig that fanned straight up. In contrast, the closing speaker of the other team had simply raced through his disorganized notes. He and his teammates were defeated; the better-prepared team and the blue wig won.

Today's vote was to go with the proposition *We aliens should take knowledge scrolls from the Celestial Library and allow Earth's top scientists to have them for ten weeks before returning them.* Next they formed the "for" and "against" teams, and each debater was given a number. The meeting ended with everyone committing to be there Friday night, on time, with their speeches and costumes ready.

As Will, Darius, and Audrey headed to the parking lot, Will looked at the huge flatbed trucks casting long shadows in the hazy twilight. All was quiet. The workers were gone. "Did you find anything out about the drilling equipment?" Will asked Darius.

"Yup," said Darius, "and it's just as incredible as any fusion reactor. What do you think you can both get *from* and put *into* the ground that's valuable?"

"Darius," said Audrey, her tone one of exasperation, "we've got tons of homework and it's *full* of questions. Can't you just tell us?"

"Yeah," said Will, "just tell us." He didn't have a clue what Darius meant. *You could get gold or silver out of the ground*, he thought, *but you wouldn't put it back.*

"I'll give you a hint," said Darius.

Will rolled his eyes. "Go ahead." Expecting to get a ready answer from a Lego-master-builder was hopeless. "What's the hint?"

Darius swept his arm in front of him. "The ground's full of it."

"Grass?" said Audrey.

"No, what I'm talking about is buried."

"Worms," she offered.

"No."

"Hmm . . . people?" said Will.

"People!?" Darius put his hands up in mock revulsion. "No! Taking people out of the ground? Gross! I'm talking about heat energy!"

"Heat energy?" asked Audrey, puzzled.

"Right," Darius went on. "Heat energy. One of the most promising energy sources is right under us. It's the temperature of the earth." As they climbed into Darius's jeep, he went on. "Mr. Bentley drew it out for me on the board, which is what took so long. He had that enthusiastic, wild look on his face."

"You mean like when he explained density and the freezing point of water?" said Will.

"Yes! Exactly! Anyway, the trucks are here to drill ninety wells. They'll go to a depth of three hundred feet."

"Okay," said Will, "ninety wells, three hundred feet. Then what?"

Darius started the jeep. "Let me begin with a bigger picture. A ground-source heat pump system can pull heat energy out of the ground because the ground is at a certain temperature. That temperature is usually between 40 to 50 degrees Fahrenheit, or 4 to 10 degrees Celsius. But what's really interesting is that the big systems, like the one here for our school, can store cold or heat back into the ground and then take it out later. It's like money in a bank! You can put it in, and you can take it out. Of course, in this case, to answer your question, it's done with pumps and long sections of liquid-filled pipes in the ground. Look—when we get to your house, I'll draw you a picture like the one Mr. Bentley drew for me. I could even make a Lego model out of it."

When they got to the Chambers' home, the three pulled chairs up to the kitchen table, and Darius sketched a diagram.[14]

"In winter, the liquid mixture of methanol and water in the underground pipes gets pumped up into this building," he explained, drawing a small structure and pointing to it. "This is a pump house. It's twenty feet square. The wells are vertical. Here," he said, pointing to a pipeline that came into the building, "is a horizontal trench with a pipe from the well heads to the pump house. From the pump house the mixture goes into the interior of the building,

---

14. For Footnote Link go to Captain Glow Website

and through a heat exchanger here. The heat exchanger transfers the underground temperature to glycol. In winter the glycol can be warmed further by electric heat pumps, getting the air inside to a nice, comfy 72 degrees Fahrenheit, 22 degrees Celsius. In summer it works in reverse, moving the hot liquid down into the ground and bringing up the liquid from the ground, which is much cooler compared to the hot summer air. It's all a continuous loop."[15]

"Wow!" said Audrey. "Good explanation, Darius!"

Will pushed aside a small pang of jealousy. "Does it save money?" he asked.

"Oh, yeah! At least, that's what Mr. Bentley says. This kind of system is . . . how did he put it? Twice as efficient as top-rated air conditioners and close to 50 percent more efficient than the best gas furnace, all year round. Plus, there aren't many moving parts, so it should last a long time." All three fell silent.

Finally Will said, "Guess we can say 'drill, baby, drill' again, only this time it's for ground-source heat pump wells." Audrey laughed and rubbed his arm. Suddenly, he was ridiculously happy. He stood up and stretched. "Darius, I think you *should* make a Lego model for a ground-source heat pump system."

Darius grinned, completely oblivious to the ups and downs of Will Chambers' feelings for Audrey Carter.

---

15. For Footnote Link go to Captain Glow Website

CHAPTER
9

O N THE THURSDAY NIGHT before the debate, Margaret came over to the Chambers' home just after supper. Weeks earlier she'd asked whether she could use Comox as a sidekick for her debate character. They'd said yes immediately. Since they planned to attend the debate, they offered to bring Comox home afterward. Now Margaret was here to do the last fitting of the dog's Yoda costume.

"It's made for a dog," she said. "You see? It goes over the back and then hangs loosely down in front. He'll look adorable!" She and Mrs. Chambers slid the lightweight, loose-fitting costume over the husky. Everyone in the room burst out laughing; even Comox looked amused. Margaret had cut larger holes in the fabric to accommodate his ears. They stuck straight up in contrast to the green fabric ears, which flopped down on either side.

"I think Comox might take the best costume prize, eh?" said Mrs. Chambers, wiping away her tears.

"Yes," Dr. Chambers agreed, "I'll have a hard time voting for anyone but him, kids."

Margaret hugged the good-natured dog and said, "See you tomorrow, Comox, and remember: a vote for you is a vote for me." Comox wagged his tail.

———

ON THE NIGHT OF The Great Alien Debate, excitement was running high. Will had decided to skip the tiger costume and chose instead to wear a Star Fleet officer's shirt of gold and black, based on the well-loved television and film series, *Star Trek*. This indicated he was an engineering officer. Darius rang the front door bell at six p.m. to pick up Will and Audrey. He'd chosen similar attire, wearing a Star Fleet officer's shirt of red and black. The pips on his collar indicated he was a Captain. His normally bushy black hair was slicked down in place and it made him look very grown up. He'd also brought in a self-designed Lego model of the *USS Phoenix* star ship, which he'd created several years earlier. He showed its intricate construction to Will and Dr. Chambers.

Darius and Will were on opposing teams. Will would be against raiding the Celestial Library, and Darius would be for it. Audrey was on the same team as Will and was still being secretive about her costume. Every night for the past week, she'd disappeared into her room when she finished her homework so she could work on it.

Moments after Darius's arrival, Mrs. Chambers dashed into the kitchen. "I'll be bringing Audrey. She has one last section to attach, but it's tricky. Go on and pick up Margaret and take Comox—he's ready." Comox jumped up when he heard his name.

Will and the dog climbed into the gold jeep. Will buckled his seatbelt and then asked, "Do you have your speech done?" Darius was standing at the rear of the jeep, tucking the starship model into a padded cardboard box.

"Yup," he answered cheerfully as he got behind the wheel. They backed out of the driveway and headed for Sterling Court, the street where the Clayberrys lived.

It was a beautiful fall evening; the cool air was filled with the dusky smell of autumn. Margaret was already waiting on the front steps of her house, surrounded by pumpkins.

Her costume was made entirely of the same fabric in tawny pale beige, the color of sand. The flowing top layer came down from her shoulders, tunic style. It split into two sections, crisscrossing her upper torso and ending just below the knees. Looped twice around her waist was a brown leather belt with a pouch that rested on her hip. Her arms had snug cloth coverings extending from shoulder to wrist. A T-shirt and loose pants that came to her knee completed her garb. On her feet were short, black, flat-sole boots. Her dark mass of hair was pulled back into three knobby sections, giving her a strong resemblance to a young female from a galaxy far, far away.

She slid into the jeep's back seat and immediately began to coo over Comox, patting him on the head and saying, "Good boy, you ready to win this thing?" She turned to Darius and Will. "Where's Audrey?"

"She's coming with my folks," said Will, staring at her transformation. "Great costume," he offered.

"Yeah," agreed Darius.

"Thanks," said Margaret, grinning, "You too." As they pulled away from Sterling Court and onto the main road, Will noticed Margaret holding tightly onto her speech, which was tucked inside a clear sheet protector. *She's practiced it,* he thought. She was on the other team with Darius. Will's speech was on a crumpled sheet of paper stuffed into his pocket. *I did run though it twice,* he thought. *Well, almost twice.* He'd focused a lot more on his precalculus homework than he had on his debate speech.

Audrey was on his team. *She's probably practiced too. Come on*, he told himself, *this is really about learning to debate and the voting process.* Actually, he preferred the idea of raiding the library to gain knowledge on behalf of Earth. But there had to be two opposing teams, and he understood that they were practicing how to communicate the pros and cons of ideas. *At least I look credible in this uniform.*

"Is your dad coming tonight?" he asked Margaret. He hadn't talked to the detective since their meeting concerning the license plates.

"Nope. He's picking someone up at the airport and won't be home 'til late. My mom's visiting family in Denver, but Jackie's coming; she's got the car, and she's bringing friends!" Darius pulled into the parking lot at the school. They climbed out of the jeep, and Margaret slipped the Yoda costume onto Comox.

They'd almost stopped laughing when the sight of Lynette Goodhardt and Natalie Porter got them going again. The two wore a single, giant, stretched-out, lime-green T-shirt that ended just above their knees. In black leggings, with their inside legs bound together, they'd become a three-legged, two-headed creature. They heightened the illusion by using red hairspray paint, which made Natalie's brown hair and Lynette's blonde hair closer to the same color. They were also on Margaret and Darius's team. *We might stand a chance,* thought Will, seeing how Lynette and Natalie couldn't stop giggling.

The walkway to the school entrance was lined with a dozen carved pumpkins that had lit candles inside. Most had come from TR's garden. Some had noses and ears made from cut-out pumpkin pieces; others were carved with spaceships and star shapes.

The school's entryway had clouds of white mist rolling low along the ground from two fog machines. These were concealed in the base of two large papier-mâché rockets set on either side of the glass double doors.

Will entered first. The inside doors were decorated with a silver arch of material, which framed the top and draped down the sides. Beyond the archway were two curtains made from a fabric of colorful planets in space. These were held open on either side. "Wow," said Will, "the student activity team delivered on the decorations."

"Best ones I've seen!" agreed Darius.

"Awesome," said Margaret, coming through the curtains with Yoda/Comox.

Floating inside the auditorium were nearly a hundred green balloons tethered to the walls and the stage. They were transformed with black electrician's tape to look like alien faces. Some were smiling; others were stoic; a good number of them were scowling. A few looked like bad-guy Minecraft creepers. The stage was covered with a massive orange drop cloth. Items of various heights had been placed underneath it, giving the stage a rocky-landscape appearance. A dark velvet curtain hung as the backdrop. On it was the image of planet Earth, floating like a jewel in the blackness of space. There were ten simple padded stools set out, making it easy for anyone who wore a bulky costume to sit down. A tall, thin, plastic pole was attached vertically to each stool with zip ties. Large emerald-green cards were fastened to the top of the ten separate poles. Each card had a gigantic black number on it. Starting from left to right, the numbers went in order from one to ten.

The podium for the moderator was in the middle, which split the padded stools into two sections of five stools each. The podium had a very large placard that fit perfectly over its front. The placard bore a photo from the Hubble Telescope of a real galaxy and also included the words *The Great Alien Debate.*

A buzzing of voices filled the auditorium as guests arrived. Most were students, but a number of them were parents who'd brought along young children. Matt Simons appeared, dressed in black. He had extra arms attached in additional black sleeves, which rose and fell as he moved his real arms. His light-brown hair was now sprayed a vibrant blue. He and TR had joined creative forces to be from the same species, since TR—who'd also just arrived, wore identical garb.

"These extra arms will come in useful," said TR, waving his additional arms. "We'd be the most valuable guys on any sports team."

"Well . . . not on a soccer team!" said Matt, motioning to his double to go up the steps in front. Climbing onto the stage, they attracted attention. They waved cheerily to the audience and went to opposite sides of the orange "rocky" terrain, since they were on opposing teams. They found their assigned numbers and sat down on the padded stools.

"Hey TR!—TR!" a child's voice called out. TR scanned the crowd. It was his eight-year-old brother, Denzel, sitting in the front row along with Mr. and Mrs. Bartson. Denzel had come in costume. He looked to be from the computer game *SPORE* and was portraying a walking, talking, four-foot plant. He had two large, dark-green, fiddle-leaf fig tree leaves sticking up from the back of his head like giant glossy ears. They were held in place by a green headband with five plastic eyeballs glued to the front. He also wore a flowing green cape, green sweatshirt, and green pants, and he was waving a neon-green light sabre that glowed from within. Denzel's mother had ironed the words *Botany Man* onto his sweatshirt.

"Hey, Botany Man!" TR called to his brother.

Denzel raised his sword and hollered, "Trick-or-treat!" People around him laughed.

Jace Spurlock was the next to appear, wearing a gray, black, and white camouflage shirt and trouser combo. The shirt had white-and-gold braided loops on the shoulders, and he wore protective football gear underneath. The shoulder and thigh pads gave him the look of an immense space warrior, and his hair was spiked up as high as it could go.

Chris Craddock followed Jace, also wearing football gear underneath but looking more like a scientist in the biggest white lab coat Will had ever seen. Chris had a gold badge pinned to his coat, and he carried a blue plastic clipboard. In typical Jace and Chris fashion, they physically sparred with each other in front of the stage before going up the steps, drawing laughter from the audience members who were sitting in front.

At five minutes to seven, all but one of the debaters had taken their places. Matt Simons was on the outer-left edge in seat number one. Natalie Porter and Lynette Goodhardt sat together in seats two and three. Next was Darius in seat four. He'd placed his starship model on the stage in front of him. Next to Darius and closest to the podium in seat number five was Margaret, who had Comox sitting next to her. To the right of the podium, in seat number six, sat Will. Seat number seven, reserved for Audrey, was empty. TR Bartson was in eight, Jace Spurlock was in nine, and Chris Craddock was in ten.

As the students faced the audience, two large, floating, silver "wagon" wheels came through the auditorium doors. The wheels were on either side of a gleaming frame with a figure rising up between them. The apparatus moved forward. Only the upper torso was visible; the figure's lower half was obscured by sparkly silver netting. The elevated silver wheels rotated forward. A slim horizontal axle connecting the wheels was threaded through a small, gray backpack worn by the person within. The spokes of the wheels sparkled too. Strands of tinsel the length of a pencil wafted away from the edges of the wheels, adding to the illusion that it was gliding through the air.

That has to be Audrey, thought Will, but her face was unrecognizable. It was painted white; there was a powdery turquoise oval painted above one eye and a pale pink oval above the other. In symmetry, on either cheek, was a perfectly drawn black spiral, and her lips were a light purple. The effect was very other-worldly.

The figure in the floating cart smiled, and Will instantly knew her. As Audrey approached the stairs leading up to the stage, Jace jumped forward to help. Wishing he'd thought of it first, Will came along beside him. *No wonder she'd been busy,* he thought.

Audrey wisely took the arms of both Will and Jace. It was unsteady work to climb the stairs to the stage. She reached the top, regained her balance, and surprisingly sat down with no problem. Her design wasn't wide, but it was deep.

Will leaned over and whispered, "Very impressive!"

"Thanks, Will" she whispered back.

Mr. Compton came to the podium. He wore a long, tailored, black gown with a stretchy black-stocking cap. It had no brim, but it was structured and rather boxy, and it almost covered his ears. The front of the cap had an official-looking emblem. He tapped the mic and called out, "Welcome guests!" Then he banged a gavel down on the podium several times; with that, everyone in the room settled down. He turned around, gave a thumbs up to the alien debaters, and turned back to the microphone.

"Welcome, distinguished space visitors and voting members, to our Ninth Annual Great Alien Debate. To many of you, I am a local high school teacher. But tonight, I am the Honorable Beri Den-Rod, leader of the Intergalactic Federation, and I'll be your unbiased moderator for tonight's debate. We know many of you have traveled long distances to get here. We ask that your spaceships are parked and you don't let them idle. If you need assistance, see Mrs. Keller, over to my right; she's helping out tonight." Mrs. Keller waved from the side of the stage. She was wearing a pair of red antennae.

The audience gave a round of applause. He continued, "Please turn off or silence your communication devices. That said, let's begin. Tonight, we aliens are debating for or against the proposition that we should take knowledge scrolls from the Celestial Library and allow Earth's top scientists to have them for a limited time. "Team A, on your left, supports borrowing from the Celestial Library, and Team B, on your right, *opposes* borrowing from the Celestial Library."

As he gestured to the teammates, some of them gave a wave to the audience. "We'll start with introductions and then flip a coin to decide which team begins. Our debaters will alternate giving their speeches, which are limited to three minutes each. I'll be watching the clock. Remember that, please," he said, turning to the students as he picked up a brightly colored plastic ray-gun that lay alongside the gavel. "Otherwise, you'll be vaporized. Three minutes; that's it. Then we'll accept questions from the audience, and once that's done, we'll take the final vote. You, the audience members, will decide which team has made the best presentation, which individual made the best speech, and which costume is the most creative. Ballots are being passed out even as I speak."

Sure enough, Mrs. Keller and Mr. Bentley were handing out small sheets of white paper. The Honorable Leader Beri Den-Rod held one up. "You'll see that our ballots have the large letters *A* and *B* printed on the top. Those letters represent the two teams. To vote, make a tear through the letter of your choice. Next, the numbers one through ten on the right will let you vote for best costume; tear through the number to make your best costume choice. Finally, on the left are the numbers one through ten for best speech. Again, tear the number for the speech you think is best. You only need to make a tear through the two sets of numbers and then through a letter to cast your vote. At the end of the debate, we'll collect the ballots and count them. Then we'll announce the winning team and award the trophies and cash prizes for best speech and costume. Thank you! We are ready to start!"

The audience applauded and whistled. Mr. Compton/ Beri Den-Rod took the cordless mic out of the holder and gave it to Matt Simons who looked alarmed at having to go first. He regained his composure and spoke clearly, introducing himself as Mobox from the Gamma Galaxy and pointing to TR, on the other side, as his copilot. TR lifted his wobbly arms and waved. Lynette and Natalie introduced themselves as coming from the planet Legantula, taking turns and trying not to giggle as they spoke. Darius held up his starship model and gave his name as Captain Darius Cameron of the *USS Starship Phoenix*. Margaret introduced herself as Rey and introduced Comox as Yoda. Mr. Compton then passed the microphone to Will, who gave his name as Starfleet Officer Will Tigers, taking his name from the tiger costume he'd mentioned earlier to Audrey.

Audrey stood and introduced herself as Omega from the constellation *Pictor*. "I'm a holographic projection sent from a solar system that's forty-two light-years away. The Pictor Constellation is known to Earth through instruments used at the La Silla Telescope in the country of Chile." She held up a large poster. It showed an observatory captioned with the words *ESO La Silla Telescope*.[16] She set the poster down and said, "From there, you're looking at us, *and* . . . we're looking back! It's great to be here, even if I'm only a projection—thanks!" She sat down. People applauded, including Mrs. Chambers with great enthusiasm. TR was up next. He introduced himself as Jobox. Wiggling his extra arms, he waved to Mobox/Matt, who waved back, making the audience chuckle.

---

16. For Footnote Link go to Captain Glow Website

Next, Jace Spurlock introduced himself as Jace Grinder, a mission leader in the Intraspace Police Force. Going last, Chris Craddock presented himself as Chris Grinder and pointed to Jace, saying, "I'm Jace Grinder's senior officer *and* grandfather, though we look the same age. I'm actually seventy-seven in Earth years. We're aging differently because I live on the other side of a wormhole where time is moving more slowly. Check out the work of Dr. Kip Thorne, the Nobel Prize-winning theoretical physicist[17] who grew up right here in Utah." That mention got a round of applause.

Now that introductions were finished, the Honorable Beri Den-Rod took the microphone back from Chris, pulled out a quarter, and said "Rey, will you call it?" Rey/Margaret chose heads for Team A. Beri Den-Rod tossed the quarter and it landed on tails. Team B was up.

Will, who'd been going over his crumpled piece of paper, stood up, took the mic, and looked out at the audience. "I oppose taking scrolls from the Celestial Library for one main reason. It's against the prime directive of not interfering with the progress of species on other planets. Such interference includes sharing more advanced knowledge or technology.

"This applies to Earth also. Simply handing over information on how to construct space elevators or fusion

---

17. For Footnote Link go to Captain Glow Website

technology interferes with our ability to figure it out on our own. The knowledge could make us weaker and expose us to the dangers of not being able to safely use technologies we don't fully understand."

He looked down at his notes on recent human innovations.

"We are capable of making achievements ourselves. Look at Earth's Middle Eastern countries where the United Arab Emirates Abu Dhabi Future Energy Company[18] has clean energy projects all over the world. Look at the Scandinavian countries in which about 83 percent of electricity generation is low-carbon—63 percent of it coming entirely from renewable sources.

"In the United States we have a brilliant company that produces rocket launchers that return to earth and land in perfect synchronization. That same company set up an Australian commercial-scale solar PV installation with battery back-up that was done in record time. That's a postcard from the future.

"The Hanford nuclear waste site in the state of Washington is the biggest challenge the Department of Energy has ever faced. Now, an inventive procedure and smart leadership from the Bechtel Corporation will guide the plant through a recently developed process where low-activity radioactive-tank waste will be converted into a

---

18. For Footnote Link go to Captain Glow Website

stable glass form. Read up on vitrification of nuclear waste if you're interested in how we humans can stabilize radio-active by-products.[19]

"Not so very long ago at Houston's annual Cambridge Energy Research Associates Week, known as CERAWeek, Robert Dudley, a group chief executive of British Petroleum, said, 'Renewables are growing faster than any fuel in history—five times faster than gas. That makes them a really exciting investment prospect—particularly where you can partner wind and solar with gas to counter the intermittency issues.'

"As for that intermittency issue, which means when the sun doesn't shine or the wind doesn't blow, labs, universities, and countries around the world—such as Sandia National Laboratories along with Canada and Germany—are collaborating to improve and scale-up a process called power to gas. Power to gas uses synthetic methane gas to store excess electricity generated by wind and solar in our already existing underground methane gas pipeline infrastructure.

"All the facts I've presented just now show that we human beings are able to find solutions. Our history proves this. We don't need to invite punishment from other star systems by having a lack of faith ourselves. On that basis I agree with Team B and oppose bringing the scrolls to Earth. Thank you."

---

19. For Footnote Link go to Captain Glow Website

Will sat down, grateful for the modest applause, and gave the mic back to their moderator, who passed it to Margaret.

Margaret stood. Comox stood too. The audience loved it. "Down through the ages," she said, standing tall, "we've noticed that the greatest achievements of self-aware beings happen when we are brave and want to share knowledge. Why? Because this urge taps into the divine longing to create something good and to share the good that is created. This is why I choose not to follow the prime directive rule. When beneficial knowledge is shared, it's a win for both sides and creates alliances that last beyond centuries."

She paused. Comox sat down again. She glanced at her paper and continued. "Our Galactic panel is fortunate in that we have obtained the library access codes to get these scrolls. We can give the scrolls to Earth and get them back before the Celestial Library becomes aware that they have been borrowed and their librarian goes on a destructive rampage. It's time to ask our attending twenty-first-century humans if they want the beneficial knowledge." She swept her arm toward the audience, indicating she meant them.

"If you vote yes, the next three steps are: one," she held up her index finger, "co-create the guidelines for the use of these new technologies; two, formulate a schedule to integrate the technologies; and three—the toughest part—assist in growing the skills needed to put the technologies successfully into action without peril."

Margaret paused. "Guidelines, schedule, skill-building. And, my dear fellow space travelers, I believe we can get the scrolls back into the library before the ten weeks are up, without detection and without punishment."

Comox, still sitting, scratched vigorously at his ear, pulling the costume sideways. The audience began laughing, and Margaret knew to end there. Kneeling down, she readjusted the costume and said quickly, "Vote for Team A to share the scrolls. Thank you!" Comox barked, and Rey/Margaret sat down to enthusiastic applause.

The microphone came to Audrey. Her objection to bringing the scrolls to Earth was based on the spread of diseases. "I urge you to realize that until rigorous studies have been done on the contact of humans with materials and beings from another star system, it's too high a risk. We may share diseases with each other that spin out of control. We're not ready right now." She went on to recount how in different times in the history of Earth this had accidentally happened, citing the way cholera wiped out most of the indigenous peoples of Vancouver Island in Canada. She closed by saying, "Please vote for Team B. Don't take the scrolls. Thank you." She gave her wheels a spin and sat down to polite hand-clapping.

Darius was up next. His thoughts echoed Margaret's win-win point where both sides would benefit. He talked of how the holders of knowledge became the most expertly skilled when they shared it with others. "Once we study the scrolls and we know who designed the technologies we need most, we'll contact them directly. This ship," he said, holding up his model, "uses a well-designed warp-speed engine. But what most of you don't know is that the propulsion sections are based on a design from the radiation harvesters used on a K2 exoplanet circling the star EPIC 2-0-1-1-3-6-7-0-6-5 in the nearby Leo Constellation. That star was found thanks to NASA's Large Binocular Telescope Interferometer, also known as LBTI. That one's down in Arizona, and it's another great telescope," he said, giving a nod to Omega/Audrey.

"But back to the warp-speed engines," he continued, "the inhabitants of that far-off planet got their design team together with our Star Fleet design team, and the result? Warp-speed technology that surpassed anything the design teams could have done on their own. That outcome proves sharing technology can bring greater results! We should get the scrolls. Vote Team A! Thank you."

The mic went to Team B and TR, who brought up the harsh topic of weapons. "We must think about whether any of the technologies the scrolls reveal could be turned into weapons of mass destruction! If so, there could be a tragic ending where all life on earth perishes, or—or— the Earthlings could start attacking us! Humans can be deceptive; think of the Trojan horse. Think of the humans who claimed that 'No, no, cigarettes don't cause cancer' or humans who claim the Earth is only six thousand years old, when all evidence proves that to be too short a time. Humans are too unstable. I support the prime directive to not interfere by giving them technology they did not develop!" He waved his many arms and said, "Vote for Team B against taking the scrolls." He handed the mic back to the Honorable Leader and took a bow.

Lynette and Natalie gave a surprisingly coherent speech, avoiding the fits of laughter they'd been prone to earlier. They took turns finishing each other's sentences and claimed that giving humans new technologies would allow them to quickly regain a stable climate system. Then humans could develop transportation to come and go from Earth, which would give a boost to earth's economy and morale. "Taking a holiday is such a pick-me-up," said Lynette. At this point they stood and burst into song with a three-legged kick like in a chorus line. They sang, "The gift of sharing is brave and daring, to make a better galaxy for all!" Then Lynette began to giggle. Natalie managed to close with "Please vote Team A to get the scrolls."

Jace, on the opposing side, supported TR's idea that the sharing of technology could lead to the development of deadly weapons. "But," he said, "my grandfather and I do want to share something exciting that is less danger-ous. And this is technology *we've* developed. We're offering remotely guided robotic building systems. These robots cannot become weapons, and they will make it possible for Earth to colonize Mars. As spaceships we provide to Earth orbit around the red planet, humans would control the robots. After that, we'll assist with our *never-fail* method for growing atmospheres, and we'll throw in partially melting polar ice caps for free, which will create oceans and also create a stable water cycle. Mars will be habitable for humans in fewer than fifty years. How's that?"

The audience was momentarily stunned. "Are you ready for the ultimate adventure? Hiking and biking on Mars? Ready to make it happen? We can do it! Skip causing trouble in another galaxy. Vote for Team B. Don't take the scrolls!" Several committed mountain bikers gave a cheer. The rest of the audience caught the enthusiasm, and Jace received a round of applause.

With the floor back to Team A, Matt took the microphone and began speaking in a clear, thoughtful voice. "You actually don't need help with remotely guided robotic building systems. You're going to be able to make those by yourselves in few years! Don't take that in place of the knowledge scrolls. The scrolls' information is too valuable; you'd be making a bad bargain."

With a glance at his notes, Matt took the debate in a fresh direction. He spoke of how the more highly developed technology would greatly reduce the costly process of carbon fuel-extraction from the Earth. As the new technologies are implemented, he said, they would likely lead to a more equitable distribution of resources needed for all human, animal, and plant life. The increased human creativity would then lead to more positive global interaction.

"The trick is to get the scrolls in the hands of the best hundred minds on the planet that can accept the new information and then accept that these scrolls are going to go away," he paused. "I agree that we don't want to bring war to Earth, so these scrolls have to go back. I'm willing to take the risk of getting them from the library and returning them without detection. My team, the brave Team A, can do it. Vote Team A. Thank you!" With that, he handed the mic over and sat down.

On the other side, Chris said, "In my seventy-seven years of life, I've seen many good plans fall apart. It's easy to start a war when you take things, even if you plan to return them!" He pulled a phone out of his lab-coat pocket. Jace said, "Hey, that's my phone!" The two began to spar in a comical manner, with Chris getting Jace in a headlock. The Honorable Leader banged the podium with his gavel; when that didn't work, he went over and banged the gavel on Chris and Jace. Finally they separated, laughing, and he retrieved the microphone.

"Do I have to remind you—you're on the same team?"

"Right," said Chris.

"Just a little feud," said Jace, taking back the mic.

"But d'you see my point?" asked Chris, giving the phone to Jace. "A small act of thievery can lead to a fight!"

"We know these Celestial Library people!" said Jace, pushing his hair back up into spikes. "Yes," said Chris, wiping his hands, which had hair goop on them. "Remember the Library of Alexandria that was destroyed by fire in 48 BC? That was the Celestial Librarian havin' a bad day! Some of his scrolls had found their way to into Alexandria and—whoosh, up in flames! That's what happened."

"Yep," said Jace. "Tell 'em about the Moses thing."

"The Ten Commandments were written on tablets and given to Moses as a gift. But that part about Moses getting angry and breaking those tablets? Nope. It was that same guy. He thought they were from *his* library, and even though it turns out he was wrong, kaboom! He busted 'em up."

"And put it on Moses," said Jace. "Who was probably freakin' out about the tablets getting' busted up!!"

Chris nodded. "We think our friends on Team A could get hurt or killed, and we also think people on Earth could get hurt or killed—because it does happen when you mess with the Celestial Library. So Jace and I ask you to vote against the proposition, and that means we're asking you to vote for Team B. Thank you."

The two young men sat down.

The Honorable Beri Den-Rod was back at the podium. "It's now time take questions from the audience."

Margaret's sister, Jackie, raised her hand and was given a microphone by Mrs. Keller. Jackie addressed her question to Matt/Mobox, which was no surprise because they had just started dating. "Would you want to lend the scrolls only to scientists, or would you lend them to scientists *and* political leaders?"

He answered thoughtfully. "Well, Jackie, I'd lend them to gifted scientists and to political leaders who have a clear record of good leadership."

Then Fletcher Stiles, leaning against a wall, popped one of the green balloons. "Sooorry." Fletcher said sarcastically. "Stupid things. Anyway, I have a question. Why are we wasting our time with this?" The question wasn't addressed to anyone; Fletcher just wanted to bring down the mood.

Will said, "I'll take it." He was given the mic. "Debate and voting are part of our lives and it's also mathematically likely we share this universe with other beings. The question doesn't relate, so it should be thrown out."

"Along with him," whispered Audrey. It was silent for a moment then other hands shot up.

"That's settled then," said Mr. Compton, "and we have more questions."

Mr. Compton/Beri Den-Rod's teenage daughter, Francesca, raised her hand and asked, "Captain Darius, given people are always in search of medical advances, does the pro-sharing team think we'd gain medical advances by taking a look at these scrolls?"

Darius took the mic. "Yes! We can make a special point to borrow medical scrolls."

Audrey waved her hand for the mic. "How could that work? The other species will likely be different enough that their medical treatments won't apply to Earthlings." She handed the mic back.

Will noticed Fletcher Stiles had moved to the rear of the auditorium with his friend, Delbert Korbelak. The two were helping themselves to refreshments meant for the upcoming break when the ballots would be counted.

The debaters took a few more questions then the Honorable Beri Den-Rod brought down the gavel to end the debate. "Please tear your votes into your ballots and pass them to your right." He looked at his assistants. "Mr. Bentley, Mrs. Keller, please take the ballots to be counted in the side office." The crowd dispersed to the rear of the room, snacking on fresh fruit, cookies, apple juice, and water. The debaters, still on the stage, stood up and moved around, feeling energized by the excitement. Audrey gave her silver wheels a spin.

Mrs. Keller and Mr. Bentley returned in fewer than ten minutes with the results. They gave the results to Mr. Compton, who banged his gavel for attention. The debaters returned to the padded stools with their numbers. Not all of the audience returned to their seats, but everyone quieted down so they could hear the results.

Mr. Compton boomed out, "Both teams did very well, and we want to thank them for their efforts. The winning team is Team A, which favored going to borrow the scrolls!"

Applause rang out. Team A jumped up, congratulating each other. Mr. Compton went on with the other results. Darius and Margaret tied for best speech. They agreed to split the cash, and Mr. Compton promised to have a second trophy made for best speech. Darius gallantly gave the existing one to Margaret. It came as no surprise that Omega/Audrey won for best costume.

As other family members surged forward to join the debate participants, Dr. and Mrs. Chambers also came onto the stage. "Both teams did a great job!" said Dr. Chambers. "It had to be a close vote."

Turning to Margaret, Mrs. Chambers said, "Do you want us to take Comox home now?" Margaret was aglow with her victory.

"Oh, Mrs. Chambers, they're taking pictures for the yearbook! May I keep him for that? I'll catch a ride with Jackie and bring him back then."

"Perfect," said Mrs. Chambers. "We're heading home now. Just tell Darius he'll have to make room in his jeep for Audrey's costume." She continued, "Can Will get a ride home with you? And congratulations—you did a great job!" Margaret said thank you and was swept away as other friends crowded in to offer praise.

The *Aberdeen Courier,* a local newspaper, had sent a photographer and reporter to cover the debate. Mr. Kresher, the photographer, was rounding up the debaters and Mr. Compton. His goal was to get a group shot. Audrey's costume size was presenting a challenge, and Mr. Kresher quickly decided he'd take one of her separately. The reporter, Gabbie Patterson, took down the names of the participants, interviewing them about their thoughts on the debate and their confidence in human space exploration.

"Audrey," said Margaret, speaking up over the phone cameras clicking away, "you're supposed to get a ride with Darius. Dr. and Mrs. Chambers have left. Comox, Will, and I will catch a ride with Jackie—" but then she was interrupted.

"Rey and Yoda," called Gabbie Patterson, "can my photographer and I get you over here for a few words and a close-up?" The group broke up and Margaret was pulled out into the hallway along with Comox, away from the hubbub of the student activity team as they dismantled the stage.

Will looked around for Audrey. She was in a corner of the stage, trying to wrestle off the backpack that housed the axle for the silver wheels. The effort was throwing her off-balance. This time Will was the first to come to her aid and he helped her remove the costume. Jace had noticed this too, watching from where he and Chris Craddock were lined up for a yearbook photo. Once the structure of the wheels, axle, and backpack were on the floor, Audrey put her arms wide in the air and stretched. "Oh, that feels good."

"Does your face paint itch?" said Will, studying the intricate design.

"No," said Audrey, "I got the paint from a good theatrical company. But still—"

"Ready to wash it off?" said Will.

"Yes!"

"Let's go find Darius and—"

At that moment Jace came over and said, "Audrey, can I give you a lift home?"

Caught by surprise, Audrey stammered, "I—I think I'm supposed to go home with Darius and Will . . ."

"Yeah, that's right," interrupted Will. "That's the plan. We, uh—need to find Darius."

"Okay then," said Jace, looking disappointed. "Audrey, your costume was great. It was fun doing this with you."

"Thanks, Jace—you were good too," Audrey answered. Even through the white paint, Will could see that she was blushing. He looked at Jace with a poker face. Why hadn't he realized before how annoying this guy was? His YouTube animations weren't that funny.

"We gotta go, Jace," he said, picking up the aluminum wheels and backpack. "Audrey and I need to get the dog home." Jace looked over his shoulder at Chris, who was standing with two pretty senior girls.

"C'mon, Jace," Chris grinned and waved. "Breanna and Chelsea wanna have a photo taken with us." A tinkling laugh came from Breanna and she beckoned Jace to come over. He looked self-conscious but went to rejoin Chris.

"Will," said Audrey, "I think you're supposed to get a ride with Margaret and Jackie, because Margaret still has Comox. Your mom and dad have gone home already." At that point, Darius appeared. He had his spaceship in one hand and the jeep key in the other.

"Ready to go?" he asked.

"Yep," answered Will, glad that Audrey had shown no disappointment about not riding home with Jace.

"I'm going with Margaret and Comox," answered Will. "But you take Audrey home. I'll help load her costume stuff into the jeep." He set the wheels back down. "I'm going to tell Margaret I'll be back." He walked over to the hallway and poked his head out to where Gabbie Patterson was interviewing Margaret. "See you soon, Margaret; just helping Audrey move her stuff." Margaret nodded back.

Will returned to the almost-empty stage and grabbed Audrey's wheels, swinging them up onto his shoulders. He, Audrey, and Darius went out through the silver archway, which was being taken down by two students on ladders. The night air was chilly as they walked across the parking lot. Will noticed Jace getting into a shiny, new, all-electric car.

"Whoa! Look at that!" said Darius, stopping to stare at the vehicle. "No tail pipe. Cool."

"So what?" said Will. "He probably doesn't even know how it works."

Darius snorted. "What?"

Will ignored him. It *was* a great car. Luckily Audrey had been clutching her poster and trophy while fumbling in her purse and hadn't heard Will's comment. Prying open a small box of raisins, she said, "I'm starving! Debating with aliens makes you hungry!" Will and Darius grinned. *Tonight was fun,* thought Will.

After loading Audrey's costume into the jeep and seeing them pull away, he headed back to the school. Approaching the building, he heard loud whoops. It was Fletcher Stiles and Delbert Korbelak. First one, then the other, tossed a pumpkin out onto the pavement. The big orange globes landed with a thud, smashing apart in heavy chunks. Six other pumpkins had gone the same way. Seeing Will, Fletcher barked a rude comment and took off with Delbert. Will didn't care. Audrey wasn't going home with Jace, the debate had gone well, and the night air smelled wonderful.

Suddenly he realized that he was parched. *I'll get something from one of the machines in the commons area,* he thought. Entering the building, he turned right and jogged down a long hallway to the vending machines.

The building was mostly empty. He dropped coins into one of the machines and chose a raspberry-apple juice. He unscrewed the top and gulped it down. It tasted great.

At that same moment, Margaret walked out of the building along with Comox; Gabbie Patterson, the reporter; and Mr. Kresher, the photographer. The two journalists thanked her and drove off.

Margaret peered around the parking lot, trying to spot Will or Jackie's car. She removed the costume from Comox and held on to it along with her trophy and Comox's leash. Not seeing Will or the Clayberry car, she headed farther east with the uncomfortable realization that most everyone was gone. There were only two remaining cars in the parking lot, and neither of them looked familiar. It was occurring to her that Jackie must have left.

As she halted with Comox on the eastern edge of the lot, something small and brown shot out from under a bush and tore past them. It was a rabbit. Comox went wild, jerking the leash out of her hand. "No, Comox!" she cried, but it was too late. He dashed around the corner of the school. Margaret stuffed the Yoda costume and trophy under her arm and raced after him.

At that same moment Will walked back down the corridor. He heard the last of the auditorium lights click off, and two students emerged from the doorway along with Mr. Compton. "Hi, Will! Good work tonight," said the teacher, who had shed his moderator costume.

"Thanks! Are Margaret and my dog in there?" asked Will.

"No, they left a couple of minutes ago," said Mr. Compton. "Now, which one did Mr. Robinson give me?" He was flipping through keys on a ring. "Sorry, Robinson's out late with the wrestling team so I'll be locking up tonight." He looked up. "Did you check outside?"

"Not yet," said Will.

"Yes!" said the teacher, finding the right key and locking the doors. They left the school building together. Will peered across the parking lot.

"Any sign of them?" Mr. Compton asked.

Will shook his head.

"Guess they left already." The other two students headed for their car.

"D'you need a lift?" Mr. Compton asked.

"Yeah, I guess so," said Will, thinking Margaret and Jackie hadn't realized he was riding with them.

When Will got home, he was surprised to see that Comox wasn't there.

"Did you see Margaret leave?" asked his mother.

"No," said Will. "I tried her phone, but she's not answering. Maybe she didn't bring it." They called the Clayberry residence, and Jackie answered. She said Margaret and Comox weren't there, either.

"I didn't know I was supposed to bring you and Margaret home, Will! I'm sorry!" she said. "And yes, Margaret's cell phone's here. I'll go back to the school and get her."

"No, Jackie, I'll get them," said Will. "I'll call you as soon as I see them. I probably just missed her, and now she's locked out, hoping someone'll show up."

"My folks wouldn't like this," said Jackie. "They'd be worried."

"Well remember," said Will, "Margaret's with Comox. He won't let anyone hurt her."

"I guess not," she said.

"I'll call as soon as I find them; you call me if she shows up, okay?"

"Okay," said Jackie, and he gave her his cell phone number.

"Do you want me to go with you?" asked Audrey. He did, but not for the reasons she was thinking.

"Audrey," interrupted Mrs. Chambers, "let's get your costume stuff cleaned up. Will and Comox'll be back in no time. Will, take my car."

Will sped along the shadowed streets of Aberdeen, passing homes with Halloween lights glowing in the dark. He pulled up to the school. There was no one in sight. Cruising past the front doors, he moved along the sidewalk, heading to the east side. Suddenly he heard a loud engine. Parking the car, he got out and went onto the grassy field toward the construction zone. Something glinted a few feet away. His heart plummeted. On the ground, near a tree, lay Margaret's trophy and the Yoda costume.

"Margaret! Comox!" he hollered at the top of his lungs, but his voice was drowned out by the engine. A backhoe was moving on the field. The vehicle jolted as though the driver didn't know how to work it. Then it began to move forward toward a huge stack of high-density polyethylene pipe that was piled up beside a trench.

"Hey! Stop!" hollered Will. He ran toward the backhoe, but the driver didn't see him. Ca-runch. The first few pipes splintered. As he ran closer, the driver saw him. The machine stopped and turned, coming for Will, its lights blinding him. Moving backward, he tripped over a stake in the ground. The machine kept coming. He got up and tripped over another one. Rolling onto his side, he tumbled into a narrow trench just as the machine reached him. He pressed himself down into the earth as far as he could go. The machine thundered over him. Shaken and barely breathing, he realized he hadn't been hurt. The backhoe lurched to a wider part of the trench and became lodged there in a deafening roar.

His heart pounding, Will pulled himself up. A silver-haired man was racing away. Will regained his balance and tore after the man, who'd reached a truck and was climbing into it. Spraying dirt chunks, the truck shot off the field and raced out of sight.

Will was sure it was the same truck he'd seen at Beyond Hair. He'd caught the first two digits of the license plate: 3, 4—then it was gone. *Different numbers now.*

He called his dad, who said he'd be there right away; then he called 911, asking for Officer McGuiggan. He didn't ask for Detective Clayberry, since he knew Margaret's father was coming back from the airport. He jogged back to where the truck had been and picked up Comox's leash off the ground. He realized with horror it was drenched in blood. *Comox,* he thought, *where are you and Margaret?*

Officer McGuiggan and one other policeman arrived at the same time as Dr. Chambers. Will's teeth were chattering. His father put a blanket around him after checking for any injuries. Luckily, Will had only a few scrapes. The officers issued an attempt to locate (ATL) order on the truck and Officer McGuiggan shut off the backhoe, being careful to preserve any fingerprints.

Principal Parker, who had been contacted by the police, arrived next, accompanied by Mr. Robinson, who was back from the wrestling match.

"Hey, I've seen that kid before," said Mr. Robinson. "He and his friends were messing around with Drivers Ed cars."

The accusation snapped Will out of his stupor. "No, I wasn't!" he shouted. "I had nothing to do with that!"

"Calm down, Will," said his father. He turned to the shop teacher. "Mr. Robinson, why would my son report himself vandalizing school property? And more seriously, there's a girl missing."

"Right!" said Principal Parker, clearly concerned, "Margaret Clayberry." The officers radioed in a missing persons alert and all six of them fanned out over the grounds, calling for Margaret and Comox. There was no reply.

Will answered all the questions the officers had and Officer McGuiggan told Will and his father they were free to go. Dr. Chambers called the Clayberry home; Jackie, in tears, confirmed that Margaret and Comox hadn't shown up yet. Detective Clayberry was still on his way home from the airport.

Will and his father felt someone should stay with Jackie, and Dr. Chambers offered to go. "You've been through a lot, Will. I'll drop you at home. You should rest."

But Will insisted on coming, saying, "Dad, I wouldn't be able to sleep."

"All right,' his father said, "I'll follow you there."

When they rang the doorbell at the Clayberry home, Jackie answered immediately.

"Is Margaret with you?" she asked.

Will shook his head.

As Jackie ushered them into the living room, a car pulled into the driveway. It was Margaret's father, Detective Clayberry. He came inside followed by a younger man wearing camouflage fatigues. There was no time for introductions, and the stranger stayed quietly in the background as Dr. Chambers and Will told the detective that his daughter was missing and what had happened at the school. Detective Clayberry's eyes hardened with rage as he listened.

"Sir, it was the same truck," said Will. "It had different plates, but I'm sure it was the same truck—I think it was Sainos." Jackie burst into tears just as the Clayberrys' home phone rang. The detective answered it and turned to face the kitchen where the phone's cradle hung on a wall inside the doorway. His conversation was short.

When he turned around, his face had flooded with relief. "It's her—Margaret. She's at the south Sentinel Gas Station. She says she's fine but to come quickly—Sainos just left, and Comox is hurt."

Will, his father, and Detective Clayberry took Dr. Chambers' car, and within minutes they were pulling into the gas station. They entered the food mart and looked around. It was filled to the brim with snacks and merchandise, but no Margaret. The female clerk looked at them, warily taking in Will's roughed-up Starfleet uniform.

Detective Clayberry spoke. "Have you seen a teenage girl with dark hair dressed in a tan costume? She called us from here."

The clerk's eyes lit up. "Oh, yes, she asked to use the phone so she could get a ride. She said she'd wait outside. Her costume was a little scary. Isn't she out there?" They bolted back through the front door and began yelling for Margaret. Suddenly they heard a voice calling out from around back, "I'm here, Dad—back here! Comox is hurt!"

All three rushed behind the building to find a bedraggled and terrified Margaret. Her hair was tousled and her tunic was stained with blood. She cradled Comox in her lap. He was breathing heavily and gave a whimper as Dr. Chambers lifted his muzzle. The dog had a nasty gash between his ears, and the blood had started to clot. Margaret insisted that she was all right, though she looked exhausted. Both of her hands were smeared with blood.

Will and his father bent down, gently lifting Comox up and allowing Detective Clayberry to pull his daughter to her feet. He wrapped her in a bear hug. Dr. Chambers held Comox as Will dashed to their car and drove it around to the back. They loaded Comox and Margaret inside. Detective Clayberry noticed the young clerk standing at the back door. She looked very concerned. He flashed a detective's badge and gave her his name, explaining that Margaret was his daughter.

"He's my dad," Margaret called from the car. "It's okay. Thank you for your help." The clerk nodded, still a bit shaken.

As they drove off, Margaret assured them she had no injuries, so they headed to the zoo hospital, where Dr. Chambers could take care of Comox. When the car was parked, the doctor went ahead to unlock the hospital and disarm the new alarm system. Will and Detective Clayberry carried the limp dog into the building.

As the doctor hooked Comox up to an IV tube, Detective Clayberry turned to Will and said, "I'm taking Margaret home." Will nodded. "Come with me, Will. Your other car is there, but I'll take you home and then come back for your dad." Will's father nodded in agreement without taking his focus from Comox.

As they approached the Chambers vehicle, the detective was firm. "I'll drive." Will gave him the keys. As they left the zoo, the detective said carefully, "Margaret, we think Sainos was at the school tonight. Can you tell us what happened?"

"I—I . . . where do I begin? Because . . ." she took a deep breath, "because I may know where Sainos is living." The detective pulled the car over to the side of the road to give Margaret his full attention.

"I don't have the address, Dad. I could only look out from under a tarp where I was hidden when he stopped. It's close to the store I was at." Her voice quavered. "I would recognize the house if I saw it again." She pulled at the messy tangles in her hair, which seemed to calm her down. "It's a small, gray house—there's a canal on the left and there are two large trees out in front. There's a huge black-and-white checkered mailbox in front of a red brick house on the right."

The detective put the gear-shift into park. "I'm sure we'll be able to find that house, Margaret. I'll send your information in now. Good observation—I'm proud of you." He dialed a number, and Will and Margaret heard him relay the description to an officer on the other end. When he finished, he turned to her again. "I'm going to start driving, is that okay?" She nodded. He went on, "What happened from the time the debate ended to when you called us?"

As the car moved through the empty streets, Margaret began to talk. She described the brown rabbit bursting out from the bushes. "Comox chased it for like—forever! Finally, I gave up and was going to head to the pizza place nearby to use their phone. I knew I'd missed you and Jackie," she said, turning to Will. "Then I saw the rabbit dive into a trench, and Comox dove in after it. He was digging furiously, and I thought, 'Well, he's in one place and I can grab him now,' but then a big truck came onto the field. The driver stopped by the trench where Comox was and shut off the engine. When he got out, Comox left the trench and . . . he—he crouched down and began to growl! The man went to the back of his truck and I was afraid he was getting a gun! I just froze! Comox came closer to the man, and the whole time Comox was growling! The man had a crowbar. Comox charged and the man hit him with it! I saw Comox drop—and—then the man threw him in the back of the truck like a rag doll! Next, the man went over to that small bulldozer—"

"Backhoe," said Will.

"Whatever—and he started it up. While he was busy with that, I went over to the truck." Tears were pouring down her face. "I had to find out if Comox was okay." Will patted her shoulder, feeling guilty that he hadn't gone straight to both her and Comox in those few minutes after the debate.

"Go on," said her father in a kind tone.

"When I got there, I climbed into the bed of the truck. I was so glad to find Comox still breathing, but he was hurt and not moving." Here she paused. "I know I was crazy to get into the truck, but what else could I do?"

Will spoke, "And I'd just come back to find you."

"Go on, Margaret," said her father.

"Sainos—if that's who it was—drove the backhoe across the field," she continued. "I was with Comox, telling him he'd be all right and trying to think of how to get us out of there. I unhooked the leash and tossed it. Then I heard a horrible grinding noise—a crash! I saw the man rush back to the truck, so I hid under a tarp. I know it was crazy, but if I hadn't, I don't know what would have happened to Comox and me."

Will was grateful for all Margaret had done and could feel himself flushing with anger.

Margaret went on. "He jammed the truck into gear. It was awful! Even though I pulled Comox toward me, we were thrown all around. I held on tight," she sobbed. "It was terrible! Finally he stopped. When the man got out, I hid under the tarp again, pushing myself as close as I could to the front. He came around back. I heard the jingle of Comox's tags, but I didn't hear Comox move at all. Then I heard the man walk away. So I peeked out and looked around. That's when I saw the canal, the mailbox, and all that. Halfway to the house, he stopped. I ducked under the tarp again. I could hear him coming back to the truck, cursing and saying something about 'finding out.' He got in and started the engine again. This time he drove carefully. We didn't go far. When we were parked, I heard him get out and walk away, so I looked out. We were at the Sentinel Gas Station, and he'd gone inside. That's when I climbed out of the truck.

"I don't know how I did it, but I was able to get Comox down too. Thank goodness for this tunic. It worked like a sling—I pulled it around him and somehow it held him up." She pointed down to her lap where the fabric was drenched with blood. "I got behind the store before he came back out. When he did, thank heaven, he didn't check the back of the truck. I was so scared he'd come back to the gas station to look for Comox and—and find us both! I left Comox and went inside. I asked the clerk if I could use the phone and she said I could, commenting that 'everybody needs to use our phone tonight.' I called you, Dad, and you came. You came." She started to cry harder, and Will patted her arm, not knowing what else to do.

Her father looked grim but said, "Margaret, you were very brave. You're safe now."

They arrived at the Clayberry house. The other Chambers car was still there. Jackie rushed out as soon as she saw them pull into the driveway. Will told Margaret he couldn't thank her enough. With a burst of new energy, Will told the detective he wanted to go back and pick up his father.

"No, Will. I'll drive you home," the detective said, but Will had rallied and convinced Detective Clayberry that he was fine to drive. Then he asked the detective for two favors.

"First, could you or Jackie get that car back to our house?" Will pointed to his mother's car. "I'll give you the keys."

"Sure," said Detective Clayberry, helping Margaret out of the car. "We'll bring it by early tomorrow."

"Margaret," said Will, touching her shoulder before Jackie led her away, "I promise to let you know how Comox is doing. You saved his life."

"What's the second favor?" asked Detective Clayberry.

"D'you have anything I could eat?" As he drove back to the hospital, Will chomped down huge mouthfuls of a thick roast beef sandwich. When he got to the hospital, he punched numbers into the gate's numeric keypad, pushed the gate open, then knocked on the hospital door and went in.

Inside, his dad was putting away disinfectants. Joe, the anaconda, was wide awake, watching with good-natured interest. Comox was resting peacefully in the large enclosure that had previously held the tiger cub.

"I had to put in two rows of stitches," said Dr. Chambers. Comox had a gauzy, white bandage that wrapped up around his head and in-between his ears. The doctor went on, "We're lucky, Will. The wound isn't deep enough to cause lasting damage. He bled a lot, because that's what head wounds do." The doctor stretched, arching his back. "He won't be chasing rabbits for a while, but he'll be okay."

The doctor snapped a drawer of bandages shut. "Comox woke up while I was working on him and his eyes looked good. I gave him a sedative, and he's sleeping. Laura's coming in at five a.m. to check on Gracie, and I'll have her check on Comox too."

After hearing Comox would be okay, Will hardly heard another word his father said. Every bone in his body ached. "Can we go home, Dad?"

"You bet," said Dr. Chambers, putting an arm around his son's shoulder.

As they drove, Will relayed all that Margaret had told him. "She was very lucky," said his father. "The police need to catch that guy." Will heard the controlled anger in his father's voice as the man continued, "I wonder what he was after at the Sentinal Gas Station?"

Will didn't answer. He'd been thinking about that too. He had a theory but didn't want to say anything. He'd check it out at home.

They pulled into the driveway. There was a dim glow from one small kitchen light, which meant no one was waiting up. "I, uh, didn't give any of the details to your mom; she would have been very worried. When I called, I told her Margaret and Comox were safe but that Comox had chased a rabbit and needed some stitches. Luckily that seemed to work; she and Audrey can learn the grisly truth tomorrow." Dr. Chambers turned off the car, leaving it in the driveway to avoid opening the garage door, which would be noisy. They entered the garage and went through the side door that led into the kitchen. "Off to bed," said Dr. Chambers.

"Some water first, Dad, then I'll come up," said Will. His father climbed the stairs. The house was quiet. It felt strange not having Comox in the kitchen where he normally would have been. Will drank some water and then went to the phone to check out his theory. There was a phone number listed on the caller ID. He called it back. The voice of the store clerk answered, "Sentinel Gas Station." He muttered, "Sorry, wrong number," and hung up. He knew who had called. Comox's tag didn't have the family name and address, but it did have the Chambers' phone number on it.

Nothing he could do now; the left side of his face ached, and he was exhausted. He trudged up the stairs, pulled off his muddy clothes, and fell into bed. Moments later, he was asleep.

CHAPTER
10

THE FOLLOWING MORNING WILL woke to the jangle of a telephone. He grabbed the upstairs extension in his parents' room. It was Detective Clayberry calling to say he'd dropped off the Chambers' car on his way to work. He asked whether Will had heard from the captain.

"No," said Will, then he shared the good news about Comox. He also explained that last night Sainos had phoned the Chambers' home from the Sentinel Gas Station.

"I'm guessing," said Detective Clayberry, "he wanted to use a phone that couldn't be traced to him." In a gruff tone of voice, he added, "I'm glad he did, for Margaret's sake." He took a deep breath, then went on, "given your father's connection to the zoo, Sainos might be wondering if you came to the school because you have some information about him."

"Yeah . . ." Will mumbled, still waking up.

"I hafta go," the detective said suddenly. "We've located the house Margaret described." He sounded hopeful. "We might have him."

"Great!" said Will. That news woke him up.

"If anything happens," the detective said, "call!"

Will headed downstairs. He saw two plates stacked in the sink and realized his father had already left for work. His mother was at her Saturday nine a.m. fitness class and probably still knew nothing about last night.

Wanting to eat something hot, he slid a carton of eggs out of the fridge. The noise of gushing water in the pipes indicated a running shower, so he knew Audrey was up. He cracked enough eggs for them both into a mixing bowl and threw in some grated parmesan cheese, pepper, and a teaspoon of milk. And after lightly whisking the mixture with a fork, he poured it into a smooth skillet. Waiting for the eggs to cook, he took an apple from the fruit bowl. He grabbed a knife, peeled it, cut it, and began to eat. It tasted wonderful. He devoured his share of the eggs and put Audrey's on a plate in the oven to keep them warm. Then he grabbed the phone and called Darius.

"He's on his way to *your* house," answered a buoyant Mrs. Cheng. "Big news—you're in the newspaper this morning! I wanted to go last night, but I couldn't get off work!"

Will had forgotten all about the debate. "Oh, that's all right. It . . . it went really well," he answered awkwardly.

He wondered whether the paper had also reported the school's vandalism. Just then he heard the front doorbell. He interrupted politely saying, "Uh, Mrs. Cheng, I think Darius is here. Bye!"

He hung up the phone and sprinted to the front door. Darius had an odd look on his face, but his jaw really dropped when he saw the large purple bruise on Will's face.

"Wow! What happened to you?"

"Come back to the kitchen," said Will. "I'll tell you all about it." He turned to see Audrey coming down the stairs, fresh from her shower.

"Will," Darius called after him, "did you know there's a knife with a note stuck to your front door?"

"What?!" Will swung around, and Darius stepped aside to let him pass. A piece of paper at eye level was fixed to the doorframe with a pocketknife. Will dashed back inside. He grabbed a glove from inside a coat pocket and laid it over the pivot point, unseating the knife and the note. Taking them to the kitchen, he laid them on the table, making sure he didn't smudge possible fingerprints. Then he put the glove on, opened the note and read it. His friends waited.

"Well?" asked Darius. "Is it from the captain?

"No," said Will. "It's from Sainos."

Audrey was horrified. "How did he find you?"

Will told them about the previous night, starting with the mixed-up car ride and ending with Margaret and Comox's narrow escape. "He got our phone number from Comox's tag. When he called, he got the message with our name. He looked that up and that must be how he got the address."

Darius frowned. "What does it say?"

Will read out two sentences that were scrawled in jagged writing. "It says, 'The money at Little Brush Creek Cave is mine! Stay out of this or you will get hurt.' There's no signature." Will's brow furrowed. "The money at Little Brush Creek Cave? He thinks I know more than I do. This note has to be from Sainos!"

Darius and Audrey were quiet. Will looked at the scribbled note again. "The money . . . What does he mean? The only money I can think of is the money the captain's been using."

"That would make sense," said Darius. "The captain's funds have to be coming from somewhere. And the captain said Sainos really hates him. Maybe the money belongs to Sainos."

"Wow," said Audrey. "I hope it's not stolen money, even if it's being used for good."

"Like——Robin Hood?" said Will. Darius looked puzzled and Will let it go. "What does he mean about Little Brush Creek Cave?" Will murmured. "I'd better call Dad and Detective Clayberry."

He phoned the hospital. Laura, the zoo nurse, picked up. "Hey, Laura, it's Will. Is my dad there?"

"He's with Gracie."

"Who?"

"Gracie! You know—Gracie, our *very* pregnant polar bear?"

"Oh, yeah, Gracie!" said Will. "Uh, Laura, would you tell him to call me when he's free? And how's Comox?"

"Comox?" she paused, "Oh, your dog! He's doing fine! What *happened* to him?"

"Long story," said Will. "But—he's okay?"

"He's groggy—but his wound is clean and his vital signs are good. Was he hit by a car?"

"Not sure," said Will, dodging an explanation. "We're trying to figure it out. Hey, I gotta go, Laura."

"Okay," she said, "I'll give your dad the message."

Next Will called Detective Clayberry, who picked up right away. Will told him about the note.

"I'm not happy he knows where you live," said the detective.

"Can't be helped," said Will. Then he asked eagerly, "Did you find the house?"

"We found it," said the detective dolefully, "it was abandoned. Sainos had cleared out. He left food in the fridge and empty boxes, and that was it. No information, no fingerprints—he covered his tracks."

"Who owns the house?"

"A guy named Ferguson. He said the rental was done over the phone, and the tenant's name was Ray Smelting. This Smelting—or, most likely, Sainos—used a cashier's check sent through the mail. The copy of the driver's license and employment pay stub he gave Ferguson were both fakes."

"Wow," said Will. "He must have felt threatened to leave that quickly."

"Yup," growled the detective. "When I think of what could have happened to Margaret . . ." He took a deep breath. "We'll come by and get the knife and the note. Maybe we can get a lead there." He paused, "I'm counting on Sainos to trip up somewhere."

"Hope so," said Will. "I'll let you know if anything else happens."

"Right," said the detective. The call ended. Will turned to Darius and Audrey, giving them the discouraging news of the abandoned house.

Then they heard a garage door go up. Will slid the edge of his plate to cover the note and the knife. The kitchen door banged open. Mrs. Chambers came in with her gym bag and a copy of the *Aberdeen Courier* tucked under her arm. Her face was glowing, and she was keen to see the news story on the debate. She tossed the paper onto the table and pulled a carton of pineapple juice from the fridge.

Will noticed the oven was still on warm. "Audrey," he said, "there are some scrambled eggs in the oven for you." Audrey rescued the eggs, which were just short of rubbery, and grabbed a fork. She came to the table and began to eat.

Mrs. Chambers pointed to the newspaper. "Open it," she said, pushing the gym bag to the side to make room. The *Aberdeen Courier* had done an exceptional job. One of the best pictures showed Margaret and Comox beaming at the photographer. Another showed the participants with Mr. Compton. Audrey's picture was excellent, though she was completely unrecognizable. They liked the quotes lifted from Darius and Margaret's speeches. Then Will turned his head and Mrs. Chambers gasped.

"Will, where did you get that bruise?!"

"Well, Mom, something happened last night . . ."

"Yes?" said Mrs. Chambers, taking in his somber tone.

He explained the events of the previous evening. Sliding his plate to show her the note and knife, he finished by telling her what the note said.

At first Mrs. Chambers was stunned; quite quickly she became furious. "This man—he has to be caught and put in jail! He's—he's horrible! And now he's threatening us?" Her voice swelled. "He'll learn we don't take well to being threatened! And poor Margaret!" Her voice changed and her hands went to her forehead. "I'm so glad she's all right! And—Comox!" She gripped the top of her gym bag. "Poor Comox!"

"Mom, it's all right. Comox is gonna be fine," said Will, and he put his arm around her. "I just called the zoo and talked to Laura, and she says he's doing great. Well, not exactly great, but he's gonna be fine."

Mrs. Chambers asked what seemed like a million questions and then engulfed Will in a bear hug. "You might have been killed! Look at you; you still have dirt in your hair!" It was true. He rubbed his scalp and could feel the grit.

"I'm fine, Mom—really!" He got another hug. His mother finally went upstairs after he promised to take a shower in the next few minutes. He turned back to his friends and shrugged, with some embarrassment.

"Well, it *is* unnerving," said Audrey, looking at Comox's untouched food dish. "Horrible Sainos right here at your front door!" She shivered.

Will lifted the mood. "Detective Clayberry's right. At some point Sainos is going to make a mistake—just like in that summer camp chess game."

"Hmm," said Darius thoughtfully. "We should make a list of everything we know." He pulled out a small notepad.

"Great idea," said Will. "Hold on." He grabbed more paper from the study and slid the sheets onto the table. They set to work listing everything they knew about the captain and Sainos. "I wonder where Little Brush Creek Cave is," said Will.

The front doorbell rang. When they answered it, there stood Officer McGuiggan, sunlight streaming in behind him. "Hello, Will Chambers. You're looking better today. Detective Clayberry sent me to pick up a knife and a note."

They brought him back to the kitchen and pointed to the scrap of paper on the table. Will explained how he'd carefully used a glove to protect any fingerprints that might be on the two items.

"If we do find a print, I'd bet we'll find a match for it," said Officer McGuiggan. "This guy likely has a criminal record."

"I hope there's a print," said Will. "So far he's been really careful."

The officer agreed and then asked, "What about your neighbors? Could one of them have seen him?"

"Well," said Will, "maybe the Lundstroms right across the street did. Or the Hansons next door. Depends on what time he was here." Then he quickly added, "Officer, may I get a picture of that note before you take it?"

"Sure," said Officer McGuiggan. Will took a picture with his phone, and the officer used a pair of tweezers to lift the paper and put it in a plastic bag. He picked up the knife with a glove, bagged it, and labeled both the knife and the note before putting them into a briefcase. Will led him to the front door, where the officer said he'd go and check with the neighbors.

Will returned to his friends in the kitchen. "Let's keep going with this," he said, referring to the list.

Five minutes later, Dr. Chambers came through the front door with the good news that Gracie, the polar bear, had given birth.

"We have two healthy new cubs: a female and a male," he said buoyantly. "They're named Kayla and Apollo. Gracie's a wonderful mother!"

"Did she do okay?" asked Audrey.

"Yes, she did. Thank goodness I didn't have to assist; she'd have torn me to bits!" He slipped off his jacket and flopped onto a chair. "I suppose if we'd needed to help, we'd have used a mild sedative, but I didn't want to—anyway, we're giving her and the cubs time alone. It couldn't have gone better!"

"Dad, that's great," said Will.

Darius grinned.

"Oh, I wish I could see them right now!" said Audrey.

"Did you see Comox?" asked Will.

"Yes, he's doing well. He'll come home tomorrow," Dr. Chambers said, stifling a yawn. "I'm going to take a rest."

Will thought of the note. "Dad—we've had a message from Sainos."

"What?" said his father, his voice completely changed. "What kind of message?"

"A written one. It's . . . a warning. He stuck it to the front door with a knife. The police picked up the knife and note, but I took a picture of it. Here," Will handed his phone to his father.

Dr. Chambers read it aloud. "The money at Little Brush Creek Cave is *mine*! Stay out of this or you *will* get hurt."

He looked up. "Does Little Brush Creek Cave mean anything to you?"

"No," said Will. "Never heard of it."

"And you let Detective Clayberry know about the note?"

"Yeah," answered Will. Then he shared the bad news about the vacant house Margaret had described and how Sainos must have found their address from Comox's tags. Just then Dr. Chambers' phone buzzed. After checking the number, he answered.

"They're fighting *again?*" From his look of exasperation, the others knew the answer must have been yes. "I'll be right there." Will's father was all business again as he put the phone back in his pocket. "Two of our colobus monkeys have been brawling over mangos, and one of them bit the other. He'll likely require stitches." He grabbed a container of leftover chicken curry from the fridge, pulled on his jacket, waved goodbye, and left.

Will looked at his friends. "At least the polar bears are doing well."

Audrey laughed, "I'm so happy about that." Her eyes were glowing. "I can hardly wait to see them!"

"You can soon," grinned Will. "There's a new webcam at the top of their den, remember? It'll be on in a few days."

Darius teased her. "They'll be okay until you move in, Audrey."

"I'd like nothing better," she said. "I'll dress like a polar bear so I fit in."

Will shook his head and laughed.

Darius looked down at the list, his face somber again. "So, Sainos has moved, but just how far?" They looked up Little Brush Creek Cave on Google. It was about twenty miles north of Vernal, Utah—a town with a varying population that averaged ten thousand. It didn't connect to any of their other information.

"The cave is the longest in Utah," read Will. "It often floods from spring to late summer with snow melt."

"Not a good place to hide something," said Darius, adding that to the list.

Will underlined his note about Sainos being a clumsy backhoe operator, then said, "Wonder why the captain didn't give a warning about last night's attack."

"Maybe he didn't fund the high school's ground-source heat-pump system," suggested Darius.

Will raised his eyebrows. "But the attacker has to be Sainos. That note is definitely connected to what happened last night. What else could it mean?"

Darius tossed in another idea. "Could Fletcher Stiles have been in the backhoe in disguise? He was there earlier—"

"No, absolutely not," said Will. "I'm sure of that. It was an older man—plus I'm sure it was the same truck we saw at the café."

Audrey spoke up. "Maybe Sainos has found the captain. But the captain spent all the money and . . . now—oooh."

Will finished her gruesome thought, "Maybe the captain's dead?" The room went silent. *Had something happened to the captain?* Will exhaled. "Maybe he left to keep from being discovered." He stood up and stretched. "The captain definitely wants to keep his identity a secret."

"Let's hope he contacts you or Detective Clayberry soon," said Darius.

Will nodded. "I'd like to ask him about the group called Students for Ecosystem Justice and find out if the captain was at the Green Valley Project." He tossed his pen onto the table and headed upstairs for a shower. When he returned, free of grit and feeling better, he saw that his friends had merged the lists into one and set it aside. Calculus textbooks were open and the two were moving with determination through a particularly tough assignment that was due Monday. Will joined in and the three of them worked on it for more than an hour.

Taking a break, Audrey returned to their earlier conversation with more optimism. "I bet the captain would appreciate knowing Detective Clayberry's willing to keep his identity a secret."

"True," said Will.

"Just maybe," said Darius, "Sainos got to the captain but the money's still missing—and he thinks we have it."

"I hope not," said Audrey, stiffening. "I wouldn't want him thinking we have *anything* he wants!"

"No, Darius, I don't think so," said Will. "Wouldn't he have demanded the money if he thought we knew where it was? That note is to scare us away. He mentioned the cave because he thinks we already know about it and that we know more than we do. He doesn't know why I was at the field last night, though it was just a weird twist of fate." He spun his pencil in his fingers. "Maybe he recognized me, then when he connected Comox to our address, he thinks we're helping the captain so he's warning us to stay out of it. That's ironic—the captain's also telling us to stay out of it."

"Now that Sainos knows the police are closer to finding him, maybe he'll leave," said Audrey.

Will raised his eyebrows. "I don't know; the captain and Detective Clayberry both said Sainos doesn't let go very easily."

"Not the 'going away' type?" said Darius.

"Well," Will said, "I guess we'll find out."

They did another hour's worth of calculus. When they finished, they moved on to a chemistry assignment. Once that was done, they put their school bags away and polished off a delicious, thick, black bean chicken soup along with salad.

As he put bowls into the dishwasher, Will said, "We ought to see how Margaret's doing." His friends agreed. Putting the phone into speaker mode, they called the Clayberry household.

Jackie answered. "Here, you can talk to her yourself. I'm trying to get her to rest, and she won't listen at all!" Jackie meant for Margaret to hear the complaint, but then she added in a lighter tone, "It's good that you called."

Margaret came to the phone. "Everybody wants me to stay in bed, but really, I'm fine! Mom's coming home from Denver tonight, and Dad went to the airport to pick her up. She was upset when he explained what had happened. I know they want me to rest, but you guys can come by. Jackie'll be okay with you coming over, won't you Jackie." It was more of a comment than a question.

They heard Jackie's muffled, "Sure."

"We have one thing we have to do first," said Will, "then we'll be over." Within minutes, he, Darius, and Audrey piled into the gold jeep.

When they arrived at the Clayberry home, they rang the doorbell and Jackie answered right away. "Come in! Margaret's on the couch in the family room."

Will, Darius and Audrey followed Jackie to a cozy room with a high ceiling, wood-paneled walls, a green corduroy couch, and two large brown leather chairs. Margaret rested on the couch. She looked much better than she had the night before.

Darius strode across the room and took her hands in his. "You are very brave, Margaret." Then he bowed. "I award you the U.S. Congressional Medal of Honor for a Brilliant Dog Rescue." He grinned, "If Congress actually has one of those."

"Oh, Darius," she laughed, her cheeks turning pink. "They probably have more important things to do than give me a medal."

Will smiled at his friends' banter. Then it struck him: maybe Darius had a soft spot for Margaret, and maybe she felt the same.

He sneaked a sideways glance at Audrey, but her back was to him. Will had gotten used to Audrey and Darius bantering with one other, but last night it had been the power-house team of Margaret and Darius who'd won the debate. Maybe the two had a connection. Then Audrey turned around, and her face was all smiles. He wondered whether it was only because Margaret was fine or something else. *What goes on in that head of hers?* Then they began to talk about the events of the previous night and the note that had been left on the door.

"Oh, no!" said Margaret, disappointed to learn that the house she'd described was now abandoned and offered no clues.

Will changed the topic. "This should cheer you up." He handed over a thick, brown-paper bag that held something heavy. Margaret looked inside and whooped.

"Fantastic!" she said, pulling out her trophy and the Yoda costume, both of which had been retrieved from the police.

"Thanks, guys," said Margaret. Then her face fell. "I wish I'd held tighter to Comox's leash. If he hadn't gotten away, he wouldn't be hurt, and Sainos wouldn't know where you live."

"Forget it, Margaret," said Will, thinking of all she'd been through. "You rescued Comox, and you and I got away too. I think we did okay. Anyway, we should let you rest now." Margaret and Jackie walked them to the front door, Then Will thought of something else. "Hey, who was that guy with your dad last night?" The girls exchanged looks.

"Dad kept that kind of quiet," said Jackie.

Margaret added cautiously, "With Dad's work, he has to keep a lot of things confidential. But . . . well . . . we know his name is Lieutenant Vahriman, and he's here about Sainos."

"What?!" said Will.

"They were careful when we were around—and they kept their voices really low, but this morning I heard the name Sainos more than once," said Margaret.

"And," Jackie added, "they did a lot of work on two different computers. For sure they were researching something."

"Lieutenant Vahriman has left," said Margaret. "I think Dad took him to the airport because Dad was going to pick up Mom. At least I . . . *think* he's going to the airport. I'm not sure. Lieutenant Vahriman put his computer and other stuff in Dad's car. He—well . . . he kept pretty much to himself."

"Did your dad ever call him by a first name?" asked Will.

Margaret shook her head, "I don't think they knew each other before last night."

"Dad mostly called him *lieutenant,*" said Jackie. "But I did overhear another name this morning—a woman's name—Marylou." The other four looked at her then Will spoke.

"If they were talking about Marylou Hansen, they're probably looking for the captain too."

"Please," said Jackie, looking worried. "Don't say anything to him until he's ready to tell you. Oh, he'd be so irritated if he knew we'd told you this much."

The friends told Jackie they wouldn't say anything to her father. She looked relieved. But on the ride back to the Chambers' home, Will wondered. *Could the secretive houseguest be the captain?* If that was true, their part in this was over. Will texted Margaret, asking, "Was the man at your home last night the captain?" She answered that she'd check with her father when she found the right time to ask him.

———

COMOX CAME HOME ON Sunday, less than forty-eight hours after his attack. They looked after him, making sure he was comfortable. Dr. Chambers was pleased with how well the wound was healing. "His internal stitches will dissolve in the next two to three weeks," he said. "The external ones will too, but I'll remove them sooner or he'll scratch at them."

"Great, Comox! You've avoided the cone of shame," said Will.

"Agreed, he doesn't deserve that," said Dr. Chambers, laughing.

That night in his room, Will felt good to see Comox

asleep in his bed. Then his thoughts turned to his brother Michael, in Germany, where so much was happening. Germany had given refugee status to many lost and desperate people even as Germany pulled forward to be a world leader in the area of clean energy. He hoped his brother was safe and able to do the work of a peacemaker.

———

THE FOLLOWING MONDAY AT school, just before the first bell rang, Margaret caught up to Will and Darius in the hallway. Audrey had just dashed off to the administrative office. "I need some elementary school info," she'd said before disappearing into the crowd.

Will turned to Margaret. "Did you ask if that guy was the captain?"

"I . . . I asked him," she hesitated, "but he said no and then changed the subject."

"That's it?" said Will, sliding his pack to the ground. "Nothing more?" He tried to conceal his irritation.

"Hold on, Will," she said, "my dad doesn't want to talk about it with me or anybody." She spoke in a rush, "My mom was really surprised that he had been a *member* of the Green Valley commune. I asked her if she knew he'd been there, and she said yes, but she'd thought it had been for only a couple of days!"

"Oh, I see," said Darius. "some missing pieces of history

coming up?—Awkward."

"Yes," said Margaret, flashing him a look of gratitude. "So, anyway, can we back off? They're not fighting or anything, but this topic is, well—off-limits. Of course if anything new happens, tell him; he'd want to know. But, guys, we have other stuff to focus on, like our midterms. Jackie says it's impossible to raise a grade-point average in your senior year if you do poorly as a junior." Darius straightened up when he heard that.

"Okay," said Will, lifting his pack and pushing his irritation away. She was right; they did have other things to think about. The second morning bell rang, and they joined the rush of other students to get to class.

In the week that followed, nothing eventful happened at the school's construction site. The police wrapped up their investigation, and by Friday morning, work had resumed. Reward posters went up for any information leading to the arrest and conviction of persons involved in the vandalism. The reward was for one thousand dollars.

HALLOWEEN EVENING ARRIVED WITH its usual flurry of activity. In the kitchen, Audrey and Mrs. Chambers used serrated drywall saws to turn three pumpkins into jack-o-lanterns. Will carried them out to the front steps. Mrs. Chambers placed a bulky candle inside each one, lit the candles, and put the tops back on. A moment later the whiff of scorching pumpkin filled the air.

Comox, almost healed, had a Frankenstein-like appearance. That evening he sat by the front door with Will and Audrey and several children asked, "Is your dog like that for Halloween?" Will nodded rather than explain. Hudson, the cat, had already found a place to hide away from all the commotion.

The assortment of costumes the trick-or-treaters wore ranged from well-known superheroes to the absolute one-of-a-kind. Dr. Chambers complimented one little boy who wore a cardboard box over his torso with a chest X-ray glued to the front. He said he'd made the whole thing himself.

The treats at the Chambers' home were small pre-wrapped pieces of dark chocolate with sweet orange bits—Mrs. Chambers felt dark chocolate was one of the healthier choices. At eight o'clock, Will convinced his parents that he and Audrey could handle the last hour. As his parents retreated, Will said in a hushed voice, "Glad she moved on from the toothbrushes."

"What?" said Audrey.

"Yeah, that's what she gave out two years ago. You shoulda seen the looks we got."

Audrey laughed, "Did the kids take 'em?"

"Oh, yeah—they didn't complain, but we found a few tossed in the bushes the next day—well, maybe just one." Audrey grinned.

At around nine-thirty the chocolate was gone, and they turned the porch light off. Will carried the empty bowl back to the kitchen. As he turned around, he bumped straight into Audrey. He hadn't realized she was behind him. His faced burned as they both mumbled an apology. It felt awkward and wonderful at the same time.

Mrs. Chambers called cheerfully from halfway down the stairs. "All done?"

"Yes, Janet!" Audrey answered.

"Right, Mom—" said Will. "Just shutting the lights off." Audrey was already starting up the stairs. "Night, then," he called.

"Night, Will," she said over her shoulder.

Will turned to Comox. Giving his dog a carefully placed rub to the ears, he said, "Come on, Frankenstein. Time for bed."

———

IN EARLY DECEMBER, WITH no messages from the captain and no sign of Sainos, Will became determined to get one mystery solved. He went to see Principal Parker during a lunch break. The attractive red-headed secretary, Mrs. Rayner, sat at her desk in the main office. After hearing Will's request, she walked to an inner doorway and asked the principal whether he was available. Returning to her desk, she gave Will the nod to go in.

He entered the office and looked around. It was the first time he'd been there. Principal Parker's university diplomas and teaching certificates were on the wall along with an aerial photo of the school. Two tall bookshelves held bulky three-ring binders, assorted books, and one small potted plant. In front of the only window was a large mahogany desk, behind which the principal sat. His no-nonsense look prompted Will to speak without delay.

"Hi, Mr. Parker, thanks for seeing me. I—I have a question. Were there any anonymous donations made for the school's new ground-source heat-pump system?"

The principal was clearly surprised. He regained his composure. "Why do you ask?"

Will was prepared. "The zoo hospital where my dad works was given a donation that could be used only for a solar-PV system. The donor remained anonymous. After the installation, the system was almost wrecked. A friend and I chased off a guy who was trying to smash it with a sledgehammer. He wasn't caught, and the police are still trying to find him."

Principal Parker cleared his throat and asked, "When did that happen?"

"This past June."

"And you're telling me this because?"

"Well, sir, I—I thought the two attacks could be related, that's all." Then he added, "I don't think the police have gotten closer to arresting the guy who was here, have they?"

"No," the principal answered brusquely, "and yes, there was a very generous anonymous donation."

"Did it come with conditions?" asked Will.

The principal decided to return honesty with the same. "Our donor had two specific rules. The first was that the money could be spent only on our new ground-source heat-pump system." The principal folded his arms. "And since we'd already approved and planned to put in a ground-source heat-pump system, that was fine. The other request was that the donor would remain anonymous." They sat quietly. Then the principal asked, "I imagine the authorities are aware of the similarities in these two cases?"

"Detective Clayberry—Margaret and Jackie's dad—is aware," answered Will, unsure whether telling this to the principal was a mistake.

"I would have thought so," said Principal Parker. "He asked me the very same question you did, and I told him yes, we had a mysterious donor. However, I *didn't* know about the other attack and its possible connection to ours."

Will's insides churned.

The principal looked out the window for a moment and then sighed. "I suppose when information's held back, it can be useful." Will's face was turning red. The principal went on, "If a suspect reveals details only the criminal would know, it can help authorities dig deeper to prove he or she is connected to the crime. You follow?"

Will answered, "Yes, sir." He was very glad he hadn't

said more. The bell rang, signaling the end of lunch. Will shifted uneasily. "I—I hope they catch this guy."

"I agree. I'm in contact with Detective Clayberry. May I discuss this new information with him?"

Will paused then said, "Yes," hoping Detective Clayberry would be all right with it.

"Is that all?" asked the principal.

"Yes," said Will, standing up. "Thank you, sir." He bolted out of the office and down the hallway to his next class.

———

A FEW DAYS AFTER THE meeting with Principal Parker, Will got a call from the detective. "Will, I can understand that you want to know more about the attacks . . . and you might not like what I'm going to say, but you are not to have any further involvement in this investigation."

Will was stunned, "Why?" He knew he sounded churlish, but he'd been involved from the start. He pushed back. "That guy wearing camouflage at your house—the night Sainos was at the school—is he the captain?"

"Forget you saw that man, Will. I'm using complex security channels to find Sainos, and because of that, secrecy is the rule."

"Are you any closer to catching him?"

"Well—I hope so, but I can't discuss it with you. Not for now, anyway. So here's the deal—you kids are out of this, understand? Unless you hear something from the captain or Sainos—then you let me know."

Will paused then repeated back, "I'm out of this unless I'm contacted?"

"Right," was the reply. "Thanks." And the phone call ended.

———

THE FOLLOWING SATURDAY, WILL and his father pulled shovels out of the backyard shed. The first winter storm was on its way. The forecast predicted more than a foot of snowfall in Utah's Wasatch Mountains by the next morning.

"Any news from James Clayberry on capturing Sainos?" asked Dr. Chambers.

"Nope. No news," said Will. He explained that the detective had taken him and the others out of the investigation. The first snowflakes drifted down.

"Well, I'm relieved," said Dr. Chambers. "I'd rather have Sainos thinking you and your friends are not involved!"

Will said nothing. He understood his father's concern. But still, saving the newly installed systems had felt good—even if it had been accidental in one of those instances. He, Audrey, and Darius had been useful, along with the installers and inventors who'd worked hard to get these new energy systems in place.

His father closed the shed door. "Focus on school, Will. That—and getting the electric bike project ready for the science fair." They entered the garage from the back.

"Yup," said Will, propping up two smaller blue shovels by a big red one. Wiping their feet, they came in through the side kitchen door. It was lunchtime. Mrs. Chambers and Audrey ladled out steaming bowls of Thai chicken-curry soup, along with crackers, Greek yogurt, and mandarin oranges.

"It's official," said Mrs. Chambers, turning off the stove. "My sister Delores just phoned. She and her husband, Mitchell," she elaborated for Audrey's benefit, "are coming from Vancouver, Canada, for Christmas!"

"Oh?" said the doctor.

Mrs. Chambers went on briskly, "Well, Lloyd, we haven't seen them in more than five years." She bent down and put food into Comox's bowl, and the husky started eating right away. The hairs on his head were mostly filled in, and other than a slight indentation in the fur he was his usual happy self. Mrs. Chambers continued, "Delores said she probably wouldn't even recognize Will if she bumped into him on the street!"

Dr. Chambers made a long slurping noise with his spoon, much louder than usual. "All right, Janet. Mitchell probably won't behave himself, but they're always welcome to visit."

Mrs. Chambers didn't miss a beat. "Don't let him push

your buttons, Lloyd. That's the key."

"Very well, Janet." Another big slurp. "If he gets too annoying, I'll just feed him to my polar bears. I know they'd love eating a famous Canadian." He winked at Audrey and Will. Mrs. Chambers came behind him, ruffling his hair and giving him a hug.

"So that's settled," she said. "Audrey, we'll have to get your room changed over; this works perfectly with your parents coming!" Audrey's eyes sparkled at the mention of her family. Her parents and her sister, Bette, were coming for the holidays. Their home in San Diego was rented out for their entire two-year stay in Santiago, so they'd decided to spend Christmas in Utah. After New Year's Day, Audrey's parents would be going back to Chile, but Bette would stay on with Audrey and the Chambers family.

Though doing well in Santiago, Bette was still catching up from the delays in her early education caused by the pandemic. So the Carters, with the Chambers' help, had worked out a plan where Bette would stay with them until at least next summer. By attending John Adams Elementary School as a second grader after the holidays, Bette would have a better academic recovery.

"I can hardly wait," said Audrey. "I miss them so much! And I know Bette will love seeing Apollo and Kayla." The newborn polar bear cubs and their mother, Gracie, were still in seclusion to give them plenty of bonding time with each other. Only the zoo staff saw them, vowing the cubs were so cute they caused polar-bear-induced delirium. This idea was further supported by the many internet hits to the polar bear cubs' webcam. Thousands, including Audrey, checked on them regularly.

For most of the holiday, Audrey would stay with her family, who'd booked a large, nearby cottage that was usually rented by people planning to ski in Park City. It was close to a canyon entrance and was a half-hour drive from the Chambers' home. With a sharp jab of annoyance, Will realized it was close to where Jace Spurlock's family had just moved. *She'll be too busy with her family to see anyone,* thought Will. *So what if Jace is in some new, huge, overbuilt home?* Will liked where he lived. It was close to the high school and the university—and, best of all, it felt like home.

CHAPTER
11

THE PRE-CHRISTMAS ATMOSPHERE AT Aberdeen High crackled with energy. Students were excited for the holiday break, which started right after exams. Will, Audrey, and Darius often stayed at school until five p.m. to get homework done and receive peer-tutoring on difficult assignments. When exam results came in, Audrey, Darius, Will, and Margaret had all received good grades. As usual, Darius got the highest marks; Will, Audrey, and Margaret had more variety—some up and some down in different subjects. Will's language grade suffered, while Audrey had an *A* in Spanish; they both had received an *A* in physics. Margaret's physics grade was lower, but she had top marks in English and history.

When the bell rang on the last day of term, rowdy students flooded through the school doors. Fletcher Stiles and

Delbert Korbelak were having an argument just outside as Will, Darius and Audrey passed them. Delbert looked fearful. Fletcher was angry. They clammed up as Will and Darius slowed, waiting for students in front to move. Will noticed a crumpled-up reward poster in Fletcher's hand. *Did they know something about the attack?* The mob of students leaving the building pushed Will and his friends forward. When he looked back, Fletcher and Delbert were gone.

At the Chambers home, the Christmas tree had been up for two weeks. It was decorated with tiny colored lights and bright ornaments, more than half of which were familiar, having been accumulated over the years.

Cheery Christmas cards were clipped onto a garland that framed the doorway leading into the kitchen. One of them from Mrs. Chambers' sister Delores and her husband, Mitchell, showed them sitting up on the back seat of a blue, vintage convertible in the most recent July 1st Canada Day Parade. Mitchell Watson was a successful syndicated radio talk-show host and was well known in the Vancouver area. A hastily scribbled message on the card read, "See you soon! Can't wait for that greeeeen Utah Jell-O!—Mitchell." Alongside that, "Love, Delores" was written in a more graceful script.

Two days before Christmas, the Carter family arrived. Will answered the door with Audrey right behind him. She flung her arms around her father and then hugged both her mother and her sister. All three were bronzed from the sunny weather of Santiago, Chile. Mrs. Chambers rushed out of the kitchen and gave her longtime friends a warm welcome.

Exchanging hugs and shaking off snow, Mrs. Carter pointed at two large suitcases and said, "These are Bette's things—her shoes, clothing, books—all the things she'll need for the school year. She has a backpack too, but she'll be using the backpack while we're here." She let her arms flop down to her sides and said with absolute sincerity, "Thank you, Janet. This is so kind of you and Lloyd! We really appreciate it!"

"Lisa, we're happy to have Audrey and Bette stay with us," said Mrs. Chambers. "Really, your kids are great; we love 'em!" Smiling, she turned to Will. "Sweetie, would you put these suitcases in the downstairs closet, please?" She turned back to Mrs. Carter, "We'll put Bette's things upstairs right after my sister and her husband leave."

Bette let out a squeal of delight as Hudson, the cat, came strolling down the hallway. Audrey picked the cat up and introduced him to Bette. He purred loudly, enjoying the fuss.

That evening, the Chambers served a succulent pot-roast supper along with a green salad, quinoa mixed with rice, and a butter-roasted parsnip dish that was a Chambers' holiday favorite. Between bites of food, the Carters explained what they were working on and where they lived in Santiago. After that they were keen to know all about Audrey and how things were going in school, asking her what classes she liked and what she thought of her teachers. When Lisa Carter timorously asked Audrey whether she'd gone to any dances, Will realized that Mrs. Carter was curious to know if Audrey was dating someone.

"No, Mom!" said Audrey, a pink tinge coming to her cheeks.

"Well, that's fine—lots of time for that later," said her mother, looking relieved. Audrey's blush deepened, and she stared down at her plate. Mr. Carter came to the rescue by changing the subject.

"Lloyd, your new polar bears look great!"

"Oh, yes," Dr. Chambers agreed. "Absolutely thriving!"

Bette sat up, eyes sparkling. "I watched them roll around—they're so cute! Can I go see them?"

"Oh, not for a while, Bette," said Dr. Chambers. "In four months—that's about a hundred and twenty-one days—you can visit them."

"That long?" said Bette. She slumped down and poked at her chocolate-mousse tart.

"Afraid so," said Dr. Chambers.

Dan Carter gave Bette a hug. "They need time alone, honey, but they'll be so happy when you see them, it'll be worth the wait!"

The Carters said their goodbyes when dinner was finished, since they were scheduled to meet up with relatives that night. After quick hugs, they were off to their holiday cottage.

An hour after she'd left, to Will—the home seemed empty without Audrey. He'd forgotten to give her the Christmas present he'd gotten her—a box of mint-flavored chocolates that were still on his bedside table. There hadn't been time, and it wasn't even wrapped. *Better to wait*, he thought. *Her parents might think I'm pushy.*

―――――

JUST BEFORE NOON ON Christmas Eve, Will's aunt and uncle arrived. It had been so long since Will had seen them that he hadn't really known what to expect. His aunt's resemblance to his mother was unmistakable, right down to their mannerisms. Mitchell was of medium height with a solid build. He was pleasant and considerate to his wife.

"I'm counting on you to make conversation, Will," his mother had told him earlier. "Please? They remember Michael pretty well; now they can get to know you."

"Sure," Will had replied. He hoped his uncle wouldn't mind that he was much more interested in science than sports.

He took their suitcases upstairs to the guest bedroom recently vacated by Audrey and came back down for lunch.

The Watsons were not frequent church-goers, and Mitchell liked to poke fun at the Chambers' position on alcohol, which was basically not to drink any. Mitchell had brought along a case of beer and politely asked whether it was okay if he drank it during the holidays.

Dr. Chambers said, "If you want to drink dead yeast organisms swimming in their own waste, Mitchell, that's your choice."

Mrs. Chambers held her breath, but Mitchell simply roared with laughter. "Always the scientist, aren't you, Lloyd?"

Dr. Chambers answered, "Not always, Mitchell, but that's what it *is*."

"I'll keep that in mind, Lloyd. Now when are we going to get around to a worthy topic? Hockey!" Janet and Delores visibly sighed with relief.

Dr. Chambers was a committed hockey fan, and Michael, in Germany, was an avid hockey player. The two older Chambers males had watched every single Stanley Cup Series and Olympic hockey match televised in the past fifteen years. *It was possible*, thought Will with a grin, *Michael was missing hockey more than being at home.* Tomorrow they'd be doing a Skype call with Michael at ten a.m. It would be seven p.m. in Germany, and it would be the first time they would see his face or talk to him since he'd left the country.

Attempting to connect the next day at exactly ten a.m., they had two failed efforts. Then, amazingly, there he was from the other side of the world in Hamburg, waving at them through the screen, wishing them well, saying how much he missed them and how he was still working hard to master the German language.

"Man, I love these people! They're great!" said Michael. "Course, some of them think I'm crazy, but a few are showing interest. My companion's terrific! He's from Owen Sound, Canada. And we both love sauerbraten! It's delicious, Mom, it's, it's—like pot roast! And we eat tons of vegetables here." Mrs. Chambers laughed—she knew her son had said that just to make her feel good.

"One of the Germans I'm meeting with is a federal transport ministry guy who's working on the hydrogen fuel-cell transportation market, and he's so stressed—he's really a smart guy. Sad to say he had to cancel our meeting two days ago."

"Why's that?" said Dr. Chambers.

"Work emergency—he writes firewall code to prevent hacking. He usually doesn't comment on his job, but the last time we were at his home he said he wished he had a better way to store data to prevent it from being stolen or corrupted."

"Wow—that does sound stressful," said Will. "Who's doing the hacking?"

"He's not sure, but he says his team is great. Anyway—he invited us back."

"Good!" said Mrs. Chambers. "Do they have any kids?"

"Yup, two boys, just like us, Mom. He and his wife are super nice. They make us feel very welcome."

They were allowed forty-five minutes for the call, and they used every last one. Mitchell and Delores were invited to join in. They expressed their good wishes, and Mitchell even brought up the Stanley Cup matches scheduled for spring, along with his pick for the winner: "The Montreal Canadiens, of course!"

"They love hockey here," said Michael. "Someday I'm coming back to see the Thomas Sabo Ice Tigers play!"

"I'm sure you will," Dr. Chambers chimed in, gently elbowing Mitchell out of the way. Nearing the end of the call, they finished with the cheerful news of Gracie's polar bear cubs. Mrs. Chambers sniffled, unable to hide her tears. Dr. Chambers put his arm around her shoulder, they waved goodbye, and the connection ended.

Later that afternoon they sat down to Christmas dinner, which included a huge, juicy baked salmon, which Mitchell had brought packed in an ice chest. He'd caught it days earlier, up near the town of Campbell River on Vancouver Island, and it was delicious. They ate more roasted parsnips, green Jell-O salad with cottage cheese, rice, and a side dish of steaming broccoli. Will hadn't liked broccoli as a child, but he liked it now—something about "taste buds changing as you get older," his mother said.

They moved to the living room, sitting on couches in front of a warm fire to let their meal settle in place, agreeing they'd do the dishes later. Will felt a singularity realizing he was the only person in the room under the age of forty. *It's Christmas Day. This is fine*, he thought. He wondered about Audrey. *What was she doing at this moment?*

Back to his surroundings, Will thought his aunt and uncle were actually quite interesting. Mitchell may have been combative in previous visits, but this time he was benevolent, possibly due to his success as a radio talk-show host, or maybe his wife had coached him to be more charming.

Delores and Mitchell didn't have children of their own, and from an overheard conversation Will knew that was not by choice. They'd thought about adoption, but until recently, Mitchell's radio career had necessitated frequent moves, so adopting hadn't been possible. By the time Mitchell was established in Vancouver, they felt their time for raising small children had passed. Happily, Mitchell's sister also lived in Vancouver and was raising three teenage girls by herself. Delores and Mitchell had become their second parents.

Mitchell pulled out his phone to show off photos of his nieces and was as proud as any father could be. "They're smart, way too cute, and will absolutely keep you on your toes!"

Delores pointed to the tallest girl. "Nancy's in her second year of college. She has an internship lined up with a great information-technology company." A thought struck her. "If you guys come to visit, we'll all go together to Stanley Park and the aquarium!" Settling back to enjoy the warmth of the fireplace, she turned in Will's direction. "I hear you have a friend who's a very talented Lego builder."

"Yes," he answered, "That's Darius. He probably got a new set for Christmas."

"Will," said Mrs. Chambers, "give Darius a call and see if he and Jing can join us for dessert." She turned to her sister and explained about their good friendship with Darius and his mother.

Will's call connected. "Hey Darius, what's going on? Did you get a new Lego kit?"

"Yep! Auntie Lin came through. I'm working on the Tower of Orthanc."

"The what?"

"One of the towers from *Lord of the Rings*. It's great! Almost twenty-five hundred pieces. Mom loves it 'cause it goes straight up instead of out—takes up less space."

"Right," said Will. "Hey, you and your mom wanna come over and have dessert here?"

"Auntie Lin and my mom are looking through old photographs, so I don't think they will, but I'll ask if *I* can." Darius covered the phone for a moment and then said, "All good. I'll be over in fifteen minutes."

By the time Darius arrived, the dining table and kitchen were cleaned up, the dishwasher was running, and a variety of gelatos were laid out on the kitchen counter. Will and Darius both took a scoop of caramel-salt gelato and a scoop of green chocolate-chip mint.

"I think my favorite is berries and cream," said Mrs. Chambers, making sure everyone else was served first.

Her husband laughed. "Janet, I think most of them are your favorite."

"You're right," she laughed, "let's eat in the living room. We can enjoy our tree and just—be thankful." As the six of them sat down, Comox, who'd been sleeping by the fire, stood up to see what they were eating. He should have stayed asleep. Hudson, the cat, was on the couch. The cat, being older, liked to show the husky who was boss. He reached out to give Comox a cuff on the head as the husky passed by, but the pat on the head didn't go as planned. Three of Hudson's claws got stuck inside the metal edging of the dog's collar. The cat slid off the couch and onto Comox's back so fast, no one knew what had happened. Comox began to arch and jump. Hudson, growling and spitting, sank his remaining claws into the dog's back.

Mitchell jumped up and began a rodeo count, "One, two, three," as the cat flew up and down on Comox's shoulders. The entire room burst out laughing. Will and Darius got on either side of the desperate dog and managed to hold him down long enough for Dr. Chambers to lift the cat up and get his claws out from under the edge of the collar.

Mitchell, on his knees and cracking up, had reached a count of twelve. "Pretty good, Hudson," he yelled after the cat, who streaked out of the room, "You've got the record!" Everyone erupted in laughter again. Comox calmed down, accepting hugs of sympathy from Will and his father.

———

THE NEXT MORNING WILL came into the kitchen to find Mitchell and his father eating breakfast. Eyeing his plate of hot food, Mitchell commented, "Hormel is once again feeding a hungry world. First Spam during World War II— now precooked bacon. Bless 'em."

"On that I agree with you, Mitchell," said Dr. Chambers, checking to see whether his wife was nearby. He added, "Janet thinks two slices of bacon are enough, but not me; this stuff is pure genius!" The doctor munched his third piece with relish. Will grinned. He could hear his aunt and mother coming downstairs, so he added two empty plates to his own and put them in the oven to warm.

Mitchell usually led the morning conversations. Being a talk-show interviewer, he always ignored the rules of "Don't talk religion or politics" and dove right in to any controversial subject. That particular morning, the capability of clean energies was on the table. Will asked his parents, in front of Mitchell, whether it was bad manners to argue with his uncle. His aunt Delores burst out laughing.

"Mitchell loves a good argument! It's whining he can't stand!"

"That's true," said Mitchell. "I get paid to argue. So, Will, what about solar-generated power—can it compete?"

Will grinned. "As Elon Musk points out, solar energy is *already* the source of the majority of earth's energy. Otherwise we'd be sitting on a frozen rock." Elon Musk was a phenomenal engineer and planetary thinker who was the creator of PayPal and the CEO of Tesla Motors, Space-X, and other global enterprises. "But I know you're meaning electricity and heat power generated from solar. So—to answer that, we should look at Germany, a world leader in solar cell efficiency."

"And we owe Germany a great deal for their work on this," said Dr. Chambers. "The German people made an impressive financial commitment to support that research."

Will grabbed a science journal out of his pack, flipping to a page he had marked, and read, "As *Inhabitat* points out, 'The accomplishment proves once again that a lack of sunshine is no obstacle to scaling up solar energy—and if the Teutons can produce record amounts of solar power under grey skies, then the potential for countries with sunnier weather and more land mass (like the United States) is limitless.'"

Mitchell took the article and scanned it. When he looked up again, Will said, "Solar panels don't have mercury emissions like coal—so right now solar is pushing along with wind power to supply as much residential and commercial electricity as possible. Will continued, "The electrical grid is expanding between England and Brussels to make use of England's excess electricity—showing how grid design is an area of great development."

Dr. Chambers added, "That push is essential to fill the gap until the next generation of nuclear reactors are up and running. —And Bill Gates is backing remarkable inventions that are likely to bring clean energy online."[20]

"I've heard about that," said Mitchell, "and I interviewed a Canadian environmentalist who *strongly* supports molten-salt-cooled reactors.[21] My understanding is water-cooled 'bad'," Mitchell did a thumbs down, "and molten-salt-cooled good," he changed to a thumbs up. "The guy felt it was the cleanest energy possible." Then Mitchell turned back to Will. "What else interests you?"

"The new technology of concentrated solar thermal—CST is the acronym." Mitchell looked puzzled then his face lit up.

"Concentrated . . . is that where mirrors focus sunlight onto a tower to gain ultra-high heat?

---

20. For Footnote Link go to Captain Glow Website
21. For Footnote Link go to Captain Glow Website

"Yes," said Will, pulling out his phone. "This YouTube video is good. It explains how this low-cost, zero-carbon technology can replace the emission-intense processes of making cement, steel, petrochemicals and other stuff that put out more than a fifth of our greenhouse gas emissions." He showed his uncle the minute-and-forty-five second video.[22]

His uncle whistled. "Okay, that's looking efficient and clean, points for that!"

"Lots of CST, also called CSP, is under construction now—there's a huge plant in Israel and one in Dubai."

"Okay, Will," said Mitchell. "Let's talk about how cheap natural gas is."

"I'm good to talk about natural gas," said Will. "Seventy to ninety percent of natural gas is methane, right?" said Will.

"Yup," said Mitchell.

"And the natural gas that reaches our houses is almost pure methane, right?"

"That's right," said Dr. Chambers.

"So, picture this, Uncle Mitchell," Will explained, "systems that currently work independently are getting joined together in a specific new way—like a LEGO set. It's called 'power to gas,' or P2G for short. Electricity generated by

---

22. For Footnote Link go to Captain Glow Website

wind or solar goes into fuel cells that split water into hydrogen and oxygen. The next step is methanation, where the hydrogen is merged with carbon dioxide, which we want to use up—well, get rid of, anyway—and presto! You get synthetic natural gas, also known as E-gas or syngas." Will tapped his phone. "I can show you a good P2G diagram." He clicked on a link and handed it to his uncle.

Mitchell looked over the diagram.

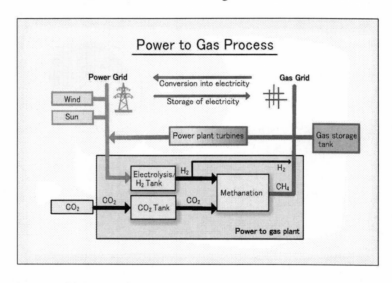

"And here's a three-minute P2G YouTube link."[23] After watching it together, Will said, "What's good about power to gas is that now you don't need to frack in order to get methane. See, fracking generates huge amounts of contaminated wastewater, which is a real loss here in the West.

---

23. For Footnote Link go to Captain Glow Website

And it's for real that Germany and Europe are working hard to scale P2G up to utility-size production."

Mitchell's response surprised him. "So you don't store the electrical energy in batteries, or on the grid. You store it in the chemical form of methane, and our methane-gas pipeline infrastructure is already in place. What heats our houses and our water right now is the natural gas we extract from the earth. We could replace the extraction process with P2G. Hmm, that does seem pretty smart; makes me feel like us humans are using our brains—but I'd want to see a scaled-up system that is actually working."

My uncle's a quick study, thought Will, who had been expecting his uncle to be argumentative. Looking at the diagram and the YouTube videos probably helped.

Suddenly Mitchell got an angry glint in his eye. "Well, I have to admit, the tar-sands people have me riled with some of the propaganda they've generated." He crossed his knife and fork on his plate. "I did an interview recently on how the Alberta government was blaming declining caribou population on wolves. Independent scientists, *every* one of them who studied it, agreed the caribou were suffering from habitat loss caused by the tar-sand industries." He slid his plate away. "But rather than confronting the tar-sand industries, some Alberta officials hired a bunch of guys to shoot wolves. It was a complete waste of money and did nothing to help the caribou."

"That was terrible, Mitchell," said Delores, "but you know, honey, your 'let's get real' broadcast probably helped put a stop to it."

"I think it might have," said Mitchell, rubbing his chin. "Tar-sand development's hard on water too; each barrel of tar-sand oil uses two to six barrels of water. But anyway . . ." He looked at Will. "Send me that link on power to gas. I'm interested."

"You bet," said Will. He brought up a screen on his phone. "Type in your email." Mitchell did, and Will sent him the link. Just then Hudson strolled by. Comox, who'd been resting in the corner, eyed the gray cat warily.

"Speaking of wildlife," grinned Mitchell, "what about that snowshoe hike you promised us, Lloyd?"

As Mitchell, Delores, and Dr. Chambers left to get their snowshoe gear ready, Mrs. Chambers leaned over to Will and said, "This has been the best holiday with Delores and Mitchel that we've ever had! Thanks, Will; I think a lot of it is because of you!"

"No problem," said Will, who helped clear away dishes.

———

DURING THE HOLIDAY INTERVAL, Will went up to the university and worked on his project, which now had its title: "The E-bike-to-Microgrid Ratio." He was carefully compiling data from the phone app that he and twenty-nine other e-bikers had used. They'd started recording data in mid-August and had ended after the first week in October. The total of forty-nine days equaled a seven-week span. Will worked by himself after he and Dr. Sheffield verified that the algorithms were correct and would enable Will to derive a ratio of the number of e-bikes that could be supported, to the size of a solar PV microgrid.

Will was looking forward to the night of December twenty-eighth, when he and his friends, including Audrey, planned to meet up at an indoor skating rink. The recently built rink hosted both college and junior-league hockey games and offered figure skating classes. At certain times in the early evening, it was also open for public skating, and that's what Will and his friends were going to do. On the morning of the twenty-eighth, he called Audrey's phone to confirm the plan, but it went to voicemail.

That night Will, Darius, and Margaret arrived at the rink at seven, running late due to relatives on Margaret's side. Will went to the edge of the ice rink, hoping he'd spot Audrey and they'd be able to spend time together. He'd brought the Christmas present, which he'd finally wrapped. There she was, gracefully skating backward. She was good. He hurried to the rental counter, got sport skates, pulled his shoes off, yanked on the skates, and laced them up. Stepping out onto the ice, Will's stomach lurched. Audrey glided by, hand-in-hand with Jace Spurlock. Will was stunned.

Darius skated over, and after a moment he waved his hand in front of Will's face.

"Hellooo . . . You okay?"

"Huh?" Will came back to life. "Yeah—yeah, I'm fine."

Darius looked out at the ice and then said, "Oooh, guess she must have asked Jace. We didn't invite him, did we?"

"Who cares?" said Will, shoving his gloves into his pockets. "Free country."

"Yeah, that's true," Darius nodded.

Just then, Margaret skated up and did a flawless pirouette. "Want to circle the rink, anyone?"

"I will," said Darius, looking pleased, and off they went.

Will started to skate too; it was better than just standing there. He felt a tug on his shirt. Looking back, there was Bette grinning at him. "Hey, Bette, how ya doing?"

"Hi, Will," she answered. She looked like a younger version of Audrey, only still goofy. Then she slipped and would have fallen if Will hadn't caught her arm. The eight-year-old wasn't much of an ice-skater yet; ice chopping was more like it. Still, the two of them circled around the rink three times. *Agonizing*, thought Will, *but kind of sweet*. Bette took a break off the ice to warm up, so he skated alone.

Jace monopolized Audrey, and soon the public skating hours were over. At eight p.m. the crowd began to exit the ice sheet in droves. Will was finally able to talk with Audrey, learning that she and Bette had come there with Jace, and he was taking them back to their cottage.

Will looked at the gift in his pack. He wasn't going to give her the chocolates in front of anyone, especially Jace. He pushed the box down out of sight. Later that night he tossed it onto the trophy shelf in his room, wondering whether Audrey thought of him as . . . well . . . kind of more like a brother.

———

ON THE MORNING OF December 30, Mitchell and Delores were packed and ready to go back to Canada. Standing in the front doorway, Mrs. Chambers gave both Watsons a big hug. They'd had a fine holiday, discussing everything from family memories to Canada's energetic young prime minister, and there was talk of the Chambers coming to Vancouver in the spring for a tribute-roast where Mitchell was going to be honored.

"Have you ever heard of Vancouver TheatreSports?" Mitchell asked. "Well, a couple of those guys are involved, and if you come, you're going to laugh harder than you ever have before! It'll be early in the season, but maybe you and I can do some salmon fishing."

"We'll see, Mitchell. I'll have to check my schedule, but salmon fishing does sound good," said Dr. Chambers as they headed outside. Delores slid in to the front seat of the car while Mitchell and Dr. Chambers split the luggage between the back seat and the trunk.

Mitchell turned to Dr. Chambers. His face was unusually serious. "You've got a couple of great kids, Lloyd. And Janet . . . well, she's so happy—you do a good job. Sometimes I might even envy you." Then the familiar grin returned to his face. "That's why I gotta give you such a hard time—you flippin' nonconformist! Have a beer now and then!"

Dr. Chambers looked stunned. He began to stutter, "I . . . I—well, that's nice of you, Mitchell. We'll see if we can get together in the spring, but no thanks to the beer."

Mitchell laughed and bounced over to the driver's side. "Too bad we don't have a video of rodeo-cat! That was worth the whole trip right there!"

"Get outta here," laughed Dr. Chambers, and with one final wave, Will's aunt and uncle pulled out of the driveway and were on their way.

———

ON NEW YEAR'S DAY Audrey and Bette returned to the Chambers' home with their parents. The Carters' flight out of Salt Lake City was scheduled for later that evening. When they arrived, Will felt awkward and quickly went downstairs to move Bette's suitcases to the upstairs bedroom she and Audrey would now be sharing. He put the wrapped box of chocolates on the bed without a note, hoping Audrey would think it was from his mom. That evening the two families sat down to a delicious Indian curry that was served with lots of sauce, steaming rice, thick, plain yogurt, and a mango fruit medley.

The Carter family was in good spirits. The time they'd spent in Utah skiing with relatives at Snowbird, Deer Valley, and Park City had gone well. While Audrey's parents were not exceptionally prosperous, her grandparents on her father's side were, and this was one of the years when Grandpa and Grandma had generously funded a holiday reunion and ski trip.

Will was quiet at the supper table that night, especially when Audrey thanked his mother for the chocolates. "You're welcome," said Mrs. Chambers, a little puzzled; then she smiled. Thankfully, she didn't look in Will's direction.

The meal was nearly over when a new subject came up. Fewer than three hours away by car was an impressive U.S. national park called Dinosaur National Monument. It spanned across the state's border, residing in both Utah and Colorado. Audrey's parents had camped there years ago when they were first married and had great memories of being in the park.

"The big Dinosaur Exhibit Hall has been remodeled recently," said Dr. Chambers, "and they did an excellent job." Audrey had wanted to visit there ever since she'd arrived.

An aspect of interest to Will was that it was close to Vernal, Utah, which was very close to Little Brush Creek Cave.

"Maybe on Presidents' Day, you and your friends could get up early and go see it," said Mrs. Chambers. "It's not too long a drive."

"I'd like to go," said Will.

"Me too," said Audrey quickly.

"Can I come too, Mom? Can I?" pleaded Bette.

"Well, no, honey, that would be only for the older kids," said Mrs. Carter, pulling her eight-year-old daughter onto her lap while fending off Bette's protests. "Give me a hug. Daddy and I are going to have to leave for the airport soon." Mr. and Mrs. Carter spent some extra moments with Bette, telling her how much they loved her and that they'd Skype often. Then the two families said their goodbyes, and Mr. and Mrs. Carter were off to the airport.

PART 5

TOO HIGH A PRICE

CHAPTER

12

SINCE PRESIDENTS' DAY—ALWAYS OBSERVED on the third Monday in February—was a national holiday, no schools were in session. It was the perfect day to go to Dinosaur National Monument. Darius could make it, but Margaret could not, so Will asked TR to come. TR replied instantly, "You bet!"

Will noted with pleasure that Audrey wasn't paying much attention to Jace, though the senior was still clearly attracted to her. He'd even given her a valentine. She declined any dating offers, saying she needed to focus on school. After the valentine, Audrey was adamant with her girlfriends that she was not going out with Jace.

Darius even asked if she and Jace were romantically involved and Audrey said, "No, definitely not!" *She's no pushover,* thought Will.

Early on Presidents' Day, when the sky was still dark, Darius pulled into the Chambers' driveway to pick up Audrey and Will. Next they went to TR's home. He was waiting outside and leapt eagerly into the warm jeep to get out of the bitterly cold air. As they sped east on the highway, Audrey and Darius organized a mini study session for an upcoming U.S. history exam where they'd be tested on each of the American presidents.

Will sat in the front passenger seat; Audrey and TR were in back. Between descriptions of Andrew Jackson and James Madison, Will thought about the note that Sainos had left. It was one of the few clues they had, and he wanted to know more. The trail from the road to Little Brush Creek Cave wasn't far, and he was sure they'd be able to find it. Even if they didn't, the adventure and the mountain views would be worth it.

They'd be passing by Park City to get to Vernal. Park City was a good-natured town known for skiing in winter, hiking in summer, and great food all year round. Once a year, for ten days in January, it became a vital film community when it played host to an important independent film festival that presented a broad range of excellent international documentaries and fictional stories.

To its great credit, Park City had recently become a nationwide leader in clean transit by having a fleet of zero-emission battery-electric buses. The city was also putting out an RFP, a Request for Proposal on developing a large-scale renewable energy facility that would power its city operations. They hoped to have it all in place in time to make a bid for future Olympic games. Additionally, it was the first city in the United States to launch a fully electric bike-share program.

As the teenagers neared the town, they could see three of the four large ski jumps, which had been built for the 2002 Olympics. TR, who was a fairly good skier, pointed to the long, white, colossal slides. "See those tiny, black dots at the top? Those are people."

"Unbelievable," said Audrey.

"Especially when they fly long distances through the air and land safely," TR murmured. Then he suggested they go into the town so Audrey could see what Park City looked like. Historic Main Street had succeeded in keeping a unique personality with its variety of buildings. Visitors enjoyed the area's Wild West charm and the surrounding world-class resorts.

"Let's get food!" exclaimed Darius, seeing several restaurants along Main Street. The others agreed. Darius parked the jeep in front of a delicatessen, where they quickly purchased breakfast.

As they devoured sausage burritos, they drove east from the city through a mixture of rugged mountain terrain and farmland. Horses and cattle grazed on large bales of hay, basking in the sunlight that now flooded the snowy countryside. Taking a break from their U.S. presidential studies, they talked of other things. TR wrestled with his decision of which major to pursue in college. Will wanted to go for civil engineering, Darius was fully committed to computer science, and Audrey's plan was to graduate with high marks so she could get into the college of her choice and hopefully get a scholarship.

She gazed out the window at the dazzling white terrain. "Instructional technology is interesting," she said, "but so is biology. My folks said I should stay with them in Santiago this summer and take some time to figure it out."

"Santiago is so far away," said Will.

She looked at him demurely. "Well . . . you'll just have to come and visit." Will's ears became warm.

"We all will," TR jumped in eagerly. "Any place with a tropical rain forest—I'm there. My legendary green thumb is crying out, 'Take me to your lush, tangled-up conflu-ences of trees and your giant bromeliads!'"

"Wow, TR," Darius hooted. Will laughed too; he'd for-gotten how much he appreciated TR's genuine enthusiasm. They entered the small town of Roosevelt, Utah, which was only thirty miles west of Vernal, and Darius called out, "Pit stop!"

TR said, "This is great! I'm in the city named for Teddy Roosevelt, my namesake! And, hey—can we get some des-sert?" It'd been two hours and many presidents since the sausage burritos, and they all agreed to stop and get some pie.

They entered the parking lot of a large frontier-style restaurant called The Western Grille. They parked the jeep, crossed to the sidewalk, and entered at the front door. Not three steps inside, they knew something was wrong. A large, abrasive woman was yelling at two men, one in his thirties and the other, who seemed younger. The men stood up in their booth. The woman's tone was shrill and vicious when she said, "You're causin' trouble, Karcher! You keep this up, and you'll regret it! You hear me? You—aren't—wanted!"

The older man nearest to the woman shot back, "You and your husband are the ones not wanted!"

The woman became louder. "My husband's the boss! And you'll shut up if you know what's good for you."

The man named Karcher stood his ground. "You're only here 'til your contract's done, then you clear off. But your lousy work stays behind!"

His companion spoke forcibly. "On Thursday, the leak-off pressure readings weren't right in those last two wells. But you forced Dave to sign it off and turn in wrong numbers. That's why he quit." He held up his phone and said loudly, "I took photos of the real pressure readings, Bargis. They don't match what was sent in." His voice rose. "The numbers you submit are a lie. Just like the spills we never report. You bust us if we write it up. You're the worst foreman we've ever worked for."

The man named Bargis had gotten up from a table and stood next to the woman. He was extremely overweight. He looked mean, and his face had gone white.

"When you're gone," the young man continued, looking at Bargis, "what happens when someone gets hurt—or killed? You don't care!" He shook his head. "I'm done—finished—I don't care *what* overtime you're paying!"

The woman looked ready to strangle the young man. All the restaurant patrons stared in silence, and a lanky person who seemed to be the manager put himself in front of the two men.

"Mrs. Bargis," he said calmly, "I think you and your husband should go."

Scowling, the man took his wife's elbow and said, "Come on, Cyndy."

But she had one more thing to say. "You Karcher brothers better watch out! We can get rid of troublemakers!"

"Come on!" said her husband, pulling her arm. The four teenagers jumped out of the way as the couple stormed past them and out the door.

The restaurant was silent for a moment then a buzzing of voices began. "Should we stay?" TR asked, looking at his friends.

The manager overheard him and said, "Hey, what can I get for you folks? You need a booth?" He obviously wanted his restaurant to return to normal.

The two Karcher brothers sat down again. *That fight may have been building for a while*, thought Will. He wasn't exactly sure what had happened, but he could feel that the two men were still welcome. No one had asked them to leave.

Will knew a lot of quick money entered towns where fracking was now happening. Often the locals had mixed opinions about it, sometimes leading to conflicts in the community. Generally, incoming money is viewed as a good thing. But Will had been told about how often young kids dropped out of high school for short-term jobs because those jobs paid so well. Being young, they usually spent their paychecks on new cars, trucks, ATVs, and expensive vacations. But if the boom cycle turned bust, they were saddled with debts they couldn't pay and the task of finding work without having much education. If they'd also started a family, they weren't keen to leave the area, so then their best hope was that a new industry would move in. But today, Will realized, they'd witnessed something very specific—something about "turning in false pressure numbers" on well casings.

The manager looked at them expectantly. TR spoke up. "Could we please see your dessert menu?"

"You bet!" The man picked up some menus and led the four over to a booth. They sat down and began to read. The dessert section said the pies were "made fresh daily" and could be served with ice cream or, in bold, capital letters, with **REAL WHIPPED CREAM**.

"Oh, boy, cherry pie and real whipped cream! That's what I'm having," said TR. Will ordered apple pie, and Darius and Audrey agreed to split a piece of lemon meringue after seeing how big the slices were. Given the stickiness of the desserts, they decided to eat in the restaurant.

They ate the pies quickly, paid their bill, and headed out to the parking lot, walking behind the Karcher brothers. The two men got into a sky-blue Toyota pickup. As the truck pulled out of the parking lot, Will read the bumper sticker on the back: "UTAH—LIVE WILD, LIVE FREE."

"That woman was horrible," said Audrey.

"You know the T-shirt with the words *Runs with scissors*?" said TR. "Hers would say *Runs at you with scissors*."

"No lie," agreed Darius.

Continuing east on the highway, they soon came to Dinosaur National Monument. First stop was the Quarry Visitor Center, where they watched a short film about the quarry and the surrounding park. Next they went to the huge Quarry Exhibit Hall itself. Coming into the large building, they were awestruck by the spectacular view of life from long ago. An immensely high, long wall with dinosaur skeletons and plants embedded in a fossilized riverbed had turned almost vertically onto its side over eons of time.

"Imagine finding that," said TR.

"Yeah," said Will, "it feels like we're at an actual dig."

"We *are*," laughed Audrey, leaning closer to him. "They just put a building around it." Then she touched his arm, and a jolt of happiness went through him.

After the Exhibit Hall, they returned to the jeep and headed five miles east. In this area of the Colorado Plateau lay beautiful canyons carved into the earth by the Green and Yampa rivers. In the warm summer months, rafters, campers, and hikers were mesmerized by the dramatic, colorful landscapes and the astonishing diversity of plants and animals.

"Hey, look at that," said TR. Eight bighorn sheep were scrambling up a tiny, narrow ledge on the sheer vertical side of a mountain.

"Wow," said Will, taking a picture. "Amazing." Given the size of the bighorns, their agility was astounding.

Because of the snowpack, the jeep couldn't go any farther than the rock-face petroglyphs and the rustic log cabin of Josie Morris, a Wild West pioneer. They'd only planned for a day trip, so it was time to turn back. They agreed to return in the summer and hike the trails that stretched east into Colorado.

As they drove back to Vernal, Will spoke up. "Let's go see Little Brush Creek Cave."

"I thought you'd say that," said Darius. Will had printed the location out from Google Maps and was already pulling out his sheet of paper.

"It's only twenty-three miles north of Vernal. I'll give you directions."

"Well," said Audrey, returning her lip-balm to her pocket, "it isn't like Sainos is going to jump out at us." She paused, "Probably good that Margaret didn't come along."

Darius agreed, "She would have liked the park, but now that we're going to the cave . . . she might be uneasy, since her dad asked us to stay out of the investigation."

TR was puzzled. "What are you guys talking about?" He knew Will had nearly been run down during the attempted sabotage of the school's new ground-source heat-pump system, but he didn't know anything about the captain or the note from Sainos. They swore him to secrecy and filled him in. He smacked his palms together. "I say yeah, let's go to the cave! Something must have happened there."

"Whoa, check that out," said Darius as they passed through Vernal, referring to an attack helicopter with a shark's mouth painted on the front. It was mounted on metal poles several yards up from the ground, so it looked airborne. They stopped at a small grocery store for some food and then headed north out of Vernal on State Road 191. Eating turkey avocado sandwiches, they drove up and down the hill-and-valley switchbacks, finally reaching the end of the local mining property. They were close now.

Will told the others how Little Brush Creek Cave connected into one of the largest underground passages in the state of Utah. In some parts it was so narrow that a person would have to crawl, sliding on hands and knees just to squeeze through. Will assured them he had no plans to explore the cave. "It's not a spelunking trip. I just want to see what it looks like."

Following directions, they pulled off the road to the left and into a dirt parking lot. The weather had become overcast, and a few snowflakes drifted down. Thankfully there wasn't any wind, so it was still pleasant. Each of them had good boots, a warm coat, and gloves. They climbed out of the jeep and began the trek west to the cave.

Crunching over the snow for a short while, they approached a downhill slope where the river cut through the landscape. Will and TR trudged through deep snow to the river's edge. "It's here!" they called to Darius and Audrey. Looking down a wide opening they stared at the large, curved entrance to the cave. All four scrambled downward on a steep rocky path using the exposed roots of trees to keep their balance. Coming to a halt on the flat snow-covered ground that stretched out in front of the cave, they surveyed its vast arch. A smaller opening, set higher up to the right, was covered with metal bars. Will and the others stood in the silence. The place was eerie and beautiful. They jumped when a great horned owl suddenly pushed off from a nearby tree, making the branches crackle. They watched as the majestic bird glided away.

"We must have ruined his nap," said TR, with a laugh. Will walked into the cave and looked around.

The others followed him. "Do you want to go farther in?" asked Darius.

"Nope," Will shook his head. "Just wanted to take a look."

"Good," said Audrey, "because we're losing the light." She was right—it was almost five in the afternoon, and the small plateau in front of the cave was completely in shadow. The temperature was dropping.

"Wonder what happened in this place," said Will.

"It's fairly remote," said Darius. "Especially back— what—forty years ago?"

"If you hid something forty years ago," considered Will, "you would've had to hide it pretty well to keep it from being found."

"We could check old Vernal newspapers," suggested Darius, "and learn if any money *was* found here."

"If it was found," said TR, "what if the finder kept it a secret?"

"Then somewhere there's a retired cave explorer living it up in Barbados," said Will. The others laughed. Will pulled his coat tighter around him. "Ready to go?" he said. The others agreed. Clambering up the rocky slope, they headed east to the jeep, piled in, and drove back to the main highway.

It was twilight as they sped along the empty road between Vernal and Roosevelt. Rounding a curve, they came upon a dismal sight. The sky-blue Toyota with the UTAH—LIVE WILD, LIVE FREE bumper sticker was smashed up and rolled over on the side of the road. Darius slammed on his brakes and pulled onto the shoulder, just behind the truck. They got out and looked into it, but no one was in the wreck or anywhere nearby.

Seeing a windbreak of trees about fifty yards off, they saw tracks in the snow leading in that direction. "What should we do?" said Audrey, squinting at the trees for any sign of movement. They called out repeatedly, but heard no answer.

"We should call the Vernal police," said Darius. He called 911 and reported the accident and their location near the closest highway mile marker, which was only yards from the truck.

After Darius gave his name and phone number, the police allowed them to continue on their way, since they hadn't witnessed the accident, and no one was there. Back in the jeep, they headed to Roosevelt. They hadn't gone two miles when a man rose out of the ditch, waving at them in the last glimmer of sunlight.

Slowing down, they recognized him as one of the Karcher brothers they'd seen at the restaurant—the older one who'd done less of the talking. He looked desperate and had a jagged cut across his forehead. When the jeep came to a stop, Will and TR scrambled out.

"We saw your truck back there," said Will, taking the man's arm and lowering him onto the front passenger seat. "Sir, I think we better get you to a doctor."

"Thanks for stopping," said the man, struggling to get the words out. "My brother and I were run off the road."

"What?" said TR.

"Yeah, they dragged him out of the truck, but I got away!"

"We need to get you to a doctor," said Will. "You'll probably need stitches. We'll call the police about your brother. What's your name?" They could tell that the man was disoriented.

"All right . . . keep . . . keep going to Roosevelt," he said. "We'll see John—and call about my brother, okay?" Will got in the back with Audrey and TR.

The man slumped down and took a deep breath, "I'm Dallin Karcher. My younger brother's Tom. Damn! It was two big fellas, and one of 'em had a gun."

As the lights of Roosevelt came into view, Dallin seemed to rally. "Take me to Dr. John Ouray-Smith. He lives—just past the Daughters of the Utah Pioneers Museum." Following Dallin's instructions, Darius turned the jeep onto 500 West and went past the museum. "There it is," said Dallin, jabbing his finger toward a large front-yard sign that read *John Ouray-Smith, MD*. Darius pulled the jeep to the curb, and Will and TR helped the injured man into the building.

Thankfully, the doctor was at his office. Once they were inside, Darius called 911 again. He identified himself and referred to the previous call, saying they'd picked up the owner of the smashed-up Toyota and brought him to Dr. Ouray-Smith's in Roosevelt. He told them that Tom Karcher had been abducted and was in danger. Dallin listened to each word. Only when the call ended would he let Dr. Ouray-Smith look at his injuries.

The doctor was a calm man, somewhere in his late thirties, part Anglo and part Native American. The medical degree on his wall was from the University of Utah. It was clear that the doctor and Dallin knew each other.

"C'mon, Dallin, I gotta stitch up your scalp," said the physician, guiding his patient into the examination room.

"Gotta find Tom," mumbled Dallin Karcher as the doctor shut the exam room door. The four teenagers agreed among themselves to stay there until the police arrived.

Will and TR looked down at the magazines on the waiting room table. There were several well-thumbed issues of *Scientific American, ener-G, Trail-Groove,* and a whole lot of *National Geographic* magazines. All the labels were addressed to Dr. Ouray-Smith. "A nature-lover, I think," said TR, pointing to the magazines.

"About this assault," said Will, "you guys thinking what I'm thinking?"

Darius answered first. "That the fight we saw today is why Dallin and his brother were run off the road?"

"Exactly," said Will. "I think we ought to tell the police about it."

"Yeah, I do too," said Darius.

TR and Audrey agreed, with Audrey pointing out, "That awful woman—Mrs. Bargis—threatened him; everyone there heard it!"

"Okay," said Will, pulling out his phone. "First, I'll let my parents know we'll be home late." His dad's voicemail picked up, and Will left a message saying everything was fine, they'd had no car problems, but they were just going to be late. Darius did the same, assuring his mother all was well. He didn't describe Dallin Karcher's situation, simply telling her they were helping a stranded motorist. TR phoned home too; his parents thanked him for the call and told him to tell Darius to drive carefully—and especially to watch out for deer now that it was dark.

The doctor came out of the exam room. "Thanks for picking Dallin up. He'll be all right, but he's got a mean concussion and seventeen stitches. He's resting now. The police coming?"

"Yes," answered Darius.

"Good," said the doctor. "So . . . what happened?"

"Do you know Mr. Karcher well?" asked Will.

The doctor nodded his head and laughed. "Yeah, you could say that. We've been fishing buddies since we were kids. But what I want to know is—did you guys see what happened?" Will and the others answered no and then explained about finding the wreck. They also told him about the fight at the restaurant that morning.

"Oh, Ken Bargis and his gruesome wife," said the doctor. "Not from around here, but I know who they are. Dallin says Bargis has been signing off on bad work to meet schedule. And local boys here, like Dallin, don't like that. A poor cement job sits badly with the locals 'cause they know it'll leak."

The teenagers looked baffled. The doctor went on. "Cement forms the barrier that seals the drilling pipe that goes inside the shaft. It forms a case around the well. So when you have contaminated water that comes from a well, it's probably a bad cement job. Then you get someone like Bargis—who tries to look good by cheating the numbers—and he could end up costing his company millions. That is *if*—the company loses in court and has to make compensation for a spill or an accident. I'll admit they work pretty hard to avoid problems. Still—some crop up."

The doctor reached over to a pile of *National Geographic* magazines and pulled one out. He flipped to a page of a woman standing in front of her sink, where a flame was coming out of her faucet. "She made money at first, until the price of natural gas dropped. So now she gets a piddly amount of lease money, and this is what she's got for drinking water. She'll have to move. But what does wildlife do?"

"That's—that's terrible," said Audrey, looking at the sad-faced woman in the photo.

Dr. Ouray-Smith went on. "I'm not against jobs, but some companies are too predatory. Big tobacco's like that. They make money, and people get cancer from what they sell." Then he smiled, "But other companies are great. In a sunny place like this, maybe some of those solar towers will come in, like those in California and Nevada."

"Oh—you mean concentrated solar thermal," said Will, "with towers." TR and Audrey looked puzzled. Will explained, "Where mirrors are focused on a tower that heats molten salt—"

"—And the intense heat replaces the use of fossil fuels—on a scale large enough to actually improve the world," said the doctor. "Glad to see you're following these new technologies. It'd be a blessing to get those CST towers here for local jobs. If we stop drilling gas wells, we'll keep our water cleaner." Then his face creased with worry. "We gotta find Dallin's brother, Tom—he's in trouble." A car door slammed. The doctor opened the front door, letting in two Vernal policemen.

The teens gave all the information they had to the officers, including details of the restaurant fight. As they got ready to leave, Dallin Karcher insisted on coming from the exam room to thank them.

"Sit down, Dallin," said the doctor, forcing his patient into a chair.

"Hope your brother turns up okay," said TR. Will and the others murmured the same as they headed through the door. As the police began taking information from Dallin Karcher, they climbed into the jeep and headed back to Aberdeen.

The next morning at home, Will's parents were fine with the unplanned trip to the cave and thanked Will for the phone call about the delay. Audrey and Will recounted the restaurant argument and how Dallin Karcher had been run off the road. At that point, Will realized if they hadn't gone to the cave, they wouldn't have been there when Dallin had needed their help. He easily could have frozen to death—which might have been what the attackers had hoped for.

"I'm not glad you picked up a stranger," said Mrs. Chambers hesitantly, "but I . . . I understand. When you saw how badly he was hurt—what else could you do?"

———

ON THURSDAY OF THAT week, news of Dallin's brother, Tom, horrified them all. Tom's body was found in a run-down barn, where he had been tied to a chair and shot. A Salt Lake City TV station broke the story, and it was also covered in Salt Lake City's major newspapers. Ken Bargis and his wife were listed as suspects. The article noted that Tom Karcher's phone was missing. Several people had come forward to report the threats they'd heard Cyndi Bargis make in the restaurant, but no solid evidence emerged to connect them to the murder. Dallin Karcher hadn't seen the men who had attacked them before that night, and no one else in the area had either.

On Friday at the lunch table, Will told Darius and TR that he wanted to go to Tom Karcher's funeral. Audrey plunked down in the seat next to Will and began looking at the news of Tom Karcher's murder on her phone. Jace Spurlock came out of nowhere and scooped the phone from her hands. Before Jace even looked at the screen, Will jumped up and lunged to take it back. Jace sprang away and held the phone high over his head. They were well matched in size but Jace was slightly more filled out.

Audrey stood up. "It's okay, Will, let me handle this." She barely moved but her words were cogent and clear. "Jace, you're a gentleman, right?" Her tone was calm. "May I please have my phone back?" Jace lowered his arm. Audrey didn't say anything more, she simply held out her hand.

Jace spoke in a teasing manner. "Why should I?" Audrey gazed first sideways then at the ceiling. She looked back at Jace with a mystifying smile.

"Because that's what a friend would do." Jace was surprised by her comment. Will knew Jace had no idea of Tom Karcher's death and how Audrey was feeling. Jace had simply wanted a game of "wrestle and rescue."

"I can't figure you out," Jace said as he handed the phone back to her.

With a warm smile she said, "I'd be worried if you did, Jace." She stepped backward and said, "Friends, okay?"

Then, doing something unusual for Audrey, she put a hand on Will's arm. The public act of loyalty was not lost on Jace. He paused. Then he looked beyond Audrey's shoulders to where he spotted a senior girl waving at him. "See you round," he said and left.

As Audrey and Will reseated themselves, Darius and TR said they wanted to go to the funeral too, even though they'd only seen Tom Karcher once. So on a cold, windy Saturday morning at the end of February, the four headed back to Vernal.

The chapel was full and the service was sacred and meaningful. Dallin Karcher spoke last. Standing tall, he finished up by saying, "Tom, to me you're a hero . . . a man who fought the good fight. We will *never* forget you." Tears flowed on the mourners' faces.

As the service ended, Dallin Karcher joined his father, mother, and two sisters. They walked silently with Thomas Karcher's widow and his four-year-old son while she carried her husband's ashes from the chapel. Dr. John Ouray-Smith sat near the back, not too far from Will, Audrey, Darius, and TR. When he came out of the chapel doors, the doctor gave them a nod, his face etched with sorrow. Will and his friends stopped to tell Dallin Karcher how sorry they were for his loss. He shook their hands and thanked them for coming.

"We people are willing to work hard. But this?" said Dallin. "The world is not the same for me and my family now." He shook his head. "I have to believe justice will win in the end."

On the drive home they remembered what the doctor had said about how certain corporations were too predatory.

"If a company doesn't use the win-win concept, where both sides receive benefit," said Will, "how much damage are they willing to inflict?" To Will and his friends, the murder of Tom Karcher was unjustified and evil.

PART 6
THE WIND FARM

CHAPTER
13

On a sunny monday morning at the beginning of
April, a maid at the Aberdeen Motel knocked loudly
on the door of a ground-floor motel room. She'd lost an
earring somewhere nearby the day before. Not getting
an answer and not seeing a car parked in front, she took a
risk and ignored the "Do Not Disturb" sign. It was lucky
for the occupant that she did, because what she saw inside
made her scream at the top of her lungs.

Stoney Korbelak, the yardman from Ropelato's Parts and
Salvage, lay spread-eagled on the motel bed. He had a long
gash on his head, and blood from his wound dripped down
onto the floor. An empty syringe lay on the carpet next to
the bed. When the ambulance arrived, the EMTs were able
to find a pulse. They stabilized him and transported him to
Aberdeen Regional Hospital with blaring sirens.

Will soon learned of the incident when an unexpected afternoon visitor sought him out the same day. Will was in the garage with the doors open, tightening up a loose screw in the arm of a dining room chair. Hearing a car engine, he raised his head and was shocked to see Delbert Korbelak pulling up in a green sedan. It had a crumpled hood and a blue replacement fender. Delbert turned off the engine and got out. They looked at each other.

"Something I can help you with?" said Will stiffly.

Delbert's face was chalk-white. "Is there somewhere we can talk that's—more private?" He looked over his shoulder nervously as though someone could be watching him.

"All right," said Will. He motioned Delbert to follow him through the rear door of the garage. They entered the Chambers' backyard, a quiet place sheltered by four large maple trees that were starting to show spring buds.

Will turned to face the lean, young man who was obviously upset. Delbert looked down for a moment, then said, "My Dad's in the hospital. He's—he's hurt pretty bad—the doctors put him in a coma so his brain can . . . I don't know—switch off and heal—something like that." The young man twisted his hands. "He's got a really bad cut on his head." Will didn't reply, so Delbert went on. "I haven't told the police what I'm gonna tell you 'cause I don't want to get my old man in trouble—but I think I know who did it." He kept rubbing his hands. "Yeah, I'm sure I know who the guy is."

Will was on his guard. "Why come to me?"

"Cuz you're friends with that Clayberry girl and her dad's a cop, right? I sure heard enough about Clayberry after he stopped by Ropelato's . . . anyway—"

Just then Darius walked through the rear garage door. He froze when he saw Delbert, who clammed up immediately. "It's okay, Darius," said Will. Then he told Darius about Stoney Korbelak's injury. He finished with, "Delbert's got more to say."

"Does he have to be here?" growled Delbert.

"Anything you tell me, you can tell Darius," Will's eyes flashed. "He stays."

Delbert paused then let out a sigh. "Okay, but I want you guys to help keep my dad outta trouble—and *I* haven't done anything illegal! My dad . . . man—he could *die!* The guy who tried to kill him is the one causing all the trouble. And he might come back to finish the job." His face knotted up. "I gotta figure out what to do—and I'll trade you something big for your help."

"Something big?" said Will. "Whataya mean?"

Surprisingly, Delbert looked at Darius. Then he said, "Something about Fletcher Stiles—but first you gotta promise to help me and my dad—I hafta figure out how much I should tell the police." He paused. "Fletcher'll know it's me talkin' but I don't care—he's a jerk!" He gritted his teeth. "If he hadn't—I mean—man! He's the reason my dad's so messed up!" He balled his fists into his pockets and looked at the two, waiting for Will and Darius to agree.

"Look Delbert," said Will, "We promise to keep the information quiet as long as we're not accomplices to a crime."

"Agreed," said Darius. It took several minutes for Delbert to explain all that had happened.

Fletcher Stiles had come over to Delbert's house the previous afternoon. The two of them headed for the Korbelaks' storage shed to find a pair of large garden shears. Delbert's grandmother, who lived nearby, had asked if he would trim some tree branches that were growing too close to her front door. Stoney, unaware of this request, hadn't expected that his son would go into the shed. When Delbert and Fletcher got there, they found it was locked.

"That was weird, 'cause it's never locked, but I knew where the key was, so I got it and we opened it up." Delbert's eyes became wild. "There was a box of dynamite in there! When Fletcher saw it, he was all over it. He looked through the whole box and then he got some wild idea. It was like he went crazy—he kept saying, 'This'll work, I know it!' He pulled out the box before I could stop him and loaded it into his truck! There were some diagrams and other stuff in there too. The whole time I was yelling at him to put it back!"

Delbert bared his teeth. "But Fletcher didn't put it back because he never listens to anybody—he shoved me away and told me to keep my mouth shut, and he took off!

I wasn't sure what to do—so I locked the shed up again. Five minutes later, my dad shows up with some guy and they head right for the shed. When I saw 'em I—I took off—I knew they were after that box! They didn't see me."

"What did the guy with your Dad look like?" asked Will.

"Older, silver hair—tough, though, like he could punch the crap out of you."

Will and Darius looked at each other. *Sainos.* Maybe this was the missing connection to the license plates and Stoney Korbelak.

"That night, when I came home, my dad was freakin'!" said Delbert. "He asked me about the box—I didn't know what to do, so I lied. I said I didn't know what he was talking about—I was gonna try to get the box back from Fletcher and put it in the shed again—under a tarp or something—and tell my dad it *was* in the shed and maybe he'd think it was there the whole time. But I couldn't find Fletcher anywhere! It was like he'd disappeared!"

Delbert went on to describe how in the last six months Stoney had come into more money than usual but had been very secretive about it. "I think the guy with him yesterday is the one giving him money, and—my dad said something about the man not trusting him anymore, and he said that was really bad. He was really freakin'! He asked if I'd seen anyone around the shed; I said no and then he took off. When he didn't come home last night, I knew something was wrong. See, after my mom died, he always comes home at night . . . but not last night—an' then this morning—they find him at that motel, almost dead."

Delbert's voice quavered but was urgent. He went on to explain that he was sure Fletcher planned to blow up the pump house for the ground-source heat-pump system at the school. "He kept talkin' over Christmas about finding a way to damage it and be able to put the blame on someone else! Then he could point the finger and collect the reward. See how this would do it for him? He'll cause the explosion and then turn the box and papers over to the police. None of that stuff's linked to him—it's linked to my dad and that other guy. Then Fletcher would collect the reward money—you understand what I'm saying?"

"When's he going to do it?" said Will.

"Well, he's not a patient guy," said Delbert, clenching his fists. "It's Monday, first day of spring break—tonight would work, right?"

Will thought for a moment then said, "Delbert, the best thing you can do is talk directly to Detective Clayberry. He's actually tracking the guy who hurt your dad—he'll want to help—and somebody ought to be guarding your dad at the hospital."

Delbert nodded then asked, "What about my dad not going to jail?"

"Logically, you and your grandma should look for a good lawyer," said Darius. Just then, Comox entered the backyard via the kitchen dog door. He walked over to Will, sat down, and looked up at Delbert. Will leaned over and scratched Comox's ears.

"The man who beat up your dad almost killed this dog," said Will. "He's a sorry excuse for a human being. I'm gonna call Detective Clayberry now; you okay with that?"

Delbert nodded.

Detective Clayberry's phone system sent Will a message saying the phone was "out of service range." He then called Margaret, who picked up immediately.

Putting her on speaker phone, he said, "Hey, Margaret, it's Will; is your dad around?"

"Sorry, Will, not back 'til tomorrow. He and Mom are with friends at a cabin outside of Lava Hot Springs. He said they might have poor cellphone service up there."

"Oh, man . . ." said Will.

"What's up?" asked Margaret quickly. Darius shook his head to indicate that he didn't want Will to say anything for Margaret's sake. Will nodded, skipping any mention of Sainos.

"Uh, nuthin' too bad," said Will, "but when you do hear from your dad, tell him I called and need to talk to him. Gotta go. Bye, Margaret."

Delbert balled his fists up again and said, "I'm going to the hospital—I'll be the guard! I don't wanna lose my dad too." He gave them a sharp look. "Will you keep trying to reach Clayberry?"

"Yep—and we'll try to stop Fletcher—but when Detective Clayberry's back, you'll have to tell him everything."

Some of Delbert's color had returned. "Deal," he said. Then he left.

Will called Detective Clayberry's phone again, and this time he reached voicemail. He left a message saying that he had new information on Sainos. Then he and Darius talked everything over and realized they needed to make a plan.

Monday was the start of spring break for Aberdeen schools, and Audrey had taken her sister Bette and Denzel Barton to an early movie. At five p.m., Audrey and the two kids arrived home for supper. The two eight-year-olds chatted happily about the movie as they helped Audrey set the table.

Dr. and Mrs. Chambers had left the day before to stay with the Watsons in Canada so they could go to Mitchell's comedy tribute in Vancouver, British Columbia. Dr. Chambers had also arranged to meet with the African penguin specialist at the Vancouver Aquarium during their stay, so they wouldn't be back until the following Saturday. Janet Chambers had left a delicious halibut chowder in the fridge along with other easy-to-heat-up meals.

Will and Audrey decided that tonight would be perfect for the chowder, and they worked together to get supper on the table. Will heated up the soup and put it in bowls while Audrey set out crackers and made a green salad.

Darius sliced cucumbers and served them along with a creamy, ranch dressing. All five ate while making light-hearted conversation with the two eight-year-olds.

Denzel was staying until eight p.m., when TR planned to pick him up. In the past ten weeks, Denzel and Bette had become loyal friends. They shared the same classroom and a love of frogs, aquariums, knock-knock jokes, and the "Life on Earth Matching Game."

Will and Darius kept quiet about Delbert's visit. They were firm that they should honor their promise, and they knew it would upset Audrey anyway. As they were clearing away the last of the supper dishes, the doorbell rang.

"I'll get it!" said Will quickly, wanting to see TR first. When he opened the door, he said in a low whisper, "What are you doing tonight after you get Denzel home?" Will and Darius had agreed TR would be an excellent third man to help them prevent Fletcher Stiles from carrying out his scheme.

At that moment, Denzel came roaring down the hall and burst out, "Knock, knock!"

"Who's there?" asked Audrey good-naturedly, following along with Bette and Darius. TR rolled his eyes.

"Nana," said Denzel.

"Nana who?" asked Audrey.

"Nana your business."

Bette burst into giggles.

"Knock, knock," said Denzel again.

"We need your help; it's really important," confided Will to TR.

"Knock, knock," repeated Denzel.

"Who's there?" said Bette.

"Noah," said Denzel.

"Noah who?" asked Bette.

"Noah good place to eat?"

Bette laughed even harder.

"Denzel, knock it off," said TR. "Yeah, I'm free—after I get Mr. Funnypants home."

"Knock it off, you say?" jabbered Denzel, "You mean more knock-knock jokes, please?"

"No!" said TR, pushing his brother along. "Just get in the car!"

"Bye, Denzel," said Bette. "I really like your knock-knock jokes!"

"I do too!" said Audrey, waving goodbye to the young boy as he climbed into the car. She went back inside.

Will hollered out to TR, "It'll be a late night! We'll pick you up at nine forty-five. Wear a dark jacket—tell your parents you're staying here tonight." TR gave a thumbs-up, indicating he understood. He checked for traffic behind him and backed out of the driveway.

At nine-thirty that night, Will and Darius left, dressed in dark clothing. Audrey was puzzled by their sudden departure, but she didn't stop to ask questions as she was putting her sister to bed. She planned to work on her history fair project—research on the rapidly growing global middle class and its contributions to a healthy planet-wide economy. She was calling it "Benefits of a Global Middle Class; Why Goldilocks Was Right." It was keeping her busy.

TR was waiting for them outside his house. He climbed into the vehicle, and as he buckled up, he asked, "What's going on?" With no delay Will explained that Fletcher Stiles was going to blow up the pump house at the school's newly installed heat-pump system.

"What?" said TR. "Why would he do that?"

"He's a jerk, that's why," said Darius, "and he's gotten ahold of some dynamite. He wants to blow up the school's pump house and then get the thousand-dollar reward by turning in some evidence that would pin it on someone else—"

"Whoa, wait a minute—dynamite? Evidence? Back up a little, please," said TR.

"Yeah, I know—it's confusing," said Will.

Both he and Darius answered all the questions TR had except the one about where they got their information. That one remained unanswered. They explained that they'd made a promise to keep that quiet. TR didn't give up. "Is it—uh—that captain—guy?"

"No-o-o," said Will, motioning for Darius to start the jeep. "Haven't heard from him since last summer—the guy could be dead for all we know."

"Then who?"

"Can't tell you, TR," apologized Will, "but I know the person is telling the truth."

"And he's got a lot to lose," added Darius solemnly, and Will knew Darius was thinking about Delbert's father.

"All right," said TR, slapping his hands on his knees, "let's go."

They parked a few blocks away from the school, knowing that Fletcher would recognize Darius's gold jeep if they left it in the school parking lot. They brought along two shovels as part of the plan. Circling behind the school, they took a route that kept them out of sight. Silently they passed behind a tall row of bushes lining the edge of the field to a place where they could be concealed yet close to the pump house.

They knew it might be a long and possibly futile wait. They pushed the shovels into the soil to get them dirty and then lay them to the side. Crouching on the ground to begin with, they soon stretched out full length and propped up on their elbows. Eventually they lay flat. Even though the moon was full, they were now nearly invisible.

By one a.m., it felt as though a century had passed. Suddenly they tensed up as the sound of an engine cut through the silence. In the parking lot at the south end of the field, they watched two headlight beams swing around and then shut off. The engine stopped. For a few moments it was quiet then a vehicle door slammed shut. Keeping still, they watched a figure emerge from the darkness, quickly heading toward them.

The three young men planned to give Fletcher only enough time to get to the small pump house. Then Will and TR would jump him. Darius moved away, low to the ground, heading for Fletcher's truck. If Fletcher shook off Will and TR, they planned to catch up with him there. Fletcher reached the pump house and stooped down, placing a small bundle at the side of the building.

"Now," whispered Will, and they crashed out of their hiding place as a match flared. Suddenly a burly arm had a viselike grip on Will—it was the shop teacher, Mr. Robinson! He shone a blinding flashlight into Will's face as the young man struggled. "Quick—over there—dynamite!" hollered Will. *Had Fletcher lit the fuse? They'd be blown to bits!*

Will heard Fletcher yell. Robinson shone his flashlight at the sound. Two forms struggled on the ground. TR had tackled Fletcher and had him pinned. Will shouted, "Mr. Robinson—shine your light at the pump house!" The man did so, and to Will's relief, the bundle wasn't lit.

"What's going on?" barked Mr. Robinson.

"That's Fletcher Stiles on the bottom—TR's got him!"

The older man understood and quickly moved in to help TR hold Fletcher down, yelling to Will, "Call the police!"

Will did. Police sirens sounded almost immediately. Robinson, keeping a tight hold on Fletcher, aimed his next question at Will and TR. Then catching his breath he said, "What're you doing here?"

Will pointed to the shovels, saying, "We were diggin' for earthworms!"

TR added, "When we saw this guy comin' across the field, we guessed it meant trouble. Glad you showed up— what made you come?"

Will flooded with gratitude—TR had the situation in hand. Mr. Robinson knew who TR was through TR's mother, Mrs. Bartson, so things would be okay.

Mr. Robinson answered "The school's new security system triggered. When a vehicle pulls in this late, it sends an alarm. I live close by," he said, "just a block away, so I came to see why."

TR and the big shop teacher yanked Fletcher to his feet as a patrol car with flashing lights stopped at the edge of the field. Two police officers sprinted over. Thankfully, the earthworm story held up for them too. They were far more interested in Fletcher Stiles and the explosives.

The bundle of five sticks of dynamite was retrieved. Fletcher refused to answer any questions, maintaining absolute silence. Will and TR watched as the officers led him away in handcuffs.

Taking a deep breath, Will let the tension drain out of his shoulders. The cool night air felt good. He and TR told the shop teacher they were going to walk home, but Mr. Robinson insisted on giving them a ride.

"We're going to my house," said Will, "on Aspen Drive."

"I'll be back; stay here," said Mr. Robinson, and within two minutes he'd returned with a car. During the drive, Will explained how his parents were in Vancouver, and that TR was staying with him. Luckily, Mr. Robinson wasn't very interested. He dropped them at Will's home and sped off.

The minute they were alone, they called Darius. As planned, he'd been waiting at the jeep.

"Great, I'll be right there," he said, clearly relieved. Comox came into the kitchen and Will ruffled his ears. The large canine sniffed at the strange smells on Will's hand. *Things could have gone better, but they could have gone worse.* They had wanted to stop Fletcher, grab the dynamite, and force Fletcher to agree to leave Darius alone—permanently—or else they'd call the police. But as it stood now, Fletcher Stiles was in much deeper trouble and likely facing a jail sentence.

Will checked in upstairs and found that Audrey and Bette were fast asleep. As he came back down, he heard Darius knocking quietly at the front door. TR let Darius in. When he heard what had happened, he punched the air and said, "It's justice, man, pure justice!!"

"Yeah, Darius," said Will, keeping his voice down, "but what about—"

"I got it! The truck was unlocked, like we thought it would be. Wait here." He bolted back outside and returned with a large cardboard box. They took it to the kitchen, where he set it on the table. It was full of new sticks of dynamite complete with blasting caps that could be electrically detonated. Will lifted one out to examine it. The papers Delbert had mentioned were jammed down toward the bottom. A large, glossy photo caught Will's attention, and he set the stick down on the kitchen counter. Pulling out the photo, he held it up. It was an aerial photograph of a wind farm next to a bigger field with more construction. At the bottom was scrawled a single word: *SPAW.*

The two other documents were printed maps. Darius studied them. "I think this one matches the aerial photograph." Circular symbols were scrawled on the large map that could only represent the wind turbines[24] because they lined up perfectly with wind tower images in the photograph. The other map was of the same locale but had been zoomed out to a larger area. Nearby was a town called Melford, Utah.

"I know where that town is—it's only three hours south of here," said Will, "One of my cousins has a hardware store there. The wind farm's a big deal for that place."

"And what's *this*?" said TR, lifting up a drawing. It was a large diagram of the inside of a wind turbine's nacelle.

---

24. For Footnote Link go to Captain Glow Website

TR murmured, "The cover is called the *nacelle* . . . there's the nose cone, the gearbox—" his hand moved over the image, "and the generator. That part's been underlined."

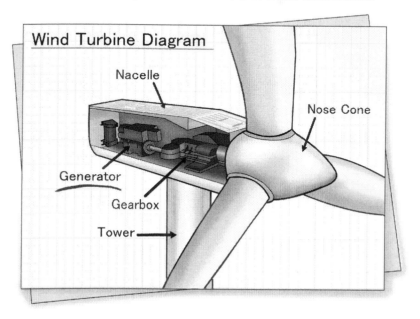

Will opened up a small, folded piece of paper and almost choked at the signature. He read the tattered email first to himself and then to the others. "Here are the maps of the SPAW target. On April 3, the site will be deserted due to off-site training. The explosions must look like faulty generators. NOTHING can be left behind to indicate otherwise. The money and false ID you need to leave the country are ready. Detonate at 1:20 a.m. on April 4. At 1:40 a.m., retrieve an envelope attached under the bench outside Dennums's Market in Melford. It will have the combination and location of a locker containing your payment and a new ID. Delete this email after reading. If you fail, the outcome for you will be prison. Varhiman." The part about the bench in front of the market had been underlined in ink.

"Varhiman?!" said Will looking at Darius, who also knew the name. "Why would he be giving orders to Sainos?"

"Who's Varhiman?" asked TR.

"A guy working with Detective Clayberry to catch Sainos," said Will.

"Guys, look at the date and time of the planned attack," muttered Darius, his face pale. "That's—that's less than twenty-four hours from now."

"If Sainos can get ahold of more explosives, he'll be able to carry this out," said Will. He quickly sent a text message to Detective Clayberry. While waiting for a reply, he and Darius took TR into their confidence after making him swear to keep the promise they'd made to Delbert Korbelak. Fifteen minutes went by with no response to Will's text. *How could Vahriman be involved?* thought Will. *Had he and Clayberry set up a sting operation?* He turned to his friends, "Detective Clayberry will check his phone the first time he's got a signal, probably in the morning."

"Can we wait for that?" said Darius.

"Maybe this is a trap that Vahriman and Detective Clayberry set up to catch Sainos," said Will, "so I think we have to wait for Detective Clayberry, or we could ruin their operation by calling it in." Darius and TR agreed. Reluctantly, the three young men held off calling the police and hoped it was the right decision.

Suddenly they were overcome with exhaustion. Will grabbed an army cot and sleeping bag from the garage. TR would sleep in Michael's bed. Will found an extra pillow for Darius, who had set up the cot in the open landing upstairs. Within five minutes all three had fallen asleep.

CHAPTER
14

A<small>T NINE-THIRTY THE NEXT</small> morning, Will's cellphone rang. He grabbed it and shook TR's shoulder, yelling for Darius, who raced in from the hallway. With Detective Clayberry on speakerphone and Darius and TR filling in, Will explained everything from the near-fatal attack on Stoney Korbelak to the box of dynamite sitting downstairs.

"Are you and Vahriman working together on this?" asked Will.

"Absolutely not! There's no plan involving Varhiman!" said Detective Clayberry, "I'm driving back now—we'll be there by eleven a.m. I'll make some calls, and by then I should know more." The detective spoke urgently. "We've got to be careful. If he *is* working with Sainos, I don't want him to realize that I know. Contact me if *anything* else happens!" The call ended.

Will hoped there'd be enough time to stop Sainos if the sabotage was still going ahead.

They raced down the stairs. A note from Audrey was on the hall table by the front door. As planned, she and Bette were already at the zoo. Dr. Chambers had let it slip that on that Tuesday morning, if they wanted to see the polar bear cubs outside, she and Bette should be at the zoo between ten a.m. and noon. They'd get to see Apollo, Kayla, and Gracie without the large crowds coming for the official ceremony happening on Friday. Margaret Clayberry, also keen to see the cubs, had already picked up Audrey and Bette earlier that morning.

"I'm glad they didn't go into the kitchen," said Will. "We should have moved that box."

The young men re-heated some sausages in the microwave and were chowing down when the kitchen phone rang. Will picked it up.

A raspy voice spoke. "Do nothing, say nothing to anyone about the explosives, the SPAW or the maps. If you want the child back alive, do nothing. You'll know her location at two a.m. tonight. Tell Clayberry—he should do nothing." Click. Will's stomach twisted into a knot as he relayed what the caller had said.

Darius's phone began to buzz. He put it on speaker. It was Margaret. She was crying and barely made sense. "Margaret, calm down," said Darius, "what's happened?"

"You've got to come; you've got to come now—someone's taken Bette!"

"Who, Margaret? Who's taken Bette?" said Will.

"I don't know! Please, come—the police are on their way!" They bolted out of the kitchen to the gold jeep, pulling on shoes as they ran. Will called Detective Clayberry as Darius drove, and TR kept a sharp eye out for traffic. It was ten forty-five a.m. Horrified by the news, the detective told them he'd meet them at the zoo and they should follow the instructions from the caller to say nothing about Sainos to anyone. Within minutes they pulled into the parking lot. They saw a police car's flashing lights.

Jumping out of the jeep and hurtling past arriving visitors, they pushed to the front of the line. Gratefully, Will spotted a zoo employee, Joe Eccles, who was at the ticket window. "Joe—we're here about the missing girl!" Joe quickly held down a button, and the turnstile in the lane nearest to them released. Will, Darius, and TR raced through it.

Dashing around the corner to their right, they spotted two policemen standing with a frantic Margaret and Audrey. Even at thirty yards, Will could see the despairing slump in Audrey's body. As he neared, she began to sway. He caught her and held her up as she crumpled.

"Oh, Will—" she said, burying her face into his shoulder.

"What happened?" he said.

Margaret explained again what she and Audrey had just told the police moments before. Thankfully, one of the policemen was Officer McGuiggan.

"We were standing over there!"—she pointed to a stone column with a water fountain on top—"and a man pushed me aside! Audrey was taking a drink, and—he grabbed Bette so fast. He clamped something over her mouth—a cloth, I think. I grabbed at him but I only caught this." She held up a broken chain with a strange gold cross dangling from it. "He went down the alley over there"—she pointed to the left—"that goes to the parking lot. We dropped everything and ran after her—but—but he pulled her into a white truck and drove off so fast we couldn't get plate numbers!"

Audrey could finally speak. "Laura, your dad's nurse, was in the parking lot. We were screaming like crazy. Somehow she got what we were yelling—and she understood that Bette was in the truck and she took off! I don't know where she went—" At that moment both Laura and Detective Clayberry arrived. Laura was completely winded and had to double over to catch her breath.

Detective Clayberry turned to ask his daughter, "Have you seen this kidnapper before? Was he the man who hurt Comox?"

"No!" said Margaret. "It wasn't him. This guy was taller." Audrey began to sob.

It was Laura who stunned them all, now that she'd caught her breath. "You can track him!"

"What? What do you mean?" asked Detective Clayberry.

She went on, "The bed of the truck! There's only one road out of here, so I ran through the houses to catch up with the truck—I went through backyards—over a fence—somehow I got close enough, and I—I just threw! My phone landed in the bed of the truck! I have the phone tracking app!"

The police and Detective Clayberry dashed into the hospital following Laura, who logged into the zoo computer and onto the app that would provide the phone's GPS location. Thankfully, Laura's phone had a strong rubber case, so it didn't shatter when it hit the truck bed. It was transmitting perfectly. Within moments, police knew its location and were after the truck.

Audrey and Margaret stood together just inside the building. Audrey was pale and trembling, but even from a distance Will could see new hope in her eyes. Officer McGuiggan took over procedures as Clayberry came out and pulled Will, Darius, and TR aside.

"We can't do anything until Bette Carter is safe—we can't risk it!"

"Right," said the young men.

Clayberry turned to Will. "I want you to go to your home. If we've got her back, we can move quickly—I'll need that box. Get it and bring it to me." Margaret had slipped out of the door, looking puzzled by their intense exchange. Her father motioned for her to come closer. "Margaret—this is very important. You'll have to think back, okay?" She nodded. "Did the kidnapper look anything like the man who was at our house in October?"

She was stunned. "The—the Lieutenant? . . . Maybe," she croaked. "Yeah, it could have been him."

He took her by the shoulders. "That information stays quiet—understand? Keeping Bette alive depends on it." He turned back to Will and his friends. "All right—go."

"What about Audrey?" Will asked.

Detective Clayberry gave him a sharp look. "We'll take care of her. She and Margaret can't leave just yet." He paused and ran his hands through his gray hair. "We're lucky your dads got a quick-thinking nurse."

"Who's got a great pitching arm," added Darius. It was the lightest moment in the next four hours.

They headed back to the Chambers home after dropping TR off first. He was scheduled to work at the EV lab. "If there's anything I can do," he said, "call me. Professor Zubner and I are doing battery testing, but I can leave if you need me." As TR got out, he said, "Let me know when you get her back, okay?"

Will gave him a thumbs up.

Pulling into the Chambers' garage, they parked the jeep and entered the house through the side kitchen door. Two steps inside, they froze. They had left the house unlocked, and the box of explosives was gone.

"CRUD!" said Will, slamming his fist on the table.

A loud scratching and whining came from the other side of the kitchen door that led to the hallway. The Chambers rarely shut that door, but it was closed, the rubber wedge that usually kept it open was kicked to the side. Will turned the knob, and Comox bounded into the kitchen. *Sainos blocked him from entering the kitchen,* thought Will. Comox sniffed all around the table and barked. Will knelt down, calming the frantic canine. He looked at Darius. "Sainos would have known to expect Comox."

"Well," said Darius, "do we call Detective Clayberry now?"

Will ignored him, saying angrily, "We should have made copies of the papers in that box."

Darius became very focused. "We didn't know we'd lose it. Will, we gotta list everything we remember right now!"

Will grabbed some paper and they pulled up chairs. As Will wrote his notes, he realized they'd barely explained the contents of the tattered email page to the detective. They'd left out the part about the envelope with the locker location containing the payment and the fake ID.

"Darius," said Will, "we can print out maps just like the ones in the box!"

"Exactly," said Darius, "let's do it." They scrambled to the study, fired up the computer, and typed *Melford, UT* into the browser search box to access an online map program. They printed out copies that were identical to what had been in the box.

They didn't have the aerial photo, but that didn't matter; they were relieved to have the maps. "Hmm," said

Will, "Sainos is supposed to start blowing up turbines at one-twenty a.m., and the kidnapper'll let us know where Bette is at two a.m. How fast can Sainos get from the wind farm to Melford?"

"What are you thinking? said Darius.

Will's eyes flashed, but he spoke calmly. "What if we head down to Melford? We stay in touch with Detective Clayberry, so we know what's going on with Bette—son of a bear!" Will lowered his face and rubbed his forehead. "He's going to be furious about the missing box."

"Then what?"

Will looked up.

Darius said, "We're in Melford—then what?"

"If they haven't found Bette, then we're really, really careful. We only watch Dennum's to see who comes there with the envelope. If we hear Bette's safe, we take it. Sainos can't leave the country without money and ID. Once she's safe, Detective Clayberry'll call in everybody—FBI, CIA, you name it. In fact, he might be doing that already."

"Go on," said Darius, listening. Will rubbed his fist where it had slammed against the table.

"So—if Bette's not safe, we just watch for the delivery person. Maybe we can identify the drop-off guy and get his license plate. Maybe Sainos'll show up while we're waiting. If it goes past two a.m. and Bette's safe, maybe we could tail him." Will stood up. "I think we should go."

"You mean leave now?"

"I do."

Darius looked at the papers on the table. "Bring these with us?"

"Yup, and this time we make copies for Detective Clayberry—like we should have before. I'll get an envelope. We'll drop them at your house; he can pick 'em up there instead of here. No use freaking Comox out twice in one day."

Please let Bette be all right, thought Will. He knew Audrey was out of her mind with fear, and he himself was angry about the kidnapping.

They made the copies and did their best to write down the exact contents of the email. They put the papers in an envelope and headed over to Darius's house.

Mrs. Cheng was relaxing in a large, comfy chair with her feet propped up, enjoying an audiobook on a peaceful Tuesday afternoon. When they told her that Darius might stay another night at the Chambers' home to study for exams, she looked surprised. "You're not going to use your break to relax? You want to study more?"

They both mumbled, "Yeah, chemistry's fun—we want good grades." Her face broke into a smile.

"I'm so proud!" she said. "If more students were like you, the world would have limitless—"

"Mom," interrupted Darius, "can we borrow the good binoculars?" Her face changed completely.

"What do you need binoculars for?" she asked, narrowing her eyes.

"We need 'em, just—we need 'em for . . ." Darius was searching.

"For an art project Audrey Carter's doing," said Will. "She needs to look at elk."

"Yeah," said Darius, "elk—in the wild."

Mrs. Cheng put down the footrest on her chair. "I'll get them for you. They're in my closet." She hurried out of the room.

"Lame," said Darius. Will shrugged. Mrs. Cheng returned in seconds with a large, black box containing the binoculars.

"Please tell Audrey to be careful with them," she said. "They belonged to your father."

"We will, Mom," said Darius. He leaned over and gave her a peck on the cheek. She brightened. "Mom, this envelope's important. It's some science stuff. Margaret Clayberry's dad'll be coming by to pick it up, okay?"

"All right," she said, taking the envelope.

"Time to go," said Darius, heading for the front door.

"Bye, Mrs. Cheng," said Will as they left.

Instead of taking Darius's jeep, they had decided to take Mrs. Chambers' car. Darius's jeep was very familiar to Sainos, but Mrs. Chambers' car was one he wouldn't recognize.

Halfway to Melford, they tried Detective Clayberry's cell phone and were surprised when he didn't pick up. Almost immediately, Margaret called back from Audrey's number. Darius put her on speaker.

"My dad's not using his cell; he thinks Vahriman could be tapping it." Will and Darius looked at each other. If that was the case, they were very glad they'd put off calling until now, though they weren't going to mention their trip to Melford anyway.

"Any news on Bette?" said Darius.

"Yes! They found the truck, abandoned. It was left at one of the malls only four miles from the zoo. The police are being really careful. They have undercover people going in. Some are FBI—they're going in as shoppers looking for Bette and showing people her photo very quietly to avoid a panic on the kidnapper's part." Her voice became lighter. "Here's the good news—a security person at the mall entrance is sure he saw her walk in with a man in a baseball cap and sunglasses around eleven a.m. There's nothing on the security cameras after that time showing two people leaving who look like them. The man may have left, but not with her. She's probably there."

"Great," said Will.

"That's good, Margaret—really good," agreed Darius. He was looking at the clock on the dash. It was two-thirty p.m.

"I'll call you as soon as she's found," said Margaret.

"How's Audrey?" asked Will.

"A little better now that we know where Bette is, but still pretty scared."

"Tell her," Will stammered—*what do you say a person who's going through this?*—"tell her—the FBI's great. They'll find Bette."

"I will. And, hey, I'm coming by your house to get something of Bette's—they may want to use police dogs to find her. See you there."

Will caught his breath, but Darius smoothed it over.

"Margaret, we had to go to my Mom's—so we won't be at the Chambers' for a while. We'll check in with you later, okay?"

"Sure," she answered.

"The door's open," said Will. "Let us know as soon as—"

"Of course," said Margaret. "Bye."

They drove on. "So is Sainos waiting in Melford now?" muttered Darius, looking down at the map of the town they'd printed out.

"I'm thinking," said Will, "if he has to be ready by one a.m., he's probably at the wind farm—or SPAW, whatever that meant."

"I'm lookin' that up," said Darius. "That term's been bugging me ever since I first saw it." He entered the words into a search bar on his phone. He read out, "SPAW—Solar Power Array & Wind farm: a combination site that has both wind turbines and concentrated solar power (CSP) thermal towers. These sites use the same infrastructure to export their energy given that both kinds of systems generate electricity."

"See what it says about the site at Melford," said Will.

Darius typed in *SPAW* with the name *Melford* and got a link to a news article from the Utah publication *Power On*.

"It's a recent article," said Darius, scanning it quickly. "Whoa—listen to this! 'The newest Solar Power Array Wind farm (SPAW) site is located near the forward-thinking town of Melford, UT. Melford high school students researched and built several small wind turbine systems, which led to a commercial wind farm that's been operating since 2009, starting with ninety-seven turbines and adding a further sixty-eight turbines in 2011.'

"Now listen to this," he whistled, "'The town has recently received a substantial anonymous donation that will allow the wind farm to upgrade to a SPAW site. The addition of CSP solar thermal towers will greatly increase the amount of electricity generated and will also make the Melford SPAW site an international leader for this combined technology.'"

"When was that article written?" asked Will.

"Uh—January something," Darius scrolled back up, looking for the date. "January third, this year!"

"Great!" said Will, and he couldn't help it. His face cracked into a smile. "Anonymous donation—it's gotta be him, don't ya think?"

"Probably," said Darius.

Will smacked the edge of the seat. "So we may be able to stop Sainos, and the captain doesn't even know it."

Darius grinned back, "We'll probably get a medal."

They pulled into the town of Melford at four p.m. Avoiding Main Street, they took the parallel road of 300 West.

They passed the high school and headed north. "If there are 165 turbines, how many of them would he rig to blow?" muttered Will.

"Just enough to make it look as if the generators are at fault."

"I agree. He's got to be out there now, Darius . . . and *we*—we gotta get gas." At the edge of Melford, they turned back to the highway and into a small service station with two pumps. As they pulled up to one of them, another vehicle, a green hatchback, was pulling out—going in the opposite direction. The driver wore a slouchy hat and stared at Will longer than usual. Will looked away, hoping the man was simply a local who was curious. It definitely wasn't Sainos. The car headed back toward Melford.

Will climbed out and gazed at the blue sky and the gray-green mountains in the distance. He twisted the cap off the gas tank, and as he pulled out his wallet, a ring tone sounded.

Seconds later, Darius yelled through Will's open door, "She's safe! They got her—she's fine! Detective Clayberry and Audrey are with her now." Darius went back to the call.

Will shoved his wallet into his pocket. A plan he'd formulated might just work. He twisted the gas cap back on and jumped in the car.

Darius was still listening and finally said, "Margaret, hold on a sec." He turned to Will. "Do we tell 'em?"

"Yeah," nodded Will.

"Margaret, we're in Melford, Utah, down near a wind farm. We have a good reason—but you need to tell your dad that, okay? He's probably gonna want to talk to us."

Darius set the phone on the dash, switching it to speaker. Margaret's voice came through clearly "—busy with FBI and police, but why does he need to know you're in Melford?"

"It's . . . it's—just tell him, Margaret, okay?" said Darius. Will gave Darius a thumbs up. He was sure if Sainos was scaling turbines, he wasn't involved with Bette's kidnapping anymore. The man would be racing along with only one thought: a locker full of money and the fake ID that led to freedom.

"It'll take a minute—" she replied.

"Thanks, Margaret," Will interrupted. "Also, call TR at the EV lab to let him know Bette's okay. We've gotta go, but remember to tell your Dad *right away* that we're at the wind farm outside of Melford; there are maps of it at Darius's home. Mrs. Cheng has them in an envelope; your Dad needs to get it. Then he should call us—K? Bye." He swiped a finger across his neck signaling Darius to hang up the phone. Will started up the engine.

"We really going over there?"

"Yep," said Will, pulling onto the road. "Darius, I know we're not supposed to hate anyone, but I hate this guy—he nearly killed me, nearly killed my dog, and nearly killed Stoney Korbelak. He terrorized Margaret, and now he's screwing up the wind farm—not to mention everything *else* he's done. He's evil! If we're not gonna stop him, what the heck else should we be doing!?"

"Are we gonna call the police?"

Will looked away and took a breath. "I figure he might escape if he sees any cop cars; maybe he'd even blow himself up. It'd be better if he was alive—then he'd lead us to Vahriman. Geez, Darius, don't you wanna know what this is all about? The cave? Who the captain is—is he alive? If Sainos escapes, we'll never know! Man, I'd hate that!"

Darius was quiet. "All right . . . Detective Clayberry might send the police."

"I think he'll call us first to find out what's going on."

"And?"

"And we tell him we're gonna try to ID Sainos's car. And we are. But then we're gonna light a stick of dynamite under the hood."

"We're going to *what*!?" said Darius.

Will explained how he'd brought along the single remaining stick of dynamite, which had been set aside on the countertop in the kitchen when they'd first gone through the box.

"Does it have its blasting cap and its fuse?" asked Darius.

"Yep, and when Sainos hears the explosion, he'll know something's up, but with no cops there, I bet he'll try for an escape."

"Then?"

"We'll be outta there, but we'll leave this car close enough to Sainos's disabled one that he'll take it and head for Melford or somewhere else—but he's not gonna get very far."

"Why?"

"Because the float's off by a quarter tank, remember?" said Will. "This car hardly has any gas in it. By then we'll have called the police, and he'll be trapped. But he won't be near any dynamite."

They saw the first view of the wind farm as they drove north. There was still no call from Detective Clayberry. He must have been busy with Bette Carter's rescue and hadn't gotten the message to call them yet.

They pulled off the highway and onto a county road, getting closer to the massive turbines swooshing through the air. The energy facility was bigger than it looked from the highway, as were the massive turbines themselves. "I think," said Will, "we're looking for a vehicle that's kinda worn. I bet Stoney got something for Sainos without the problem of having to deal with tax, title, and license."

"Yep, you're probably right," said Darius. They pulled the car to the side of the road and got out the binoculars.

Darius scanned for a car. "There," he said, pointing as he handed the binoculars to Will. In the third row of turbines was an old, brown, beat-up sedan. In the same row, a little farther along, a massive tower crane stood next to a turbine. The long neck of the crane went straight up.

At the very top was a horizontal "box," which was fixed about thirty feet away from the turbine's nacelle.

Seeing no movement anywhere, they drove down into the wind farm. They knew they were probably being watched, but the plan could still work. Sainos might be inside a nacelle right now.

Twenty yards from the old sedan, they stopped their car and jumped out. Approaching the brown car, they saw the passenger front door was open and that the missing brown box that had held the dynamite was on the front seat. It was empty.

"Let's blow the car and clear off," said Will. He wedged the stick of dynamite into a slot in the grill, then he hesitated—*should he grab the box?* Sainos's fingerprints were probably all over it.

"D'you have any matches?" Darius asked.

"Back in the glove box," said Will.

"I'll get 'em." Darius sprinted back to the car. Will waited for a moment and then made his move. As he leaned in to get the box, a man burst from behind the car and grabbed him with powerful arms. One clamped around his neck, cutting off his breathing, and the other went around his chest, pinning his arms.

The attacker smashed his head into the side of the car, and Will felt his head explode with pain. Then his feet were clipped from behind, causing him to stumble. "Should've given up!" hissed a voice in his ear, and Will felt himself being dragged away from the sedan.

Darius hollered, "Let him go," but the man ignored him.

Will yelled, "Light it!" Then he was being strangled and couldn't make another sound. Seconds later an explosion split the air.

The man paused, but only for a moment. Will caught his breath as he was dragged along. "Are you Sainos?" he gasped.

"Since we're gonna die together, yeah, I am."

Will's vision was spinning, but he still managed to choke out, "You can escape, take our car—no cops here."

"Don't screw with me, kid. It's over." The man made a harsh noise. "I hate people who interfere. I hate you! You robbed me of justice," he spat in Will's face, "every single time!"

Will smelled the stench of the man's sweat. At that moment he realized Sainos had no hope; the man was beyond a rational effort to escape.

Darius had run to the Chambers' car, probably thinking to offer it to Sainos. Will heard the engine start up, then it faltered and died. It had run out of gas.

Sainos erupted with horrible laughter. "Guess we both have car trouble," he said, moving steadily toward the tower crane, dragging Will along with him. His strength was super human. Everything he lacked in compassion he'd turned into muscle.

Will's eyes were hazy with blood. Sainos half jerked, half pulled him into the crane elevator and shoved the door shut. Will slumped to the floor. Sainos jabbed at a button, and the elevator began to rise, picking up speed as it went. It was noisy. Suddenly Will heard something else—another sound coming from higher up.

Sainos barked, "What's that?" When Will didn't answer, Sainos reached down and grabbed him by his hair, pulling him to his feet. Will wiped the blood from his eyes. His head was beginning to clear.

"Don't know," he answered truthfully.

They reached the top of the crane, and Sainos shoved the door open. He pulled Will outside onto the small steel platform at the top. Will realized that Sainos was going to throw him off the platform.

"First you need to understand why I'm doing this," Sainos screamed at him. "A woman was killed—my woman. She loved me, and she was tricked and made to believe things about me that weren't true."

Will was distracted. *What was that noise?* It was getting louder. Will looked beyond Sainos's distorted face and saw a helicopter descending. There were two people in the helicopter, and a rope ladder was hanging down. *Oh, no,* thought Will—*is it Vahriman?!* The chopper hovered over the crane platform, the rope swinging in close. Would Sainos grab the rope ladder—or would he first throw Will off the platform?

The answer came. Sainos seized him by the neck, pushing him halfway over the railing. A miraculous gust of wind caused the crane to sway in Will's favor. He used his own weight to crash into Sainos and push him back. Dropping down to the steel surface, he dove for the elevator—a good move, as just then one of the men dropped from the rope ladder onto the platform. The man looked Sainos directly in the face and then dove in after Will.

Sainos's face registered shock. He regained his balance and then looked at the person flying the helicopter. His face became twisted with hatred. Will could hardly believe what happened next. Sainos climbed over the railing. He reached for the rope ladder. He stretched out—lunging at it. The next instant, everything changed. Sainos missed the rope and fell; his death-scream growing fainter beneath the sound of the engine.

The man with Will didn't hesitate. He looked to be in his midthirties. He hunched down, peering into Will's eyes and checking for wounds.

"You injured anywhere besides that cut above your eye?" asked the man. Will shook his head.

You sure?"

"Yeah, I'm okay."

The stranger looked Will over a little longer, then agreed, "You'll be all right—take this. Don't lose it." He shoved a simple, white envelope into Will's right hand.

"Take the elevator down now—okay?" Will nodded. The man repeated the order. "Take it down—now."

The helicopter had swung back again. It turned carefully so that the rope ladder dangled just above the deck. The man stood, caught the ladder, and pulled himself up the rungs. As he climbed in, the helicopter turned and glided away, its deafening noise diminishing as it moved quickly into the hazy sky.

Will closed the elevator door and pushed the button to go down. The elevator began its descent. He reached the bottom, pulled open the door, and was grateful to see Darius standing there. Sirens sounded in the distance.

"I called 911 and Clayberry too!" said Darius. "Wow, you're bleeding, Will. Let's get that cleaned up." Will swayed and reached for the steel door. As he did, the white envelope slipped to the ground.

"Grab that envelope, Darius!" said Will. "I'm not sure what happened up there, but *don't* lose that!"

Darius scooped it up and stuffed it into his pocket.

After taking several deep breaths, Will's heart rate returned to normal and he was able to stand without support. The two walked away from the crane in the direction of the police cars that were racing toward them. Within moments, both of them were bundled into a flashing vehicle and were answering a million questions.

CHAPTER
15

WILL'S WOUND WAS SUPERFICIAL. He wouldn't need stitches, and the bleeding had stopped. He and Darius watched in amazement as the area filled with wind farm personnel and FBI Special Forces who had begun to check the turbines for sabotage and explosives.

Detective Clayberry had called in the FBI and the police the minute he'd gotten the manila envelope from Mrs. Cheng. He'd also explained that Will and Darius were there to prevent the wind farm's attack. Will gave a sworn statement that Sainos had fallen to his death; the criminal had not been pushed and also that Vahriman was not in the helicopter. Darius, who'd seen everything through his father's binoculars, confirmed that. The real mystery was where the helicopter had gone.

The investigators knew from Detective Clayberry that Sainos's ID drop-off had been scheduled for Dennum's

Market sometime after midnight. It was likely that Varhiman knew the sabotage ploy had failed, so it was likely the drop wouldn't happen. Still, there could be a lead if a local person from Melford had been hired to do it.

When the officers and the FBI had everything they needed from Will and Darius, the two young men were released. "Sir," said Will to an officer, "we're out of gas," and he pointed to the Chambers' vehicle. Just then two men walked by carrying a heavy stretcher, a bloody cloth covering the body it bore.

Will and Darius were given enough gas to get them back to Melford. Only when the Chambers' car was filled up and they were heading north on the highway did Will think to ask Darius about the envelope.

"Oh, yeah," said Darius, pulling out the envelope and ripping it open. "Hmm—you're gonna be glad we didn't look at this 'til now; otherwise, it would have been confiscated."

"What's in it?"

"An email address for a Captain Glow. It says to use it tomorrow at noon for a *Google Hangout* with you, Audrey, and me, plus Detective Clayberry."

"Wow," said Will. "Anything else?"

"Nope."

They got back to Aberdeen and Darius's house around ten p.m. "I'll tell my mom we studied enough for one day," he said, gathering up the binoculars and getting out of the car. "See you tomorrow at noon."

At the Chambers house, Will found Audrey, Bette, and Margaret waiting at the kitchen table, Comox curled up at their feet. Will gave a short explanation of what had happened, avoiding the gruesome details. He felt Bette, who leaned sideways into her older sister, had been through enough. Suddenly he couldn't do anything but yawn.

"Time for me to go," said Margaret, "we're *so* happy you're all right." She gave Audrey and Bette a hug and left by the kitchen door.

Audrey smiled at her younger sister. "Hey, Bette, it's time for bed, okay?" The little girl didn't want to go to sleep unless Audrey came with her.

"Yep, time for snooze-land," said Will, standing up. "See? Comox thinks so, too." The dog had stood up, ready to head upstairs. Audrey tucked her sister in, waited for her to fall asleep, and then slipped out to the hallway. Will had washed up, gingerly removing the traces of dried blood around the bandage above his eye. He'd also put on a clean T-shirt. They met as Audrey came out of her room, walking to the top of the stairs and sitting down there. Though bone-tired, Will told Audrey everything that had happened with Sainos.

"Oh, Will, he's dead, then, and this whole horrible thing is over. He was horrible."

"You've had a rough day, too," said Will, thinking of her and Bette. "Anyway . . . it's done now." His voice trailed off.

"You look exhausted, Will; you'd better go to sleep." She stood up and tugged at his T-shirt. "I'm so glad you weren't . . ." She couldn't finish the thought.

Will stood up, told her goodnight, went to his room and quickly fell fast asleep.

The next day Will told Detective Clayberry about the letter. He showed up at the Chambers' home at eleven forty-five a.m. Margaret had come too, and her father was firm that she be able to sit in on the phone meeting. Darius was already there. Bette was in the living room playing the "Life on Earth Matching Game" with Denzel and TR, who'd kindly agreed to stay with the two second-graders.

At eleven fifty-nine a.m., Will and the others sat in front of a computer in the study. Will opened a Google Hangout and typed in the email address on the paper. It was exactly noon.

The call was answered immediately. "Good, glad you guys could make it," said the speaker, "and good to see you, Will."

"Are you the man who was at the top of the crane?" Will asked. He clearly remembered the man's face, but now the face at the other end of the call was carefully shadowed, its features hardly visible.

"Yep—well, we were afraid we almost lost you. You look a lot better today," said the man. "Sorry you can't see me clearly—but that's how it has to be. I'm glad the rest of you are here too." The man looked down and began to read from a paper. "I'm here on behalf of the man who called himself 'Captain Glow.' That man is my father, and—and just to clear this up, Captain Glow isn't an actual person." He looked up. "In the seventies, my father and his friends used that name as a catchphrase for systems that generate electricity directly from the wind, sun or any other source in place of burning fossil fuels. Captain Glow replaces old King Coal.

"Anyway, my father and I want to thank you for your help." He looked back down at his paper. "Last June you were pulled into this fight because my father spotted Sainos in the parking lot at the Aberdeen Zoo. He knew it wasn't a coincidence. My father quickly planted a listening device in Sainos's truck—just before the first attack. That's how he knew it was going to happen. I was out of the country and couldn't help.

"Later in August, after the assault at the café and salon, the listening device had either broken or Sainos found it and threw it out. At that point, my father vowed not to contact you any further. He wanted you and your friends out of danger." The man cleared his throat. "So it seems providence smiled yesterday when my dad spotted you in Melford. You were at the service station there. He realized there was only one thing that would have brought you there. Fortunately, we had our helicopter in the area, surveying the SPAW work. Will, you're part of Captain Glow now—you're one of us. You saved that wind farm, and we're deeply grateful."

The man looked away, then said in a voice choking with emotion, "We're also grateful that you're alive."

He returned his gaze to the paper and resumed reading. "With everything you've done, you and the others deserve an explanation. Now I'm going to back up much further than June—Detective Clayberry, you already know some of this.

"My father's need for secrecy originated more than forty years ago when he was talked into accidentally being part of an armored car robbery. It was Sainos's idea. His father owned the Blooming Armored Car Transport Company, and he persuaded my naïve father that Sainos Sr. was willing to temporarily lend funds to help support the commune's ambitions. Earlier, my father had given a sizeable inheritance donated by his grandparents to the Green Valley Project—*GVP* for short. The GVP had spun off from a college group known as *Students for Ecosystem Justice*—SE-Js, or See-jays, for short. The GVP shared work, had assigned duties, and also had a goal to develop new energy systems—really hard work, because the technology was in its first phase.

"Going back to Sainos's plan, the warped idea about robbing the armored car must have occurred to Sainos after a visit he'd made to his father's estate. My father thinks

Sainos learned about the rerouting of a truck carrying a million-dollar payroll. The new route would take it across Utah on a deserted stretch of highway.

"My father agreed to what he thought was a drop-off of funds that represented an abnormal 'under the table' loan to Sainos from his father. Sainos told my father the GVP would be allowed to put the money in an offshore bank, earning considerable interest, and within months return the original sum to Sainos Sr. My father still recalls the contempt Sainos had for his father, and he says that should have been a clue that the plan was a lie.

"Sainos kept up the deception that the money was a loan and that they would return it. Only Sainos and my father knew about it; they told their GVP co-workers they were attending a meeting that could lead to funding. And that's how on one cold, spring night in eastern Utah, just past midnight, my father and Sainos waited by the side of the road. Minutes earlier, they'd put flares out on the blacktop. Sainos said the agreement was for the guards to halt at the flares, where they had instructions to deliver the loan.

"The guards did stop. But then my father realized nothing was going according to the plan that Sainos had described. Sainos went to the back of the truck and using an explosive, he blew the back doors open. Then Sainos pulled a gun and told my father he'd kill him if he didn't cooperate.

"Terrified by the explosion, the guards climbed out. Sainos threatened my father again and then lined up the two guards. Sainos doused one of them with pepper spray. Then he knocked the other guard unconscious with the butt of the gun. My father's protests made no difference. Sainos tied up both men, the second of whom was still out cold. Sainos forced my father at gunpoint to load the money into the car.

"The guard who'd been knocked out, came to and had been able to partially loosen his bonds and get to his gun. To my father's horror, Sainos turned and shot the man. The bullet knocked the man's gun out of his hand and pierced his leg. As the injured man screamed, Sainos dragged my father back to the car at gunpoint.

"In a later news report, my father was deeply grateful to hear that the guard who had been shot would make a recovery. He had been terrified that the man would bleed to death. Luckily, the other guard used snow to clear the pepper spray from his eyes, loosened his bonds, made it to the truck, and activated an alarm, which brought help.

"As my father looks back on the plan for that bizarre night, he's now certain it grew out of Sainos's obsession to gain money so he could abduct a certain woman. That woman is my mother—and, Detective Clayberry, you'll recognize her."

The man held up a black-and-white picture of a very pretty young woman. The detective nodded, clearly holding his emotions in check. The man on the screen continued, "My parents had already been married in a private ceremony before the robbery took place. Being my father's good friend, Detective Clayberry, you and your girlfriend were asked to be their witnesses."

Margaret looked at her father with surprise.

"No, Margaret, it wasn't your mother," said the detective, "I met your mom when this was all over."

The mysterious man on the screen asked, "May I continue?"

"Yes," answered Detective Clayberry hoarsely.

"Sainos told my father he would swear that my father had been in on the armored car robbery all along. In the confusion of the robbery and the shooting and the return to GVP, Sainos learned of my parents' marriage and went crazy. First, he threatened to kill my father or have him put in jail, even if it meant Sainos would go too. Detective Clayberry, I understand that you and the others held Sainos off while my parents packed their car and left. They aren't sure what happened at GVP after that."

Detective Clayberry nodded and explained, "Sainos *did* go crazy—he was very dangerous. He broke free of us and went after your parents. He was going more than a hundred miles an hour on the freeway—he even had the highway patrol after him. The Ukiah police joined in, and as I recall he actually fired on one of them."

The teens were astounded. Detective Clayberry had known a lot more than he'd let on. "Another police car had been notified to block the road ahead with their vehicle, and Sainos crashed into it. The officers weren't in the car, thank God," said Detective Clayberry. "That's what happened."

They could tell the captain's son was taking all this in. He looked down, finding his place on the paper. "Much later, my father learned that Sainos had sworn that the scheme for the robbery had been my father's idea. Sainos said *he'd* been forced into it—that my father had devised this plan because he, Edward Sainos, was the son of the owner of the armored car company. A newspaper article said Sainos swore on the stand that he'd been held at gunpoint and forced to assist at the robbery—exactly the opposite of what really happened."

"That's right—that's how it went at the trial," said Detective Clayberry, teeth clenched. "Expensive lawyers helped Sainos create a defense saying he was in fear for his life. And the guards—disoriented from the pepper spray and the concussion—couldn't give solid evidence to the contrary. When some of us GVP members were questioned, we couldn't disprove Sainos's story, though we told them Sainos was the dangerous one and that your father was a good man. I think the jury regarded us as suspicious."

He gave a wry laugh. "They didn't know what to make of us—we weren't communists, but we lived in a community that was strange by their standards, and we were young and had long hair. I think we looked—well, eccentric. But when we saw how evil Sainos was, we always felt right about what we did to help Marylou—and your father."

The detective looked around. "This goes no further than our viewer and this room. We faked Marylou Hansen's death, saying she had drowned in a water accident. We swore to it that she—" he paused and rubbed his brow, "that she was killed on Lake Mendocino. One of us, Rob Taytree, owned a sailboat there—we said the plan had been for Marylou to hide out from Sainos on the boat while her husband left to get a different car. Rob and I went to the police, unaware that Sainos had been arrested. We said we needed help—that Marylou Hansen had been on the sailboat and that as we put out from shore, the boom had swung around, knocking her off the helm. We swore we'd been searching for her and couldn't find her—that we were afraid she'd been knocked unconscious and had drowned. The Ukiah Police mounted a search to find her."

"Did they suspect anything?" asked Will.

Detective Clayberry shook his head. "Not much. Sainos had caused a lot of trouble. Not having a body turn up was strange, but with the robbery and the car chase, Sainos was a bigger focus than she was. They accepted our story, and Marylou's death was reported in the papers and on the TV news. We were glad to have Sainos believe she was gone—otherwise, I don't think she would have ever been free of him." His eyes were sad. "It was very hard on her parents."

"What happened to Sainos?" said Will.

The detective continued, "The jury didn't buy his claim of innocence in the robbery. His huge ego and the missing consistency in his testimony showed he was a person who couldn't be trusted. They gave him three years in a federal penitentiary. He also got time in the state prison for shooting at a highway patrolman." Detective Clayberry turned back to the screen. "All yours."

They could see the man was reading from the bottom of his paper. "My parents fled to Mexico and were able to obtain new identities. My mother was expecting me, and my father vowed to stay with her. She'd given up everything to be with him, and they were committed to each other.

"He did make one short trip, though. Two months before I was born and *before* Sainos's trial, my father returned to a cave north of Vernal, Utah, to retrieve the Blooming Armored Car Company money. It had been buried there after the robbery in a shallow recess. He put it into a bank account that, ironically, he had opened at Sainos's urging. It had been opened with my father's inheritance.

"Using a lawyer and a money order, he anonymously returned every cent to the Blooming Armored Car Company. Then he closed that account and put the remainder into a different account under my mother's unmarried name. He also opened an account in Mexico. So some of their funds were in the U.S. and some were in Mexico.

The original bank account being undetected was very lucky. Sainos must have kept that information back, guessing knowledge of it would prove his guilt. More importantly, my mother was finally free of him.

"My parents worked hard to make new lives. It cost them; the worst part was that for years they had no contact with their parents and siblings. When they finally let their parents know they were alive and what their new names were, they asked their families to not reveal anything, concerned it could lead to a prison sentence for my father. Their families gave their word. My mother was able to accept an inheritance using the U.S. account.

"Later my father found work and was able to invest in the newly emerging computer industry. He's actually a smart guy; though he'd point out the exception of the armored-car robbery—but luckily, he had good instincts for which new companies would do well. My father also sent money to the guard who'd been wounded in the robbery, and he feels he's paying his debt to society by funding the new energy systems. However," the young man paused, "his lawyer strongly advises him not to risk the notion that authorities would feel the same way—they might, but they might not, so he prefers to remain unknown."

The man had reached the end of his paper. "Now," he concluded, his face still in shadow, "you understand what happened. Thank you for your help. We're so thankful you weren't harmed. Please don't try to find us—but know that we're not far away. My father's grandparents were home-steaders in the Aberdeen area. We love the farmland and the red-rock deserts. So to end things, no questions, okay? This email account will be closed. Goodbye and good luck." With that, the connection ended.

Detective Clayberry turned to face the others. "Remember, what you know about Marylou Hansen must be kept secret—just as if it was a witness protection program, understand?"

They nodded.

"Do you have any other questions?"

"Yeah, what about Vahriman?" said Will. "Where does he fit in?"

Detective Clayberry's face darkened. "That's a great question, Will. That and where he is now. As soon as you and Darius told me his name was on that email, I checked very thoroughly into his credentials. If all was correct, his highest-ranking officer, General Franklin J. Grazeck, should have been able to confirm his identity. But the organization did a complete search, and there's no record of any Richard Vahriman serving now, or at any time, in any branch of the armed forces."

"So," Audrey said, "does that mean he was—"

"Correct. He was an impostor. Remember that chain and the gold cross that Margaret pulled from his neck? That's a Russian Orthodox cross. That's all we have to go on for now."

"When did Sainos become involved with Vahriman?" said Will.

"It had to be after October. I'm not sure when Vahriman actually contacted Sainos. By January, Vahriman and I weren't communicating because things had cooled off and the sabotage had stopped. Nothing had happened from January until when you contacted me yesterday." The detective paused to let them gather their thoughts.

Will spoke first. "This Vahriman . . . who's he working for?"

"Another great question," answered Detective Clayberry. "Someone who'd prefer SPAWs and wind farms to be viewed as unsafe, I guess."

"Oh, that's ugly," said Darius.

"Completely," agreed Margaret.

Her father nodded. "He's still out there, but we'll find him."

"I'm so glad Bette's okay," said Audrey exhaling deeply. Turning to Will and Darius, she said, "Has anyone told you guys how they were able to find her so quickly?"

"No," said Will.

"As soon as she entered the mall, she told knock-knock jokes to Vahriman and anyone who'd listen," Audrey explained.

"Once our team was on to it," Detective Clayberry said, smiling, "we could track them. Vahriman had no idea she was leaving a trail for us."

"Where did she end up?" asked Will.

"She was tied up in the back of a gift shop," said Detective Clayberry, "the kind that has small water fountains, ceramic art—things like that. The clerk remembered a little girl asking her a knock-knock joke. But she didn't remember the little girl leaving, and the trail ended there— so we searched the entire back of the store. There she was, hidden behind a stack of large storage boxes and tied up with a cloth taped over her mouth to keep her quiet."

Audrey shuddered. "Vahriman told her if she didn't make any noise, no one she loved would get hurt, and she'd be fine. Her friends would come to get her later if she just stayed quiet."

"What about Stoney Korbelak?" asked Darius.

"It'll be awhile," said Detective Clayberry, "but he's going to recover. Sainos jabbed him with a syringe that held a strong sedative and then—well, you know the rest."

"The syringe missing from the zoo!?" said Audrey.

"Yes, the same one, said Detective Clayberry. "Sainos might have been aware that Stoney was rescued, but thought he'd be out of the country before Stoney could give any information. It wasn't worth it for Sainos to go after Stoney again."

Suddenly Will sat up. "Has anyone talked to my parents or *your* parents?" he said, looking at Audrey.

"Can you believe it?" she said, "No—we're going to have to tell them."

"Right," said Detective Clayberry. "I'll help you with that."

They piled out of the study. Darius and Will agreed to share everything they'd learned with TR—everything, that is, except the information about Marylou Hansen's faked death. Given that Sainos was gone, there would most likely be no further contact with the captain or his family.

Comox came bounding out of the living room toward Will who knelt down and scratched behind the dog's ears. He suddenly realized there were only two months of school left. It was spring break. A week from today would be the school science fair, and he'd be presenting his e-bike project. It was time to do the improvements for his poster before spring break ended. Detective Clayberry left, promising Will and the others that he would let them know of any new developments.

Darius left with Margaret. He planned to tell his mother, Mrs. Cheng, what had really happened. "She'll flip out," he said. He was taking Margaret along for moral support.

Will and Audrey headed to the kitchen to make soup and salad for Denzel, Bette, TR, and themselves. After that, Will planned to lay out everything for his poster and to sharpen up his concluding paragraph so he could present the best possible work.

PART 7

THE CONCENTRATED SOLAR THERMAL SYSTEM

CHAPTER

16

THE UTAH REGIONAL SCIENCE Fair proved to be a mental marathon and a victory for Will. Beating out fierce competition, he was awarded first place in the category of Physical Energy-Sustainable Design, with his project topic of Sustainable Design for E-bike Microgrids. He could now participate at the International Science and Engineering Fair (ISEF) in May.

Luckily, winning a spot to represent the state of Utah at ISEF had worked well to distract and console his parents, who'd been horrified to learn of the confrontation in Melford. First they'd hugged him excessively. Then they'd chewed him out with equal energy when they learned he'd not only left Detective Clayberry out of the decision to go to Melford, but that Will had also gone with the intent of possibly trapping Sainos. Comox stood loyally by Will's side during the parental scolding.

It was the last week of April. The Chambers family, along with Darius and Bette, were heading off to southern Nevada for a weekend adventure. Audrey was unable to go because she was having her wisdom teeth removed. The appointment had been made quickly when her gums had swollen up as a result of the emerging teeth. The plan was for her to stay with Margaret, whose family would look after her following the two-hour dental surgery.

The Chambers' weekend adventure involved delivering a male wallaby to a zoo at a place called Bonnie River Ranch. For the previous two weeks, an enclosure crate had been placed in the wallaby habitat so the four wallabies would become familiar with it. Food and water were also placed inside. This allowed the male wallaby, Roscoe, the one scheduled for transport, to be at ease when he traveled in the enclosure to his new home.

At six a.m. on Saturday morning, the family drove to the zoo to meet Dr. Chambers. Roscoe was safely inside the tall metal crate, which had been placed in a large van used for small animal transport. The van was painted with beautiful, custom artwork showing the zoo's name and many of the zoo animals majestically grouped together. The vehicle was a clear invitation to come and visit the Aberdeen Zoo.

They left their family car in the parking lot. Dr. Chambers drove. Mrs. Chambers sat in the front passenger seat; Will, Darius, and Bette sat behind them. Roscoe rested calmly in his crate, which was secured to the van's inside walls with thick canvas straps.

The six-hour trip took them right past the unique and enticing city of Las Vegas.

At 1:30 p.m., they arrived at Bonnie River Ranch, an old Nevada western town that also had a motel, a restaurant, a zoo, horse-boarding facilities, cowboys and cowgirls. The site had been established in 1843 as a stop-off point for the wagon trains on their way to California.

Taking the turn-off from the main road that led to the ranch, which was now in view, they spotted three wild gray burros grazing close to the side of the road. They looked well-fed and content.

Dr. Chambers pulled up to the sign that read 'Lobby' and went in to get their room keys. Mrs. Chambers had booked a family-size suite with two bedrooms, one of which had four bunk-beds. The other room had a king-size bed. The men would take the room with the bunk-beds, and Mrs. Chambers and Bette would take the king-size bedroom.

They'd heard that the ranch hosted weddings and had a popular Friday night karaoke group, but since it was Saturday, that wouldn't happen tonight. There were also trail rides at the ranch, and on weekends there were performances of melodramas, mock comedy hangings, and the old west tradition of "rounding up a posse."

While Mrs. Chambers and the others took their bags to the room, Dr. Chambers drove the van to the service entrance and met up with his colleague, Dr. Hawkins, and his wife, Tabitha, who was the zoo nutritionist. The transfer of Roscoe went well. While the doctor was busy taking care of that, the others walked around the ranch to see the buildings and the entry to the town's Main Street.

Dr. Chambers met them back at the motel room. "Janet, we've been invited to come for supper at Tabitha and Jim's home in Blue Diamond."

"Do we have to go with you?" asked Will.

"You're invited," said his father, "but I'm guessing you'd rather stay here and see some more of the ranch."

"Yeah, Dad, we would," said Will.

"How close is the town of Blue Diamond?" asked Mrs. Chambers.

"Jim said it's about eight minutes from here."

"Oh, that should be okay," said Mrs. Chambers, turning to Will, Darius, and Bette. "Do you think you can handle being in the Wild West on your own?"

"Oh, yeah," said the three, chiming in together.

"You'll look after Bette and make sure she doesn't get scared?"

"I won't be," said Bette. "I like cowboys—and peacocks too, even if they do make that screechy noise." She was referring to the twenty or so peacocks that were up on rooftops and strutting around the ranch.

"Okay, then," said Dr. Chambers. "Here's the entrance money—go have fun and be sure to stop by the zoo. You might see Roscoe; he'd probably like that."

"Yes; now shoo," said Mrs. Chambers. "Your dad and I want a little time alone before we head over to Blue

Diamond. It's two forty-five now—say, Darius, didn't you take a photo of their show schedule?"

Darius pulled out his phone. "If we go now, we can see the melodrama at three, the hanging at three-thirty, and the sheriff form a posse at four-thirty."

"Sounds great," said Will. "Come on, Bette! Let's go see some cowboys."

"Yippee!" said Bette.

They headed to the wooden boardwalk where the ticket office was. On the boardwalk were three animatronic machines that would power up and do a short performance for a dollar. They passed the cowboy one and the outhouse one, and then Bette stopped squarely in front of one called "The Ol' Miner." A sign on his tall glass case said that he gave out words of wisdom.

"You wanna see what this guy has to say?" asked Will.

"Yes," said Bette. Will gave her a dollar, and she put it in the machine. The animatronic figure came to life.

His arms and head began to move, and he introduced himself as "Pappy." He continued, "As you go through life, sit up straight and don't tell lies. Don't underestimate the stupidity of other people, and don't do anything stupid yourself. Look around the place and then come back for more wisdom from Pappy, ya' hear?" With that, he was done.

"Sounds like my mother," said Darius.

They paid the entry fee and each got a wristband, which meant they could go into the Wild West town and see every event. They passed through the turnstile. Entering Main Street, which was the only street, they headed to the "saloon" to see the melodrama. It turned out to be pretty fun—complete with a villain, a sweet cowgirl, and a handsome sheriff.

Then it was time to leave the saloon for the mock "hanging." The sheriff led the villain outside to a wooden scaffold, where a ready-made noose hung from a crossbeam. The other cowboys, who were the sheriff's deputies, bantered with the audience as the visitors sat down on long, wooden benches in front of the scaffold. Some were people who'd been at the melodrama, and some had just arrived.

"We need to do this fair and proper," called the sheriff. "I've arrested this man and now we need to have a trial! Which one of you people will volunteer to be the judge?" The audience laughed, and then one jovial fellow raised his hand and said he'd be the judge. He went up to a bench positioned in front of the scaffold. He was given a wooden gavel and was instructed to bang it on a waist-high railing post that was part of the steps leading up to the scaffold platform.

"Now we need two lawyers," said one of the deputies, "one for the prosecution and one for the defense!"

Bette said, "Will! You go! Go on, you do it!" But the cowboy deputy had already picked two others from the far side of the benches. One was a young woman in a red dress who looked delighted to be chosen.

"Okay, we got our prosecuting attorney," said the sheriff pointing to her, "and we got our attorney for the defense," indicating a tall, chuckling man who'd been pushed forward by his friends. The two were sworn in, and the audience applauded.

The mock trial was staged for laughs, with the sheriff telling the judge to sustain and approve everything the prosecuting attorney said and to immediately overrule anything the defense attorney said. The defense attorney couldn't even get out one full sentence and his head-shaking frustration made everyone laugh. The villain acted unremorseful and mean-spirited saying, 'I'm not sorry, and I'd do it all again!"

Playing along at the finish, the "judge" banged the gavel, declaring the horse-thief villain to be guilty and that the man was sentenced to be hanged. The wordplay between the villain, sheriff, and deputies made it clear they were all having a good time. They led the guilty man up the steps to the platform and put the noose around his neck. Another rope was attached to a harness on his back and he was swiftly hoisted up, being pulled up from the back rope and not by the noose. The audience still gasped.

The sheriff told the judge to call out "court is now dismissed, sentence carried out," and the judge did exactly that. The deputies let the "hanged" man down, and he was no worse off from the deputies' theatrical performance. The audience stood up and began to disperse.

Will, Darius, and Bette headed for the museum, which was housed in one of the larger buildings. Inside was a representation of a blacksmith's shop, a mining mill, and a stamp mill.[25] There was also an area with five authentic, four-wheeled buckboard wagons.

Darius read from a plaque on the wall, "The board in front gave protection for the driver in case something made the horse buck."

"Look," said Bette, pointing to a big black-and-white, old-time photo. It showed a horse pulling a similar wagon with a couple on the front seat in their wedding clothes. The sunbaked groom wore a stiff suit and tie, but still had his trusty cowboy boots on.

The three emerged from the museum into bright sunlight.

"Let's get some food," suggested Will, and they went to the General Store that was another Main Street attraction. There were salads, ice-cream treats, fruit, and sandwiches made to order—egg salad, turkey, or roast beef. Will and Darius got roast beef, and Bette got the egg-salad sandwich.

"Look at that," said Darius, laughing. He pointed to the restroom doors. The men's bathroom door was decorated with a big pair of red long-johns. The ladies' bathroom door was decorated with a red, lace-trimmed, outsized bra and pantaloons.

---

25. For Footnote Link go to Captain Glow Website

They headed outside to eat their sandwiches. Main Street was filling up for the four-thirty posse show. They found some benches close to the saloon where they had shade and would also have a good view of the show. Bette told Will and Darius she just wanted to stay with them and eat her sandwich instead of joining the crowd of children with the sheriff and his deputies.

The sheriff said they were going to form a posse but first they wanted to go over gun safety rules. They quizzed the children on what they should do if they ever came across a gun.

"What do you do if you find a gun?" asked the sheriff.

The children all knew the answer: "Go get an adult!"

"If there isn't an adult there, what do you *never* do?" asked one of the deputies.

They knew the answer to that one, too: "Never pick it up!" "Don't touch it!" "Leave the gun alone!" the children called out from the crowd.

"That's right!" the cowboys replied. A few more wise tips were given out by the deputies and sheriff, including, "If you hear gunshots, drop to the ground and stay low as you crawl toward safety." They also shared that "a gun loaded with blanks or one that is an air gun can cause serious damage or death if it's shot anywhere close to a person's body."

The gun safety part of the show finished up, and the sheriff deputized all the young children, making them pledge to "uphold the law." With that, they were part of the posse. The cowboys handed out plastic silver stars and pencils printed with *Deputy of Bonnie River Ranch*.

One of the sheriff's deputies then did a fine demonstration of rope handling and lassoing. He threw the rope in the air and caught another one of the deputies easily, cinching the rope tight around the man. They gave the crowd a warning and then shot off their guns with blanks to signal the end of the show.

Just then, Will saw Bette freeze. Her egg-salad sandwich dropped to the ground as she stared at a man off to the left. He'd taken off his sunglasses to mop his forehead.

"What's wrong, Bette?" said Will.

"It's him," she said, pointing at the man and backing away. "It's the man who took me away at the zoo." She was whispering and still moving backward.

Will took her hand and grabbed Darius's arm.

"Bette says that's Vahriman—the one in the brown T-shirt—the one who grabbed her at the zoo. Darius, take her in the saloon! Take her there quickly, before he sees her!"

Darius picked up Bette and carried her inside. Will bolted over to the cowboy holding the lariat and yelled "Help! That man has my wallet!" pointing to Vahriman. Vahriman reacted instantly, bolting for the exit as if he was guilty.

The cowboy got the rope around him, bringing him to his knees before he could escape. Will punched 911 into his phone as two other "deputies" helped the lassoing cowboy restrain Vahriman by sitting on him. Will asked 911 dispatch to have police sent to their location. Then he quickly explained to the "deputies" that the man they were holding was wanted for terrorist acts and that he could prove it. Will called Detective Clayberry, who thankfully answered right away. Will put him on speakerphone as the men continued to restrain Vahriman. Vahriman sputtered angrily and then became quiet and wary. Clayberry made sure the men who'd captured Vahriman knew it was extremely likely they were holding onto a dangerous criminal.

By then, Darius and Bette had come out of the saloon. Darius backed up Will's information. Bette, still scared, was able to identify him as the man who'd kidnapped her. She looked relieved that a muscular sheriff and three capable young men were restraining him.

Two ranch security personnel arrived. They took Vahriman off to an employee office inside the saloon and asked Will, Bette, and Darius to wait outside the office. The police arrived, read Vahriman his rights, and told him he was being detained on suspicion of kidnapping and committing terrorist acts.

Detective Clayberry had also alerted the Las Vegas bureau of the FBI, and within thirty-seven minutes of his call, three agents arrived. Two of them took Vahriman off the premises. They'd already confirmed he was wanted by the CIA—the Central Intelligence Agency.

The remaining FBI agent, named Collins, interviewed Will, Darius, Bette, the sheriff, and the lassoing cowboy. By the time they were finished, it was just after six p.m. "Is there anything else you need from us?" asked Will. "I hafta call my parents. They'll want to know what's happened."

"Go ahead," said Agent Collins. "We've got everything we need. Good job spotting him, young lady," he said to Bette. He went on, "The man you're calling Vahriman has a room at the motel here, and we're getting a warrant to search it. You're free to go."

Before they left, it was clear that the sheriff and his deputies were delighted to have actually caught a real criminal. They insisted on having their photos taken with Will and Bette. She was laughing now, recovered from her fright and pleased with the fuss the cowboys were making over her. She was given a deputy's badge and three pencils.

It was six-thirty p.m. when they said their goodbyes to the cowboys and headed out the exit turnstile. Will called his father, putting him on speakerphone.

"Hi, Dad," said Will, "how are you doing?"

"Great," said Dr. Chambers. "You guys done with the zoo and the Wild West town?"

"I think so," said Will. He wasn't sure how to start so he decided to wait until they were actually back with his parents.

"D'you want me to come and pick you up?"

"Yeah, that'd be good." Will heard a scratchy bird voice in the background.

"They have a parrot here who cusses," said Dr. Chambers, "I think you'll like him."

Will just rolled his eyes.

When they arrived in Blue Diamond and sat down on the Hawkins' back patio, Will, Darius, and Bette described the capture of Vahriman. So Jim and Tabitha Hawkins could have the full story, they filled in their previous encounters with Sainos and Vahriman.

"Whatever could he be doing here?" said Mrs. Chambers in amazement. "It doesn't have anything to do with us, does it?"

"Detective Clayberry told me he'd let us know when they've figured that out," said Will.

"This is an odd place for him to show up," said Dr. Chambers. Tabitha and Jim Hawkins agreed.

On the way home the next day, Will got a phone call from Detective Clayberry.

"When the FBI searched Vahriman's hotel room, they found photos of Ivanpah, the CST concentrated solar thermal site that's only fifty-eight miles from the ranch. There were incomplete diagrams of the site's technology as well as photos and blueprints of a prototype cement manufacturing plant in California. It looks like he wanted to gain engineering data on both of those CST sites."

"Oh, *that's* what he was interested in," said Will.

"That's right. From what they found on his computer, he may have been trying to hack into the software used to run the site. But you stopped him! Good job."

"Thanks," said Will.

"I'll let you know what else develops—if I can. Some of this may end up being classified. You can share what I've told you with your family and Darius."

"Sure," said Will, "good to know."

───

THE FIRST WEEK OF May, with only three and a half weeks of school remaining, Will, Darius, Audrey, and TR were invited to the Clayberry home, where they met Margaret. They understood that this was to learn more about who Sainos was and who Vahriman was and how he'd become involved with Sainos.

They sat in the Clayberry family room. Detective Clayberry began, "Do you remember, Margaret, how you pulled that small cross and chain dangling from the man's neck as he scooped up Bette?"

"Yes!" she said, her eyes lighting up.

"You're brave, daughter of mine," he said. "Remember to be careful, but I have to say—*that* was a valuable clue."

"Why?" she asked.

"It's a Russian Orthodox cross, which indicated to us that we should look for an eastern European operative. That's exactly who our 'Vahriman' is. He's a mercenary working out of Sevastopol to sabotage clean-energy projects."

"Sevastopol on the Crimean peninsula?" said Darius.

"Yes," said Detective Clayberry. "Vahriman contacted me last October when I began investigating Sainos. Now that I think of it, sometimes he did use odd word choices—but otherwise his English was perfect. Anyway, now I believe he was actually contacting former members of the Green Valley Project. That's what led him to me—and to Sainos."

"Why was he doing that?" asked Will.

"I promise I'll get to that. First, let me explain what happened in October. With the help of Vahriman, whose real name is Arseniy Rotenberg—we found out what Sainos did after getting out of jail. In fact, I found out a lot—starting with the fact that Sainos was not born into wealth. His mother was, uh, kind of a well-known person, pretty tough and often in trouble with the law. She was part-owner of a bar in Cainsville, a suburb on the west side of Philadelphia."

"You're explaining about Sainos's mother?" said Margaret.

"Yes, this first," her father said. He went on. "Old court records reveal that she had a 'flat tire situation' that she was accused of *causing* to happen that blocked the entry road leading up to the Sainos mansion. Her photos show her in a lot of make-up and revealing clothing. On the flat-tire evening, when Sainos Sr. arrived, she made a play for him, and he went for it. That moment resulted in a pregnancy. She came back later to see if he'd be interested in a more permanent arrangement, even though he was a married man. According to the police files, his response to her offer was very angry, ending in threats and a restraining order that prevented her from contacting him.

"She filed complaints and petitioned the court for child support—it's all in the records. She lost her case. She appeared to be a gold-digger, and DNA paternity testing didn't yet exist. But twelve years later, when the young Sainos was the spitting image of his father, she tried again. The connection was unmistakable. When Sainos Sr. met him, he knew the boy was his son. But he still chose not to have a relationship. A gardener who worked there remembers the confrontation."

"Dang," said Will. He had seen the twisted, angry face of the man that boy had become.

"Sainos Sr.'s wife, Mrs. Sainos, went to the courts stating that while she'd been a faithful spouse, her husband had not. The local newspapers reported the high-profile divorce, and Mrs. Sainos left for Europe permanently. Then everything changed. Sainos's mother and stepfather were drunk, resulting in a car accident that killed them both. Sainos Sr. took custody of his thirteen-year-old son, and the boy's life was transformed."

"Were there any other children?" asked Darius.

"Yes. There was another son from the dissolved marriage, who would stay with the mother every summer. He was quieter and only six months younger than Sainos.

They attended the same east-coast boarding school, where they avoided each other." The detective stopped to catch his breath.

"That must have been the beginning of Camp Carthage for Sainos," said Will. "So what happened next?"

"Sainos was usually at odds with his father," said Detective Clayberry, rubbing his chin, "but he still got everything paid for in high school and college. His resemblance to Sainos Sr. could have been the trigger. That same gardener, who helped us piece together this background, said that Sainos was violently contemptuous of his father—and, in fact, *any* authority figure. The profile of a sociopath fits him well. But let's come back to your question, Will: where does Vahriman/Rotenberg fit in?

"When Rotenberg approached me, I thought he was helping me with the investigation. But now I'm sure he was really looking for any former GVP member that he could blackmail—and with Sainos he found a perfect target."

"Oh, I can see that," said Darius. Audrey and Will nodded.

"Getting someone skilled with explosives who would be completely under his control meant he could direct an attack on the SPAW wind farm in Melford. If done right, it would damage the reputation of all SPAW installations. Once Rotenberg gained the information I'm about to share with you, he used his well-funded resources to make contact with Sainos. He threatened Sainos with further prison time unless Sainos agreed to help—and we know Sainos did agree. So, in fact, the predator became the prey." Detective Clayberry sat back in his chair.

"Before Rotenberg got involved, Sainos had found a way to trace the man who referred to himself as Captain Glow. Sainos found an insider who worked at the bank where the captain had opened the account for the armored-car money. Sainos's insider at the bank was a reclusive man named Bert Gimble, a man who'd worked at the bank for twenty-two years. The two were complete opposites."

"The guy was willing to help Sainos?" Darius asked, incredulous.

"Yes," said Detective Clayberry, "Sainos convinced Bert Gimble that he was investigating for the Blooming Armored Car Company and that he was seeking to trace the robbery funds. Probably wasn't hard for Sainos to acquire letterhead papers to back his story. He was now half-heir to his father's fortune, and he used his money and family name to persuade the bank associate that he was authentic."

"Amazing," said TR. "That guy should've checked."

"You're right. Bert Gimble was dazzled by the money he was offered, and that set a lot in motion. He didn't bother to contact the actual Blooming Armored Car Company. It was enough for him that Sainos was the son of the deceased owner."

"Quite devious," said Audrey. Detective Clayberry nodded and went on.

"So with Mr. Gimble's help, Sainos discovered that a half million *had* been deposited the spring after the robbery. Gimble was able to confirm the withdrawal of that money, which was transferred to a new account. It was ill-fated that the new account the captain opened up was still with that same bank. At the time, it was the easiest thing for him to do, given he was creating a new identity in Mexico and needed to keep things simple.

"Coming back to the present, Sainos used Bert to track that account, which was now being used for the clean-energy projects. Within months of his arrangement with Bert, Sainos began to target those systems for his revenge against the captain."

"The zoo, the engineering lab, and our school's new ground-source heat-pump system." said Will.

"Exactly," said Detective Clayberry. "Around mid-December, Bert Gimble was found murdered in his apartment, strangled with a drapery cord. The authorities had no leads. Oddly, he'd just purchased a sports car and got a new membership at a country club. One bank employee we interviewed said he'd been wondering where Bert got the money for that." He shook his head. "Sure enough—the trail Rotenberg uncovered led to a security camera at the bank showing Sainos meeting with Bert Gimble. But Rotenberg deliberately kept this from me, while using my contacts to get the information. So now, Rotenberg had the most recent photos of Sainos to verify this arrangement.

"When another bank employee told Rotenberg he recalled seeing Gimble and Sainos together at a local diner, it was clear that they had some pact in place. At that point, Rotenberg had all he needed, and he continued giving me false information, saying he couldn't locate Sainos or find anything that would lead to him. I believe the opposite was true, and that he had now contacted Sainos. We know the rest. Sainos was caught in a web where he had to do exactly what Rotenberg wanted—the sabotage at the Melford site."

"What's going to happen to Rotenberg?" said Will.

"He'll go to trial," said Detective Clayberry, "and will likely get a sentence of fifteen to twenty years. In addition to his terrorist work aimed at Melford, Ivanpah, and Crescent Dunes, there's a death involved. We're sure it was Sainos who killed Bert Gimble. Rotenberg likely knew about it, didn't report it, and maybe even helped plan it. He'll also face charges for obtaining and using fake IDs. I don't know all the specifics, but he won't be leaving jail anytime soon."

The explanation over, Margaret and her father showed Will, Darius, and Audrey to the door.

On the following Monday, the news stations reported that the murderer of Tom Karcher had confessed. One of the two men who'd abducted Tom Karcher had been found guilty of arson. No one had been hurt when the building went up in flames, but to make a plea bargain, the arsonist pointed to Cyndi Bargis and the other man she'd hired to kill Tom and Dallin Karcher. The arsonist had helped in the attack, but hadn't been the one to put the bullet in Tom. He turned over the text messages and the information that linked Cyndi Bargis to the payment for the crime. The person who'd pulled the trigger and committed the actual murder was on the most-wanted list. That man was now facing conviction for multiple felonies, and with the solid murder evidence against him, he'd broken down and confessed. Tom Karcher's phone was found in his house, an irrational souvenir of a person who'd been unraveling for a long time.

Will and his friends cast their minds back to Dallin Karcher and his family on the day of the funeral, and they hoped the arrest and sentencing would bring them closure. They decided they'd stop by to see Dallin when they went back to the Green River that summer to go camping and rafting.

On the advice of Audrey's parents, they'd entered the online high-use lottery contest to be able to raft the Green River that coming summer. Summertime was when the high-use designation applied, and they'd won! The raft trip would take them through the Gates of Lodore, where the beauty of the canyons was reportedly breathtaking. They'd also be able to float through the incredible Echo Park.

The memories of the past months' adventures and struggles, which they'd been pulled into, would be with them for the rest of their lives. But for now Will would go to ISEF, they'd finish up school, and they'd head for a promising adventure—one that they'd chosen for themselves.

The End

AFTERWORD

THIS STORY COULD NOT have been written without the help and inspiration from the following industries, businesses, and research facilities. Thank you.

Gardner Engineering who installed the solar PV system for the zoo hospital at Hogle Zoo in Salt Lake City, Utah.

DWA Construction, Inc. and their excellent project manager Shane Wilde who verified the technical design aspects of the ground source heat pump system.

Milford Wind, a wind farm whose remarkable origins are the basis for the Melford wind farm in the book.

Vestas Wind Turbine Company for their leadership and contributions to the wind industry.

Goshen Wind Farm Management in Idaho Falls, Idaho, who gave us a tour of their control center, along with an explanation of how the site worked, and a visit to a tower with a technician.

Utah State University's outstanding electric vehicle ASPIRE Lab, whose work on in-motion-charging systems and microgrid focus are the basis for the technical information provided for the electric vehicle lab in the story.

The highly functioning engineers who work at this lab bear no resemblance to any of the characters in our story.

This is a work of fiction. Names, characters, and incidents are either the products of the author's imagination or used in a fictitious manner. Any resemblance to actual persons, living or dead, or actual events is purely coincidental.

ACKNOWLEDGMENTS

Thank you to my inspired husband Nick who designs structures to better channel the sun's photons, making the sun an even more welcome source of energy for our planet. Thank you to our children, Holly and Max, who supported the idea of Captain Glow and the creation of this story.

Thank you to Annie Worthen, Joe Marshall, Julie Marshall, Gina Worthen, Micah Earl, Robyn Earl, Tucker Nelson, and Brent Kelly. These were my first readers, who powered on through the early drafts. Thanks to John Flann, Rufus ZaeJoDaeus, and Holly Flann for the cover art, website art and novel's images. Thank you to Jeannie Doxee and Sharon Hinton for their sharp proofreading.

Thank you to Bill Gates for pulling Generation 4 sodium-cooled nuclear reactors toward being in use. Thank you to Elon Musk for pulling electric vehicle transportation into the mainstream.

Thank you to Angela, Lindsay, Michele, Kathy J., Anna, and Shanda of Eschler Editing for their powerful skills. Thank you to Chris B. at Scrivener for physically producing the book and making the audiobook available. Thank you to Colin Johnson for thoughtfully directing Max Flann in the narration of the book, and to John Carter of Thirteen/ Eight Productions for his skillful recording and editing of the audiobook. Thank you to Jenn and Melanie of Elite Online Publishing for their marketing talents.

Very importantly, profound thanks to all the many inventors, engineers, and technicians who create clean energy systems that support and sustain life on this magnificent planet!

NOTE TO THE READER

THANK YOU FOR READING *Captain Glow*! If you enjoyed it and were inspired by the story and the things you've learned, please leave S.J. a review, as reviews are the lifeblood of an author and critical to the success of a book!

About the Author

S.J. FLANN'S WRITING EXPERIENCE includes employment with International Business Machines, better known as IBM, a world leader in the computer industry. S.J.'s employment there consisted of repairing internal test systems and external customer systems. This skill led to writing test procedures and engineering presentations. Prior to IBM, S.J. worked with affiliates of PBS, CBS and ABC television stations on studio productions, in engineering, and also in writing scripts. In addition to *Captain Glow*, S.J. and a cowriter created a feature-length screenplay. S.J. has also self-published a children's picture book, *Solar Power Comes to My Home,* which you can find on Amazon.com.

If you want to learn more about clean energy and taking care of our planet, see the electronic Footnotes Links Supplement at the front of the book. This list and the audiobook footnote time locations can be found on the www.captainglow.com website, which makes it easy for readers to click on the educational links in the novel. Also, you can follow S.J. at amazon.com/author/sjflann. For book signings or speaking engagements, contact her here: sjflann@captainglow.com.

Made in the USA
Columbia, SC
11 March 2021